Fairy Tales
Prunk'd

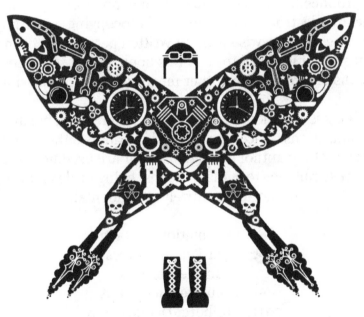

An Illustrated Mythpunk Anthology

Edited by Phoebe Darqueling

Fairy Tales Punk'd: An Illustrated Mythpunk Anthology
Tainted Tincture Press
Copyright © 2020 by Alison Weaverdyck

This book is a work of fiction. Names, characters, businesses,
organizations, places, events and incidents either are the
product of the author's imagination or are used fictitiously.
Any resemblance to actual persons, living or dead, events,
or locales is entirely coincidental.

For information contact:
Tainted Tincture Press
Alison Weaverdyck
Am Kreuzsteinacker 15A
79117 Freiburg, Deutschland
TaintedTincture@gmail.com

Edited by Phoebe Darqueling
Proofread by Crysta K. Coburn
Formatted by Daniel Sheldon

Table of Contents

Making Bones by Phoebe Darqueling   1
    Illustration by J. Woolston Carr
Star Tsarina by TJ O'Hare   21
    Illustration by Tom Brown
Steel-blue Babe by Aaron Isett   49
    Illustration by Nathan Lueth
The Sharp Mechanical Sheep by Kay Gray   59
    Illustration by Audra Miller
The Girl in the Tower by A.F. Stewart   87
    Illustration by Audra Miller
Hoods and Wolves by Briant Laslo   111
    Illustration by Tom Brown
The Great Astrolabe of Einem by K.A. Lindstrom   133
    Illustration by Tom Brown
Liberty by Crysta K. Coburn   171
    Illustration by Nathan Lueth
A Saturnine, A Martial, and a Mercurial Lunatic   203
    by Amber Michelle Cook
    Illustration by Audra Miller
The Second Mission of Azarbad the Aeronaut   217
    by J. Woolston Carr
    Illustration by J. Woolston Carr
Black Dog, Wild Wood by Thomas Gregory   239
    Illustration by J. Woolston Carr
Mirror in her Hand by Liz Tuckwell   267
    Illustrstion by J. Woolston Carr
Wound by Paul Hiscock   279
    Illustration by Nathan Lueth

Making Bones

by Phoebe Darqueling

If you've never disposed of a body, you probably won't believe me, but I prefer the tang of blood when I arrive to the chemical stench that marks my departure. The sting of bleach in my eyes from dealing with the fluids, lye for the solids curling through my nostrils, the occasional blunt force of an accelerant when extreme measures need to be taken, then the ash falling from the sky like morbid snow—none of these odors pleasant and all of them are clinging to my skin as I pull up to the Fireside Motel that night.

Not that I ever voice my complaints. Not that it would have mattered if I did.

That's the problem when you're good at your job. People keep expecting you to do it.

Angelica, my father's wife, doesn't just expect me to do my job. She expects me to smile about it. Even on nights like this when my room is given away to a "business associate" or some member of their entourage, I'm supposed to say thank you for the cheesy motel and the promise of a lackluster breakfast. The family has plenty, she could have sprung for something better. No doubt she would have if it was for my precious stepsisters. Once they finish with the hit, they get to go home to the evening's festivities and the comfort of their own beds.

And I clean up the mess.

"Only the best for my girls." I mutter the imitation of my stepmother as I glare around the lot for a place to park.

With the rain hitting the pavement harder than a heavyweight, the spaces near the row of doors are all taken. A flash of lightning illuminates a spot at the far end, and I pull in before the thunder has a chance to rumble. Most people would hurry through the cascade to save their clothes, but on my modest allowance I have nothing worth protecting. The Pontiac Streamliner is my most precious possession, but she's a tough old broad. We can both handle a little water.

My highest aspiration at that moment is to take a shower before crawling inside a bottle and chasing sleep. I keep my steps slow to let nature start the work the faucet will finish. After the heat of the fire I'd started, the coolness in the wake of the storm is a welcome reprieve. I picture steam rising off my skin as I get under the eave and dig around for the key.

I'm so absorbed with my handbag, I don't notice the fresh set of footprints leading to my door until I'm standing on top of them. My own tracks obscure the outline, and I can't guess the type of shoes, but there aren't that many people who would know where to find me. Since my mother died, there are even fewer who would bother.

My fingers finally brush the prodigal key, and I enter. Cecelia has already helped herself to a gin and tonic, and she holds a second glass out to me once I shed my dripping overcoat. I don't bother asking how she got into my room. Picking locks is only one talent in my aunt's varied skill set.

"Rough day?" she asks.

I slump into the other chair at the table and try my drink, letting the bubbles fizzle out on my tongue completely before swallowing.

"The usual."

The strands on her beaded earrings clack together as she shakes her head. "I don't know how you do it."

"Me?" I snort. "I'm not the one who kills them. I don't know how the Enforcers do what they do."

"You know how to handle a gun. Unless you've already forgotten what I taught you?"

The lime bobbing at the top of my glass spins as I swirl the contents. "I remember. But there has to be more to killing than knowing how to shoot."

"Well, I don't know about your sisters—"

"*Step*-sisters."

"—but for me, it's pretty simple. I tell myself everyone is dying from the moment I lay eyes on them. We're all just a pile of dusty bones waiting to happen. That way, it's only natural when I make it come true."

I consider asking her if that includes her current company, but I'm afraid I won't like the answer. Instead, I kick off my shoes and ask, "How was the party?"

Cecelia grimaces. "Tedious, and still going on."

"I'm sure Pearl and Lacy are having a wonderful time for the both of us."

"Dinner, on the other hand, now that was interesting." Her smile promises intrigue, but the late hour is weighing on me too much to give her the satisfaction of leaning in for the gossip. She has to settle for a couple of raised eyebrows and a noncommittal sound as I take another pull of my cocktail. This turns out to be a mistake, as I nearly choke when she says the next three words. "Bruno was there."

I hadn't seen the family's pet P.I. in nearly a decade. He'd been a strange combination of Santa Claus and the Boogieman haunting my early life, coming in the night bearing gifts, but the information he carried usually ended in something monstrous. Those were the bad old days, the bloody days, when the Families were at war over territory and bootlegging routes.

After I recover from my bout of coughing, I try to regain my air of nonchalance. "Bruno, huh? What is he up to these days?"

From the amusement tugging at Cecelia's mouth, I can tell she's not buying my casual tone. "Even though your father dismissed him for—what was the term?"

"Gross incompetence."

"Yeah, gross incompetence. That was it." She picks up the bottle and tops me off, her averted eyes hinting at something. "So even after that, he's continued as a gumshoe. Had his hands in all kinds of things."

"That so?" As I take another swallow, I barely taste it. "Find anything interesting?"

She turns to face me, and I see the shimmer in her gaze. Her eyes, my mother's eyes, my eyes, they are all the same. And they rarely shed a tear. "You're never going to believe it, baby. But he's found him, the rat bastard who killed your mama. Bruno's figured it out."

It feels as though my body is submerged in a vat of cement as I set down my glass, but my mind races. Memories clamber over each other—long, cool fingers against a fevered brow, songs half-hummed because she was no good at remembering lyrics, a waft of her perfume when she tucked me in. They're all I've got left of my mother.

The trail is nearly a decade cold. I'd abandoned any hope of learning the truth along with pigtails. Officially, the cops said she'd died in a simple car crash, but I knew too well that anyone could be bought. Being a cleaner wasn't only about ammonia and fingerprints. Occasionally, there were witnesses to silence, and it didn't have to be done at gunpoint. Doctors would be shocked to know the leading cause of memory loss wasn't a blow to the head, but a wad of hundred-dollar bills. Then again, in this town, maybe it wouldn't surprise them at all.

Cecelia allows me a few moments to absorb the news, then fills the silence with the explanation I am too off-kilter to demand from her. There's some mention of cops asking Bruno to help with an investigation, but then her words are overtaken by the hiss filling my skull, like the needle is caught between stations in my brain. At some point, her lips stop moving, so she must have finished talking.

My eyes flick to the window as another flash of lightning illuminates the curtains. The brightness forces the buzz to recede. I fight the leaden feeling and make my mouth move again. "Who was it?"

"The Enforcer himself is already dead." My heart sinks as the thoughts of revenge evaporate, then she waves away the remark as if it were nothing more than a mosquito. "But that isn't really who matters now, is it?"

I realize I'm nodding as understanding blooms. The finger that pulls the trigger isn't as important as the person who orders it to bend. She looks at me expectantly but waits for me to ask the question.

"Who ordered the hit?"

"King."

The word hangs in the air, the silence only broken by another rumble of thunder.

My glass is at my lips again before I realize what I am doing. The juniper tang helps me focus. "Father knows?"

"Yes."

"What is he planning to do about it?"

My aunt makes a disgusted sound and turns her attention to her own drink, snarling, "Vito says he needs time to think about it. All of the Enforcers are on formal notice not to take action."

"What is there to think about?"

She reaches out with a manicured hand and tucks a wet strand of hair behind my ear. "Angelica is a King on her mother's side. Third cousin or something, but she's a King all the same."

"Dammit. I forgot." I'm on my feet and pacing. My stepmother has blood ties to two of the Families, so my father's remarriage had been in service of a political alliance. At least, that is the reason I cling to. Sure, she's beautiful in an ordinary sort of way. She also has the uncanny ability to make everything she wears look cheap. Not like Mama. She could have worn a potato sack and she'd be able to glide in and light up a room.

A match flares. Cecelia's voice is contorted by her lips bending to hold the cigarette still enough to ignite. "Your father seemed keen to take action at first, but then Angelica started in with the crocodile tears and blubbering about being afraid of going back to the old days. She says retaliation now could lead to war again. And I admit, it makes a cowardly sort of sense." Cecelia shakes the match, and the flame dies in a pitiful coil of smoke.

My mouth twists into a sneer. "And with all the usual boys off fighting the krauts, it would be all you dame enforcers on the frontlines this time. Including her precious daughters." I snatch the cigarette from Cecelia's lips and breathe the poison deep into my lungs. "But the code dictates vengeance, pure and simple."

She pulls out another Lucky Strike and stabs it in the air to punctuate her words. "King is the code."

"Well, isn't that convenient?" I cross to the bedside table, then perch on the edge of the stiff hotel mattress to flick the spent embers into the ashtray. My hand is shaking, so I concentrate on the feeling of the smoke moving in and out my lungs to steady it. As only a casual smoker, the nicotine makes my fingertips tingle and my head swim. I'll have a headache when it wears off. Then again, I usually wake up with a headache. I inhale again.

"Too bad Vito asked for time." Cecelia sighs like a bellows. Always one for the dramatic.

"What difference does it make if he's going to play it safe? 'No' today and 'no' next week are still 'no.'"

She takes a drag, then waves her hand through the exhaled cloud, the ash falling to the carpet of no concern. "Because tomorrow night would be the perfect opportunity to do something about it."

"What? The New Year's Eve party? Isn't that kinda... public?"

"Sometimes the best cover is to be part of a crowd. It's one of the only ways to get into the King mansion, which is a veritable Fort Knox any other day of the year. That's how I'd do it anyway." Cecelia shrugs, a smirk tugging at the corner of her mouth. "If I were allowed to."

She's leaned into the 'I' rather than the 'if,' and it takes me a second to realize why. The alcohol is warming my belly, but my rain-soaked skin makes me shiver. Or maybe it's the notion coalescing in my brain.

I can feel her eyes on me as she continues. "Look. I'm your godmother as well as your blood, so I know I shouldn't be putting this on you. It's supposed to be my job to shelter you now that your mama is gone, but we both know that isn't really my style, or I never would have taken you to the range. I haven't always been there for you the way I shoulda been, but together we can see justice done."

She knows me well enough to let me finish my cigarette in silence while I mull over what she's proposing. The angel on one shoulder is whispering at me to tell her to take a hike. But it's the devil in my other ear who compels me to grind the stubby cigarette into the ashtray and start asking questions.

"How would I get to King?"

Cecelia kneels at my feet, clutching at my hands and kissing my knuckles. "Not King. Not exactly."

"What do you mean?"

"The code says vengeance. That means an eye for an eye, but what if it isn't King's eye this calls for? Too quick, too good for the likes of him."

My mother's eyes gaze up at me from Cecelia's face, and I nod. He needed to suffer for what he'd done to my family. "Who then? He doesn't have a mother or a wife to lose..."

"But he has got a 'prince.'"

Jimmy "The Prince" King was the next in line for a spot in the Coalition, and that was about as much as I knew about him. "What if he's innocent?"

"Who? King? Bruno swears up and down he ordered the hit."

"No, the son."

Cecelia makes a tsking sound and rises to sit beside me. "No one is innocent, not in this thing of ours. We're all guilty of something."

Now free of her grip, my hands rest in my lap, and I flex my fingers. Only a few hours ago they'd been covered in a man's blood. I could have told someone. I could have done a worse job at covering it up. But I'd never dream of it. She's right, the business couldn't help but leave its mark. The code calls for silence above even vengeance, making every one of us complicit. I may not have pulled a trigger yet, but there is no chance I'm innocent.

"If the shoe fits," I mutter.

"That's my girl." My godmother gives my shoulders a squeeze.

"You're in the perfect position. As much as I hate to agree with Angelica, a move like this could start a war. But only if an Enforcer did it. And even if they find you out, a daughter

8

acting out of grief? A crime of passion? No one will blame you. Hell, your father will probably be happy you untied his hands on the matter!"

The devil pushes aside the last of my hesitation and says, "I haven't got anything to wear."

"I'll take care of everything, don't you worry." She springs to her feet and retrieves her mink. "Dress, shoes, some heat. Oh, I know just the piece! You'll love it. Sweet little thing, monogrammed mother of pearl handle. Belonged to your mama."

I'm up and crossing over to open the door for her. "She had a gun?"

"We all carried them in those days. I bet that's why they cut her brake lines rather than facing her like a man. You make sure to wipe your prints and leave it behind, and King'll know exactly why it happened." She's got her things gathered and comes to stand before me. "Right now, get yourself a hot shower and a good night's sleep. Tomorrow, I'll have everything sent over. I'd bring it myself, but I've got to make sure I am nice and visible at home so nobody thinks I got anything cooking. Do what you have to by the time the fireworks finish up at twelve, then get out of there. Everyone will be too busy boozing and toasting to see you slip out."

The door opens onto the chill of evening, but the storm passed sometime during our conversation. Cecelia takes my face in her hands and kisses me on each cheek before stepping out into the night.

"Remember," she calls over her shoulder. "Out of there by midnight."

I expected to have a rough time falling asleep, but whether by dint of my new sense of purpose or introducing the rest of that bottle of gin to my innards, my night was damn near blissful. So blissful, in fact, that I missed the motel's sorry excuse for a breakfast. I treat myself to the blue plate special and several cups of decent coffee at a diner up the road. When I get back, the manager flags me down to give me a package. It doesn't matter how old you get, a big box tied up with a bow can't help but put a spring in your step.

Even though I don't give much thought to fashion, I can tell that Cecelia has chosen something special. The gown shimmers like champagne turned to cloth. Delicate silver stitching snakes from the left side of the hem all the way up to the right shoulder. At first glance, I didn't love the ample gathering and billowing of cloth at the small of the back. But when I read the accompanying note and find out there are laces hidden beneath it to hold my weapon, relief washes over me. Either Cecelia has been planning this for longer than she let on, or she'd commissioned the dress for some other purpose, and I happened to be benefitting.

It's an elegant solution. As long as no one gets handsy, I shouldn't have any trouble keeping the Baby Browning hidden.

The gun itself is as lovely as she'd described. I lose a few moments running my thumb over the initials engraved into the grip. It should kick even less than the Colt I'd handled under my aunt's supervision, and it hardly weighs a thing by comparison. A clutch purse, some white satin gloves, and a pair of heels taller than I would have chosen for myself

10

complete the ensemble. They'll slow me down if things go sideways. I spend a while practicing in the dress and shoes so I can make my movements seem natural, but God receives my silent entreaty that I won't have to dance.

I pull out a merlot lipstick I've never had the courage to wear before. Today, it feels right. I go just as dark and heavy on my eye makeup and even go so far as adding a pair of fake lashes. I doubt anyone would recognize me anyway, but better safe than sorry. It's been a long time since I bothered with any of the social niceties my position as the daughter of a don usually requires. With Pearl and Lacy so eager and willing to step into the spotlight, I had been content to remain in the shadows. Until now.

For one last layer of precaution, I call a cab rather than taking my own car. I hear it when the hack trundles to a stop outside, but the impatient driver also honks. The rodent behind the wheel is content to let his cargo open her own door until he looks up, then he springs out and scurries to my side with a half-assed apology and a lingering glance at my décolletage. It's not the reaction I am used to, but certainly the one I'll need to get The Prince all to myself. I pretend not to notice and purr my thanks as I slide into the back seat of the squash-yellow car.

The driver attempts small talk as we trundle into town. I give a fake name and spin a yarn about meeting friends at the opera house. It's only a few blocks from the party and a good way to explain my attire in case anyone finds a reason to ask him about an attractive female passenger later. Given the lateness of the hour, it's an obvious lie, but he doesn't bat an eye.

We pull up to 39th Street, and I tell him to let me off at the corner. The cabbie almost looks sad to take my money and let me go, but that doesn't stop him from pocketing the bills I pass him. As I step onto the sidewalk, he rolls down the passenger window and flails a card at me along with an assurance that

I could call on his services any time. I slip the card into my handbag with a smile and hope I never see him again.

Yesterday's rain has turned into a slick patina of ice. My breath hangs in the air as I pull my coat tighter. Despite the cold, a steady stream of people passes me on both sides. Lovers lean into one another to combat the chilly breeze. Rowdy groups laugh as they stumble from one bar to another. Midnight is coming, and everyone seems to feel the pressure to make something special out of the evening. I know I do.

When there's a break in the traffic, I cross the street and wend my way to the right building. Many of the windows are dark, but up in the penthouse the night shines like day. Both the doorman and the elevator operator are as appreciative as the cab driver, and I can't help but marvel over the difference a nice frock and a little lipstick can do. Or maybe it's the .25 tied to the small of my back giving me swagger. I step up to pass the invitation to the brute at the door. After a cursory glance, he motions me inside.

The massive double doors open onto an opulent hall. A tuxedoed underling takes my coat and my bag before wishing me a happy new year. I'm doubly glad for the custom dress and the weight of the gun on the small of my back as my bag disappears into the depth of the cloak room.

I keep my strides smooth and measured as I step into the ballroom, still wary of the height of my shoes and the strength of my ankles. A torch singer pours out her heart next to a ten-piece band in the corner. Her voice climbs as a waiter passes me a glass of champagne, and I soak in the room. Floor-to-ceiling windows reveal the glow of stars at the far end. A dozen or so couples are cheek to cheek in the space near the band while knots of people linger over their champagne at high-top tables assembled around the edges.

As I take a few steps deeper into the party, my eyes are drawn upward. A balcony overlooks the festivities from above the entryway, and a gaggle of men are gathered there, surveying the scene. I recognize the King patriarch, head bent in quiet conversation with a white-haired man. Most of the assembly are in their forties or older, but a few young men are mulling around among them. My heart sinks as I realize any one of them could be The Prince, and I have no idea how to tell which one. He could just as easily be one half of a dancing couple before me. The hulking clock to my left says I've got about an hour and a half to figure it out.

I feel like tossing back the whole flute of champagne, but restrain myself to only tiny sips as I drift between groups of people. The snippets of conversation tell me plenty about current affairs—which prize fighter is the favorite for next week's match, and what people think of the newest Betty Grable flick—but I lose a lot of time with nothing of substance to show for it. Though most of the people are strangers, I can place some of the faces from my own vague memories and from reading the society pages. A handful of recently elected politicians and their wives are spread around the room, no doubt the reason The Prince is here on his home soil rather than across the ocean with the rest of the men his age.

I also recognize a few big business owners enjoying the party. The Kings certainly have put their mark on the world since starting the Coalition. Hell, some of what they do is probably even legitimate, but I can't think about that now.

The clock strikes eleven, and my heart is pounding. Only an hour left, then the window closes. I focus on doing as Cecelia advised and practice making everyone dead in my mind. There's a lady in a stunning, white dress a few tables away. I slash her throat and watch her skin grow pale. I break the neck of her dance partner.His eyes sink into his skull, and his lips retreat, leaving his mouth a wide grimace. A red stain blooms like a carnation on the chest of a bartender as he cheerily shakes a martini for a woman in lavender with a knife in her back.

When I feel a tap on my shoulder, I nearly jump out of my skin. A man with an angular jaw and honey-brown eyes stands before me.

He holds out a freckled hand, jerking his head towards the dance floor. "Would you care to join me?"

The slight pistol at my back feels like it triples in size. "No thank you," I demur and gaze around the room like I'm seeking out someone specific in the crowd.

His smile doesn't falter. "You know, it's not polite to refuse your host."

"So, you're a King?" I ask, chiding myself for how my voice cracked.

"Are you a queen?" he teases. "Because you certainly deserve the royal treatment. People call me The Prince, so it looks like I'm your man."

I slip back into the husky tone I'd tried out on the cabbie. "Does that line usually work?"

"It's the first time I've tried it." His embarrassment shaves a few years off of his face. "So, you tell me."

I take his hand by way of answer, and we step over to the group of couples gently swaying to the music. The bassist plucks out a steady rhythm while the smooth voice of a muted trumpet weaves a tale of sorrow. His hand snakes around my back, but when it comes to rest well above the top of the train, I swallow my flash of anxiety. Luckily for me, my mark is a gentleman. He takes my free hand in his, and our bodies are close enough I can feel the rumble in his chest when he tells me his name is Jimmy.

I can feel a flux of emotions parading across my face, so I lean in until my lips nearly brush his ear and breathe, "You can call me Elizabeth." After the crack about being a 'queen,' it only felt right to borrow from the British monarch.

"How come I haven't seen you around before, Lizzie?"

His presumed familiarity tightens the skin around my

eyes, and I respond flatly, "I don't get out much."

"I find that hard to believe." He chuckles.

Ice water trickles down my spine. It's true. Any woman who wears a dress like this isn't some wallflower. I can't be myself tonight; I'm not the type to get a man to leave his own party for a quiet rendezvous away from so many witnesses. I've got to be the woman who wears this dress.

My mind reels, and my step falters as I search for a response. Damn these shoes. He deftly turns my stumble into a turn. I paint on a smile, look deep into his eyes, and say, "I just can't seem to find the right dance partner."

"It's true. The right partner can make all the difference." He runs his thumb over mine, and even through the glove I feel a tinge of unexpected heat. "Have you thought about holding auditions?"

"We're dancing, aren't we?" My false lashes rise and fall a few times. "Consider this a trial by fire."

It's his turn to lean in. His cheek rests against mine as he whispers, "I hope I don't get burned."

I favor him with a chuckle and purr, "Don't be so sure."

In the corner of my eye, my imagination begins to scorch the skin of the hand holding mine. He's a wonderful dancer, but he's still a pile of bones. The blackened blisters spread, but instead of the stench of gasoline, it's the warm scent of his skin I smell. My stomach clenches, and I nearly stumble again. The Prince pulls me so close there's no chance I could fall.

The song ends. Another begins. I lose count. We only break contact when a waiter comes by and offers us more champagne. I start to wave him off, then he says, "It's nearly midnight, you know?"

I fight to keep my alarm from shrilling my voice. "Is it now?"

"And what's ringing in the New Year without a toast, eh?"

The Prince grins and retrieves two glasses.

"What indeed?" I reply, panic gripping my heart like a

vice. A glance around the room shows that most of the other people have already taken up places at the windows. I take the glass he offers me and use it to gesture at the crowd. "I heard a rumor there would be fireworks."

"You heard right. In a few minutes, the sky will be full of them."

I take a sip of my champagne, then pout prettily. "It's too bad we didn't get to the windows sooner. I'm afraid I won't be able to see a thing. Is there somewhere more...private where we could watch them?"

Mischief twinkles in his eyes as he takes the bait. "Don't go telling anyone," he says in a stage whisper. "But I do have a favorite spot for watching them. It might be chilly, though. Should we get your coat?"

I can feel the seconds flying by, and I shake my head. "I'm sure you can keep me warm."

He takes my hand and leads me away from the throng. A nearly invisible door set into the wall swings inward at his touch and reveals a set of stairs. I take a few steps, but the ridiculous shoes are starting to pinch. At this rate, I'm likely to miss the fireworks, and my cover, before we ever reach where he's taking me. So, I lean on the railing and slip them off. I leave them behind as I follow him up the dark passage.

The Prince is waiting for me at the top of the stairs. He glances at my bare feet but doesn't comment, then opens the door. We're on the roof. I wince slightly as my soles touch the frozen surface and cross my arms to help repress a shudder. Maybe I should have heeded his warning of the cold.

"Over here," he says, pointing to the low wall that surrounds the rooftop. "This is the best seat in the house."

He all but scampers to the spot. Though we are likely similar in age, his delight renders him childlike. Innocent.

My resolve wavers.

When he realizes I haven't followed, he returns to my side.

Without a word, he removes his suit coat and wraps it around my shoulders. He uses the action as an excuse to keep his arm around me, and coaxes me to the spot he'd indicated. We stand side by side, and I nestle against his solid form for warmth.

The streets below are draped with strings of Christmas lights. It's an annual reprieve to the darkness that usually clings to the city but has very little to do with the setting of the Sun. A few stories down, the wide balcony of the King penthouse catches the pools of lights from the ballroom windows. I can make out the shifting shadows of expectant party guests, and I search the sky for the first hint of the fireworks display.

The Prince's hand leaves my shoulder and travels down my back. My stomach gives a flutter as it approaches the hidden Browning. Before I realize I've done it, I spin to face him. It keeps his hand away from my back, but puts my lips dangerously close to his. The chilly night air makes our mingling breath hang in the air like clouds.

"Tell me about yourself," I blurt, then put the purr back into my voice. "Your Majesty."

His Adam's apple bobs, then he wets his lips. "You can call me Jimmy, you know."

"Are you the next King, or aren't you?" Something in my tone gives him pause, the amusement slipping. I set down my glass of champagne and run a finger across his chest. "You are planning to follow in your father's footsteps, aren't you?"

He catches my hand in the cage of his fingers, then slides them down to the edges of my gloves. The satin slithers across my skin as he answers. "It wasn't always the plan."

His fingers trace gentle lines across my exposed forearm. Even though the skin is now bared to the cold, it burns with his touch. My breath hitches, but I manage to ask, "Is that so?"

The Prince lifts my hand to his face and brushes his lips against my palm. An unexpected murmur of pleasure escapes my lips, and he acts on the encouragement. As he speaks, he

17

is leaving a trail of soft kisses down my arm.

"I was going to get out. To leave this all behind. Everything down there may shine, but the light is...sullied by my father's dealings."

As he reaches the crook of my arm, I realize my hand is on his shoulder, my fingers clutching the thin fabric of his shirt. His coat has fallen to the ground behind me, forgotten. His lips continue their journey, and our bodies press closer. My free hand slithers to the small of my back.

"He's a dangerous man," I breathe, somewhere between a question and a statement.

When he reaches my collarbone, he pauses. His hot breath crawls across my skin.

"Yes."

I tilt my head to give him easier access to my neck even as my fingers are pulling at the laces of my hidden firearm. His kisses become urgent, hungry.

A moan escapes my lips, but I somehow manage to ask, "Are you a dangerous man, Jimmy?"

He's at my earlobe, so he barely has to whisper.

"Is that what you want me to say?"

His touch is making my heart thud like an angry downstairs neighbor with a broomstick. I could let it all go, melt into him the way my body is screaming at me to do. Then I swear, I smell a waft of Mama's perfume, and I steel myself. "I want the truth."

"Then, my answer," he breathes, "is yes."

The black sky explodes in a shower of sparks.

His chest explodes in a shower of red.

His body crumples to the ground.

The clock strikes twelve.

The spell is broken.

No longer his body.

Just bones.

About Phoebe Darqueling

Phoebe Darqueling is the pen name of a globe trotting vagabond who currently hangs her hat in Freiburg, Germany. In her "real life," she writes curriculum for a creativity competition for kids in MN, and works with both fiction and nonfiction authors as an editor. *Fairy Tales Punk'd* is her third sojourn into putting together multi-author collections. Phoebe loves Steampunk as an author, lecturer, and blogger for SteampunkJournal.org, and offers a free reference book for her newsletter subscribers at bit.ly/SteampunkHandbook. She also dabbles in a variety of fantasy and science fiction genres, and you can find all of her titles on Amazon at bit.ly/PhoebeD.

Star Tsarina

by TJ O'Hare

'Captain, if they keep up their orbit-shadowing tactics, our hydroponics are going to suffer,' growled master-at-arms Darya Golodryga Vann, thin-lipped and tight-lipped as always. 'No hydroponics, no fresh food. We'll be limping back to Clan-space on combat rations.'

Sotnik Hordiyenko barked, 'Scientznik Derkach, run a projection of hydroponics loss. I want to know what will go first and what losses we can sustain.'

'Aye aye, Captain. Running projection.' The science officer, Derkach, short of stature, which recalled his Gurkha lineage, had to stand up to deal with the overhead sensor screens.

The view-screen was filled with the underbelly of the Imperial Russian frigate *Castor*. Its hull gleamed like cathedral glass, a tribute to the orthodoxy of the captain and her crew. Golden domes capped the engine nacelles, a tracery of holy icons winking in the reflected starlight and the albedo of the world below.

Darya Golodryga Vann's lips curled in a thin sneer. *World, indeed.*

It was barely even a dwarf planet. But it was of strategic mineral importance between the Empire of the Russ and the Nation of Cossacks with the only known source of the crypto-element called R-61.

The *sotnik* sat back in his captain's chair and steepled his fingers. 'So much for intel keeping track of the movements of the Russ fleet.' He turned to glare at Vann, as if this development was her fault.

Vann wanted to reply that military intel was a contradiction in terms, but she didn't want to be busted down to deck duties.

The *sotnik* continued, examining her face for a reaction. 'We can't precipitate an interplanetary incident.'

Vann returned his glare. 'Does that mean a covert operation, Captain?'

'You know it does. And you're our highest-trained, but also lowest-ranked operative. I could afford to lose you if the Russ get stroppy and I had to abandon this orbit.'

'I can deal with that. I can get off-planet and rejoin you – if it came to that.'

The *sotnik* broke his steeple and waved her away with a dismissive hand. 'You would be stuck here until our return. These primitives have no space capability. It's purely a research mission. Just observe. I don't want to explain away any locals that die from a Cossack-related wound.'

Vann stood up and saluted. 'You may rely on me, Captain.'

As she turned her back on him, she knew his scowl would be less than trusting.

Vann was in the armoury when Derkach found her. 'What are you doing here, Tryzub?' she demanded, using his call sign.

'I'm here because I suggested to the *sotnik* that it would make sense if two of us went down. I'll be your pilot.'

'Didn't you hear him? He'd be happy leaving me behind. Why would you volunteer for such a thankless duty?'

Derkach merely folded his arms and looked at her.

She turned away and continued to inspect her travel-pack, ignoring his silent presence.

'You know, Darya Golodryga, the *sotnik* isn't as hard on you as you imagine.'

'Oh, yes he is. He's a prejudiced pig from a backward colony that still thinks of the Old Ways as the Only Ways.'

'I think you're doing him an injustice.'

'He doesn't like my *psi*-powers, and he's made that blatantly clear. Every chance he gets, he sends me into action. Not as a real agent or infiltrator, but as an expendable pawn. His father founded the Board of Probative Genetics. I'm surprised he didn't join the Spanish Inquisition and be done with it.'

'I sometimes wonder, Helianthus,' he drawled, using her call sign in return, 'whether you unconsciously activate your *psi* against him. True, he might well be...suspicious of your *psi*, but have you ever thought that your animosity towards him might well be.... What's the word I want to use? Trickling over into him?'

'Believe me, *scientznik*, I would not be "trickling" anything over into him. It would come out more like blaster fire.'

He shook his head. 'I think you've just answered my speculation.'

Vann grunted.

When she said nothing else, Derkach said, 'I'm taking you down in the drop-ship.'

'Fine. But you are not making planetfall. Take me down to the edge of the atmosphere, and I'll take a one-man *baidak* the rest of the way.'

Derkach kept his face neutral. 'At least, that way, you'll still have escape velocity from their gravity well.'

'Why are you doing this for me?' she grumbled.

'I want to make babies with you that have the *psi*-gene.'

'Good thing for me it's *not* genetic.' She smiled fiendishly back at his long-standing jab. 'And, besides, that'll never happen, you scurvy dog. You are way too short for me, you Gurkha dwarf.'

'One day, you'll learn to look up to me.'

She made planetfall three hours later. When she stepped out from her *baidak*, she was deep in a forest, with what passed for forest on Bianna-Disputed. The Russ had their own terminology, but as far as Vann was concerned, this was the first step in her nation's attempt to turn the planet into Bianna-Cossack.

The vegetation resembled a chaparral-style biome, except with greater height. Prickly bushes and heavily leafed shrubs made it a discreet landing place.

Vann had changed into her touch-sensitive kit-suit, and then donned the baggy peasant garb that would help her blend in to the local populace. She was a little too tall for a local woman, so her garb was male-oriented. She was really too tall for a local male, too, but she adopted a slouch and a crouched stance, and figured that she could handle mingling for an hour or so.

All the males wore moustaches with full beards. Hers was

amusing but prickly and readily detachable. She felt like a billy-goat Russ.

Every one of the free folk on Bianna carried implements for chopping wood for charcoal: swords, daggers, axes. No energy tools or weapons as yet, but she was certain that a smuggler had probably dropped the occasional contraband load into the local criminal population. There were petty warlords in the political set-up, but everything was tribe- and family-related.

She had a few – a pitifully few – *psi*-gimmicks, just enough to keep herself safe on a one-to-one basis. She breathed in the salty air and sought her inner calm, but where there ought to have been a pine scent, the trees exuded this briny smell. Just breathing the air dried her mouth and chapped her lips.

Calm, calmer, calmness, she told both her self and her inner self.

She set off in this state of mind, keeping to what narrow game trails the forest offered. Her *psi*-map informed her that the small city of Hhelff (the local appellation) lay a few *versts* off.

Settling into her mind-meditation, she started to jog at an easy pace. Her kit-suit scanners pinged in her earbuds as large members of the local fauna drifted past her. None presented a threat.

Within a half-hour, she found herself at the city walls. Horizontal sections of tree trunks comprised the walls, perhaps three metres in height, and its gate was another hollowed out tree trunk. She wondered where such giant trees grew; there was nothing like them in the local forest.

Other than that, there was no security. She walked warily through the gates and into the marketplace. Several Russ personnel in their shakos and greatcoats flaunted interplanetary laws by toting light artillery.

The Russ were always pushing the envelope, but ready to

jump on the slightest infraction from the Cossacks.

All the buildings inside the city were built from hollowed out tree trunks, similar in girth to the one that had provided the gate, all roofed with local grasses and sedges. The marketplace was poorly paved, with sediment collected in what might once have been drainage gullies. There was a rank, animal smell in the air. Mounds of dung had been brushed off to the side, and young boys and youths filled handcarts with the stuff before trundling it off.

The citizens were pretty much of human origin, with the squat, almost inbred features of a small gene pool. Their language had Slavic elements, but their features were all rounded, as if they had become pebbles in a stream of genes for generations. There were no records as to how they had found themselves on such an out of the way planet.

Sorry, dwarf planet.

The universe was full of mysteries and conspiracy theories, theologies and mythologies, all too tangled to make much more than interesting tabloid reading.

The Russ patrolled the marketplace, but kept it subtle – for them. The locals all gave them a wide berth. Vann slouched past them, following the widest route out towards what her overhead view had told her was the city forum.

An open plaza to her left showed yet another Russ infraction. They had landed a small corvette, its flanks gleaming in the soft Bianna sunlight. A corvette held ten crew and up to thirty troops. Not exactly armed for bear, but not an insignificant force if their commander decided that the folks needed a little intimidation to massage them into giving the Russ what they wanted.

Russ spy-drones buzzed around the square. She slipped into a doorway and changed her garment so that it was inside out. Now it had a different colour and texture; it would delay discovery for a little while if a drone chose her from the crowd.

Several broad avenues fed into this forum plaza, and she found herself mingling among a sizeable crowd of the locals.

One or two were as tall as she was, so she didn't feel too out of place.

A neighbour in the crowd looked at her, a man with a huge, bristly bush of hair on his upper lip. In a glottal and guttural accent, he asked, 'What's the gathering?'

Vann shrugged, hoping that would be a sufficient answer. The citizen on her other side answered for her. Twigs weighed down the plaits in his beard. 'Some sort of space delegation. They call themselves "Imperials."' His accent matched her databanks as that of a townie.

'Never heard of them,' grunted the first interlocutor. 'What d'they want?'

The person in front of Vann, an elderly woman with a fierce gaze, turned and answered. 'They want mineral rights.'

Bristly said, 'They'll never get them, Zem-mother.'

Zem-mother?

Vann filed the term away for future consideration.

The old woman replied, 'They aren't taking a simple and gentle no for an answer. The *hetman* has already said "no thanks, now move along," but these Imperials aren't listening.'

Plait-beard stroked the twigs in his oiled locks. 'Those don't look like toy weapons. We can't have them desecrating the lands of our *Dodomu-svit.*'

'They've promised blandishments of credit. Credit in excess, from what they say.'

'Credit won't buy anything in the Afterlife.'

Someone quite far ahead of them in the crowd bellowed, 'Go home, Imperials! Our lands are sacred.'

A chant swept through the crowd. 'Sacred lands! Sacred soil! Sacred world!'

The Russ officer on the platform raised his hands for silence. His voice, amplified and connected to various drones,

27

carried itself to Vann's ears.

'Good citizens of Hhelff, we have come to you to be good neighbours. All we wish is for our drilling and mining operations to be permitted to commence.'

A hover-carrier hummed over the head of the crowds. A static discharge from its anti-grav props made the hair stand up on Vann's neck. Consternation crossed various faces, their hands going to exposed skin where the hair stood up.

Someone in the carrier activated its drill, and it descended from the floating platform. People immediately underneath had to scramble to make way for it.

Several tall Russ came barging through the crowds, pushing folk back with the barrels of their carbines and separating her from the gossip of her neighbours.

The drill splayed its tripod legs and extruded its humming sonic component to cut into the ground.

A moan built up throughout the crowd.

'Desecration!' came the many-throated whisper.

'No,' cried the Russ officer. 'Not desecration – rather, manifestation!'

He stepped down from the platform and made his way towards the drilling rig.

'This world enriches you, good citizens, by providing crops and herds. But it carries other riches, riches that you spurn by not digging deeper. Let us show you how you may be enriched. Look at how the drill digs down, silent and complimentary. Is it any different from using a spade or a plough?'

Vann craned her neck to see what was happening. The soil was black and crumbly, a good loam like the rich *chernozem* of the Cossack homeland.

The old woman tugged at her elbow, a concerned look on her face: 'Come away, daughter. Your disguise won't save you if the Zem takes you.'

'The Zem?'

The cry of the Russ officer interrupted them. His amplified voice was immediately cut off, and another Russ voice spoke to calm the crowd.

Vann looked back at where the drill had raised a small mound of topsoil.

Already, the press of the crowd had pushed the Russ infantry back. Even with weapons at hand, the troops were too close to the citizens for crowd control.

Should've used hand-to-hand riot equipment.

Vann smiled grimly to herself. They had under-estimated the strength of feeling of the gathered townsfolk.

The ground rippled, and the rent in the surface widened. The drill lost its footing and fell forward, its sonic stream cutting through those nearest. Russ and locals went down in howls of agony as the drilling beam severed limbs with no distinction from its designated target. The rip in the earth widened even further, and the drill went down in its entirety, slaying several more members of the crowd as it fell.

The beam shot out beyond the crowd and started to cut a scar through the nearest buildings – and then it was cut off as it fell into the darkness beneath the soil.

For a moment, there was the jarred silence of horror, and then the crowd descended on the Russ. They tore the rifles from their hands and shot down the drones. Outnumbered dozens to one, the Russ went down like toy soldiers in a flood.

Vann dropped to her knees, hoping to avoid any stray energy blasts.

She wondered how the old woman had seen through her disguise. She had addressed her as 'daughter.' Did the locals have some sort of *psi* that allowed them to see deeper than exterior surfaces?

The crowd ran, but they weren't fleeing. An explosion from a few streets over told her that the Russ corvette was under attack.

Keeping her arms up to guard her head, she stayed where

she was as the crowd rushed past her, many exultant as they discharged the energy carbines into the air. Running knees buffeted her elbows, but her kit-suit buffers took care of most of the impacts, feeding the energy into her storage cells.

The corvette peeked over the tops of the nearby buildings as it rose, and the citizens took aim. It hadn't managed to power up its energy shields, and even the carbines were having an effect on the hull.

Within a minute, she was left alone in the forum plaza. Even the old woman had fled.

The hover-carrier wobbled a little as its source of power dwindled with the retreat of the corvette. Bodies were strewn all over the plaza, but nobody groaned in pain. Those killed by the drilling beam were dead from the merest touch of the sonic power, their bodily systems jangled by intercellular dissonance. The Russ officers lay sprawled in unseemly poses, their fine, bright uniforms speckled with dust and blood.

On her hands and knees, Vann scooted forward until she could view the pit gouged by the drill. A viscous liquid bubbled like borscht simmering on a stove, about a metre beneath the surface.

She had already activated her recording sensors, so she circled the vent, ducking from corpse to corpse. She pulled out some sample tubes and drew in some of the Russ blood, as well as several local samples. A gene-scan would prove interesting.

Then she began surveying the remains of the dead, Russ and locals alike. This was observation on a level she had never anticipated. She would need to capture as much of it as possible.

Retreating to the edge of the carnage, she stood up in a half-crouch, letting her sensors view the damage to the architecture. The walls of the tree trunks were half a metre thick, and formed a cavity wall structure. The centre filled with a black sap similar to the bubbling liquid under the soil.

She took out some canisters and inflated them to take a sample. The liquid recoiled at her advance, and it was only by using two canisters together that she was able to acquire a small quantity.

She did a quick check of the area to ensure her activities were not being viewed by any of the locals and was surprised to see that a length of the rift had started to break the topsoil of the packed earth. It was as if it was reaching out for her.

She had seen everything she needed. Running around the circumference of the plaza, she headed out towards the gate.

On her way, she got some footage of the mob over-running the landing zone of the corvette.

A hundred metres up in the air, the corvette yawed, unresponsive to its controls. Hhelff citizens had piled on the top of its hull and stabbed at it with their knives, swords, and axes.

It was perilous work even before the Russ marines exited from a port in their magnetic boots. They worked from both sides to snipe at the citizens.

Once they had their craft cleared, they would retaliate against the ground fire.

She needed to be out of here – and soon.

An energy discharge blew up chunks of dirt and stone at her feet. She whirled and saw a Russ officer with several dead citizens around him. They were cut to pieces by his energy carbine.

His blast had not been aimed at her, but had cut down the last of the citizenry surrounding him.

Then his eyes fixed on her.

The muzzle of the carbine rose.

She had no corners to hide behind because of the rounded walls of the tree trunks, but she dodged out of sight behind the nearest wall, and another blast of energy flew past where she had been only seconds before.

She tugged out her sword, but knew it would be no defence against his carbine.

Her left hand went to her belly, palm against the *khysky*-centre where her reservoir of *psi* power originated.

She could sense the soldier's life-force approaching. Not rushing, but circling the building.

She reached out through her psi paths and sent out a gut-wrench to him.

She heard him grunt with pain, and then she was around the building.

He staggered from the gut-wrench, his carbine lowered, his eyes runnelled with tears of agony.

As he saw her coming, he tried to raise his weapon.

'You Cossack bitch - what are you doing here—'

Her clumsy sword swung down and took his head off, shako and comms-unit making it roll like a spin-ball.

The head rolled towards her, and she psi-wrenched at the electronics embedded in the shako. They might have glimpsed her on his own cam-footage, but the Russ used high definition recordings which needed to buffer for a few seconds before disseminating to the corvette or even to the warship up in orbit. She stopped the head with her foot and smashed her booted heel down to make sure that nothing was left to record.

Only then did the body complete its fall.

She raced towards it and jerked the carbine from his senseless fingers.

Russ-tech was always keyed to the bio-signature of its assigned user, but she thought the sight of it in her hands might dissuade locals from challenging her. And the fingertips of her kit-suit could start to break its code. She might get lucky and get the use of the weapon.

When she turned to resume her flight, the snaking rift in the ground had almost caught up with her.

It was only a few inches wide, but since she didn't know what lay beneath the surface, she gave it a wide berth and a high leap.

Then she was running, running, full pelt towards the gate.

The voices of locals challenged her, but she gave them no heed.

She cleared the gate and came to a halt.

The old woman faced her, holding a bent walking stick for support.

A few locals ran past, but they ignored Vann. Only the old dame took any notice of her.

'Daughter, you can't run from Zem.'

'What do you mean? Why do you call me "daughter?"'

'I see with the eyes of Zem. Zem sees all.'

'Who is Zem?'

The old woman tapped her stick, and the earth cracked around Vann like an ice floe on a frozen lake. The fissure was only a few centimetres wide. Vann could leap free, so long as it didn't grow.

'Zem is the world. Zem is our life, our goddess, our mother, our provider.'

The crack widened, although Vann wasn't sure if it was because her 'earth floe' was growing smaller, or the surrounding land was crumbling. The gap was only half a metre by now - easily fordable.

The old woman went on chanting. 'Zem is the womb that gives birth to us. Zem is the tomb that takes us into the Afterlife. Zem-she is all. Zem-she is everything.'

Vann risked another glance to the ground. The black, viscous soup bubbled up around her.

'I'm - I'm not sure I want to go down into the ground - into the - into the Zem?'

The old woman smiled, radiant in her fervent belief. 'One does not ask a queen to come to visit you. You must seek an audience with royalty.'

'I'm only a soldier, a mere agent. What you need - what Zem needs is a diplomat. Someone in authority - way over my pay grade. Someone who can make decisions and discuss terms with - with Zem.'

The old woman chuckled. 'One does not decide for Zem-she. One does not discuss with Zem-she. You have presented yourself at her gates. You have emboldened yourself to walk her skin. Zem would have words with you.'

The ground quivered beneath Vann's feet. A huge bubble was forming around the little island on which she stood.

It was now or never.

She jumped, clawing her way through the air.

No pause. She landed running.

Behind her, the old woman called, 'Run, run, until you fall short of breath. Zem shall have words with you.'

As she ran, her rear sensors showed that the crack in the surface had ceased to follow her. But of course, that meant nothing.

Everywhere was surface. Even in the town, the streets had been pretty much naked soil. Packed down with foot traffic, but still an open access to the - the Zem. That was why the Russ had thought they could drill right in the town plaza and demonstrate to the townsfolk.

The ground rumbled. It went on for so long, the shrubs and bushes were shaken free of their hold on the soil. A hill appeared before her that hadn't been there before, and its incline carried her above the treeline.

Off to her left, the Russ corvette ploughed grimly skyward, limping slowly. Then, to Vann's horror, a black spout of land rose up several *versts* to the left.

She was too busy running to spare the breath for the exclamation building in her chest.

With a subterranean roar, the land opened, and a hot,

volcanic plume of liquid rock spat up into the air. It was enough to encompass the corvette, which fell like a stone from the midst of its trajectory.

It wasn't lava. It wasn't molten rock. It was more of the saplike liquid bubbling beneath the surface of Bianna. Except, this projectile had been directed by a mind. The planet itself had - volition. A sentience of some sort. A tendril of knowledge grew in her gut. Her *khysky*-centre trembled, unused to energy coming in as insight.

She reached the brow of the new hill and looked down the escarpment beyond. There was her one-man vessel, her Cossack *baidak*. It lay exposed for all the world to see, the surface around it crazed with cracks. None of the cracks were very wide, but it was almost a humorous touch. As if it asked her, *do you like to walk on broken ice?*

With her proximity to her *baidak*, she raised her comms-link and hailed Derkach in his low orbit just beyond the atmosphere.

Harsh static sounded in her ear - so fierce she tore her kit-suit from off the back of her head.

Through the interference, a familiar voice could be heard. '—calling Helianthus, come in, please. Over.'

Helianthus was the flower of the Cossack nation.

'Helianthus here." She already knew the answer, but protocol had to be followed. 'Who goes there? Over.'

'Tryzub, here. Are you requesting pick up? Over.'

As she'd surmised, it was *scientznik* Derkach on the other end. His call sign meant "trident," but at that moment, it might as well have meant salvation.

'I can see my *baidak*, but cannot approach. Can you fix on me? Over.'

'Got a fix. RV at your fix in five minutes. Non-landing. Get ready to haul your skinny butt outta there. Over.'

Before Vann could reply, a roar came from nearby. A bear-sized creature stalked out of the foliage. It was furred, but might once have been reptilian, and had moose-like antlers on its brow. It roared and pawed the earth with its forepaws

35

before rising up on its hind legs and clawing at the air.

Vann touched her *khysky*-centre. The thing was too massive for a mere gut-wrench. She dug deep and aimed a mind-blast at whatever would pass for its brain.

The creature gave an uncertain and high-pitched *Huh?* and then sat back on its haunches. It pawed at its eyes, trying to view its exterior world and finding only darkness.

Vann hoped it was cross-wired enough to lose its sense of smell. If it was anything like the extinct terrestrial bears, it would have no trouble following her scent.

She spat out another *psi*-attack, hoping for it to lose its balance.

The strongest tremors yet vibrated through her feet.

The volcanic spout, some *versts* away, shot off a fiery plume of rock and soil, trailing clouds of pyroclastic toxicity.

The force of the blast sent her flying to the ground, almost within reach of the bear-creature. It mewled like a sickly cub, looking very unhappy with its present circumstances, then wandered off in pitiful retreat

'Helianthus. I'm losing stick. Some sort of electro-magnetic turbulence from that benthic discharge. Lost stick, repeat, lost stick. You are on your—'

The static blasted itself to silence in her earbud.

She rolled over onto her back, supporting herself on her elbows, too awed to worry about her own survival.

The plume of the volcanic projectile soared up and up. She switched to the distance setting in her goggles, or she would lose track of it. The read-outs told her that it was leaving the atmosphere.

'It can't be - it can't be,' she babbled.

But it was. The volcanic plume shot up into space and targeted the Russ warship.

And hiding in the Russ warship's radar shadow, would be her own Cossack frigate.

36

Would energy shields hold against an attack of such planetary-class magnitude?

A dwarf planet, she reminded herself ruefully. But one that punched well above its weight.

The collision lit up the sky with nuclear fire. She'd seen it too many times to fool herself into believing otherwise.

She rose, buoyed by a sense of dream-like disbelief.

Behind her, the old woman's cane tap-tap-tapped.

Another creature lurched out of the forest. This was another bear-sized beast, but it had a pointed snout, almost invisible eyes, and black, very fine hair. It held out its shovel-like paws palms-out from its gigantic, barrel torso.

'I see you handled Morda Snout very well. Kindly, without damaging him too much. You won't try the same with Kopatch.'

'I think my ship is destroyed.' Vann heard her own words, but hardly believed them.

'Nay, daughter. It is safe. Damaged, but safe. It will have to land and make repairs, but you are welcome to join us.' She tapped her stick. 'But, first, you must meet Zem-she.'

Vann gulped the bile rising in her throat. 'I can't go - go under. I'm claustrophobic. I can't stand the darkness, the dark waters, the depths.'

The thing called Kopatch bent and picked up Vann, holding her in its brawny embrace as if she were an infant.

Vann struggled, helpless, as it waddled down the steep escarpment towards her *baidak*, slipping and sliding on its padded rump to fetch up beside her vessel.

It set her down and pointed towards her hatch. Numbly, Vann opened it and stepped inside, then closed it and dogged it secure behind her. She flicked on her sensor screens and saw that Kopatch had drawn a net of vegetation around the fuselage of her *baidak*.

The cracks that upheld her vessel on the surface separated, and her *baidak* sank. There was nothing to see down here, the liquid as dark as espresso.

One oddity appeared on her view screens. Her personnel file popped up, even though a lowly vessel such as a *baidak* didn't possess the access codes. Shouldn't, rather.

Despite her situation, she couldn't help from keeping half an eye on the screen and also what was happening outside her vessel. Still, nothing to see apart from the primal darkness.

As her personnel file ended, it was replaced with a star chart showing her home colony of Dnieper. An animation program began. It panned through the known worlds of the various human space-clans until it reached the planet known as Bianna.

It was depicted as a circle with a radius of ripples pulsing out Every so often and at uncertain rates, Bianna generated a single particle, which shot off into the surrounding universe. The animation ran for a minute or two, and then began running from the start.

By the time it had cycled through half a dozen times, she had figured out the timeline of the piece. A particle shot out every few years or so. She couldn't pin it down to anything more accurate than that. Once she realized the significance of the particle, she froze the program at the point where it intersected her home colony.

The timer registered as the year of her conception.

Her *khysky*-centre clenched at the thought.

Her instruments told her that she was descending at a slow rate. When she reached the thousand kilometre depth, her screens cleared, and a golden light spilled in. Kopatch was there, hauling her down with flipper-like sweeps of his huge paws.

Inside, she was a roiling sea of thoughts and emotions. Outside her vessel, the gentle flow of golden waters spilled bliss onto the skin of her kit-suit.

There were other creatures in the ambient aura, slender as otters, nimble as squirrels. Something flashed by with lynx eyes and tufted ears. A bison-like creature butted the foremost screen with its horny brow. Vann gave a yelp of fright at that, but she found herself smiling in realization, recognizing where she was.

In her mind she drew a diagram of the dwarf planet's cross-section. A thin skin of topsoil, below which was perhaps a hundred klicks of the liquid, then a new substratum of the golden buoyancy, a living biome. She scanned her console and configured the sensory array to divine further into the depths.

She saw her first humanoid. A broad-chested man, with no clothes and no shame; he was bearded and brawny, and he walked on what appeared to be a fragment of surface, as if a sphere had been broken into shards, each shard several hectares in area.

Her sensors picked up the geology she had been searching for: R-61. This was the mineral the Russ wanted to mine. And, of course, her own nation would be very much interested in exploring its unique properties.

As she sank past the shards of the spheres where the humanoids dwelt in unadulterated, bucolic pleasure, she wondered how you ask a person to be exploited and broken up into industrial uses to feed a war machine.

Below her, R-61 smiled. Inhuman, unhuman, but cognizant of a fellow form of intelligence.

Vann held her face in a mask of her fingers, peering out, afraid to see what lay below and beyond.

To give herself some distraction from the events outside, and the emotional events inside, she tried to work out the controls of the animation program. It took her a few minutes, but she was able to return to Bianna and log the number of particles that were shot out and entered Clan-space.

Going back to her own birth and beyond, she decided that there were eleven other events where a particle intercepted a colony world. Two of them were in the Russ Empire; another three were in Cossack space. The remaining six were in individual conclaves that registered no authority.

No wonder psi *was so rare.*

The Russ Empire numbered a billion citizens. Cossack space was something in the region of 700k. The others were insignificant, little more than footnotes in the current *realpolitik*.

Her sensors told her that she had reached the centre of Bianna, if indeed it even had a centre. Gravity held it stationary, and her sensors picked up a blip that had to be the Russ corvette.

To judge the timbre of her own voice, she spoke aloud. 'What are the chances that there is a Russ *psi* operative on that vessel?' Her voice sounded remarkably steady in her own ears.

She hadn't passed any signs of life forms for some time now. She wondered if she was expected to disembark.

For something to do - anything, really - she packed herself into a heavy atmosphere suit, one that could take hard radiation if necessary. Her readings told her that she was surrounded by liquid, but other than that, it couldn't process any answers.

She stepped into the airlock, and the oxygen recyclers flushed it free of atmosphere. Her craft lurched a little as it began to take on board the heavier-than-air fluid from the outside. As the level of the liquid crawled up her helmet's visor, the claustrophobia she had first experienced on looking into the cracks around her *baidak* returned.

She set her left hand on her *khysky*-centre and drew strength of will from it. She had always felt that she was connected to the universe through her *khysky*-centre, like a psychic umbilical cord, but never more so than this particular moment.

The term "more so" reminded her of Poe's Raven, who was known to quoth Nevermore. It made her smile. She felt as if she was entering literature, legend, primal time, and primal existence.

The hull doors popped their seals, and bubbles of air

floated free. She hooked her lifeline to the outer hull and ploughed her way through the water.

No, not water. Some other fluid as basic as water. Perhaps a fluid isotope of R-61.

As if she walked along a syncline of fluidic pressures, she found herself gradually approaching the fallen corvette. It had blast marks and scorch marks where the locals had given it a good going over, but it was quite airworthy. Whether it was spaceworthy was another matter.

Overhead, she saw another vessel drifting down and powerless. She recognized Derkach's vessel. At least, he had made it safely down. Not quite, however, the three-point landing he prided himself on.

The corvette's airlock was open. But there was no sign of a lifeline anchored to the hull.

She entered the airlock and attached her lifeline to the outside, then braced herself on the inside. The Russ alphabet was the same as that used by the Cossack nation, so she had no trouble deciphering the operating instructions.

The recycling action was noisier than her own. She put that down to the size of the vessel.

The inner door unsealed itself, and she found herself in a breathable atmosphere. Three Russ marines in full armour with personal poke-blasters stood outside. One waved the muzzle of his blaster, and she responded by removing her helmet.

Her eyes followed the wet footprints leading across the deck. 'I see I am not the first to arrive.'

'This way,' replied the marine in a thick, outlander accent.

She was familiar with the specs of Russ vessels and recognized that she was being escorted to the bridge. There, in the most spacious area on board, she found the commander of the vessel, two more marines, and the old woman from the surface. For some reason, Vann was not surprised.

She saluted the commander and gave out her name, rank,

and serial number.

'Commander Blick,' she responded, 'in command of Russ Corvette *Don*. I can't exactly say that you are welcome, but - you are here.'

As Vann looked around, she was aware of some sort of *psi*-tickle. Her *khysky*-centre was trying to tell her something. She looked at the old woman. 'I heard you addressed as Zem-mother, when we were in the square.'

The old woman's fierce gaze locked hers and held it. A series of images flashed through Vann's imagination: the old woman as a young girl being filled with some sort of *psi*-energy and being used as a mouthpiece for planetary consciousness.

The Russ commander narrowed her eyes. 'Stop that, you two. You are both on board *my* vessel. That makes you both under *my* command.'

A spray of sparks flashed up from a nearby console, and one of the screens went blank, only to be filled up with a particulate version of the old woman's face. The image was formed from words that spelled "Zem."

'Do you really think you are in charge here, woman?' rasped the old woman, and she tapped her cane on the deck

The rap had no great force, but a thin spray of fluid sprang up as high as Vann's knee.

The marines raised their poke-blasters, but before they could squeeze the triggers, more fluid shot out from their muzzles, adding its volume to the rest of the fluid on the deck.

'Stop that!' commanded the commander.

'Only if you will acknowledge that you are no longer commander of this vessel,' rapped the old woman. 'You are in the presence of Zem-she. What does your species normally do when in the presence of a higher power?'

Vann dropped to her knees so suddenly that the marines turned their blasters to her and drenched her in the fluid. It tasted salty and strong, and she felt a surge of *psi* from it.

Instead of feeling humiliation, she felt empowered. She smiled up at the commander.

'If I were you, I would feel a little humility.'

The commander's eyes blazed at Vann as she reluctantly knelt, gesturing for the marines to join her.

When all were kneeling, the old woman took herself to the commander's chair. The fluid ceased to squirt from the blasters and the hole in the deck. There was, however, a puddle of it, rolling around to find its own gravity sink.

The old woman glanced at the control console on the arm of the chair, admiring it. She punched in a series of buttons, and the screens around them all changed to show what appeared to be a holding cell.

A battered man was on his knees, shackled by magnetic holders. Vann immediately recognized him as a fellow *psi*-wielder. His head hung heavily, and only the shackles holding his arms kept the weary man from slumping on the deck.

Vann's words were torn from her. 'What have you done with him?'

The commander smirked. 'Unlike your Cossack pagan, rabble-like response to *psi*-wielders, we of the Russ know how to employ them to the empire's best advantage.'

Vann nodded as realization settled on her like a dark dew of despair. 'That's why your Empire is so keen to access R-61. You know of its link to *psi*-activation.'

The commander spat, her eyes blazing. 'It's not activation, you Cossack whore. It's an infestation. It's a psychic parasite. It's a genetic cuckoo in our midst.'

The old woman sighed, her hands clasped on top of her cane. 'Have the prisoner brought here. He is a member of my family, and I will not - Zem shall not - permit you to abuse him any further.'

The commander tossed her hair. 'You can have him. He's a burn-out now. You're welcome to him. The Empire knows

43

your location. Do you really think your little thought bubbles can win over hard technology?'

On the screen, the shackles dropped from the man's arms. He didn't fall to the deck, but was raised up by invisible hands and gently propelled to the hatch of the holding cell. A small puff of sparks and smoke registered the lock's ineffectiveness. He floated on through, face downward, for all the world like the corpse of a drowned man. The screens showed his progress to the bridge.

The commander shot to her feet. She pulled out her sidearm and aimed it at the old woman. 'Die, you alien bitch!' She snapped off several projectile rounds.

The slugs whistled through the air until they were only a hand's breadth away, then they stopped with an audible screech. They floated over the old woman's head like a halo.

The marines jumped to their feet, blasters levelled, but a wave of *psi* energy slammed them to their backs. They went under the fluid, where the air bubbles from their gaping mouths broke in a frenzy.

The hole in the deck opened up again, and the stream of fluid found its way into the commander's mouth. She gagged and dropped her pistol, raising her hands to fend off the gentle assault of the fluid.

Like an hourglass filling up with sands, the commander found herself succumbing to the relentless fluid. She coughed and hacked, and twisted and turned, but the liquid followed her around, always aimed at her mouth. The fluid flowed into the bridge, and soon reached the old woman's knees.

While the commander struggled, a hatch hissed open, and the prisoner came floating in, still unconscious, still borne by the invisible and mysterious psi forces.

'She's drowning!' exploded Vann. 'You can't just let her drown!'

The old woman was imperturbable. 'Yes. She is drowning. Just as a baby drowns when it leaves the waters of its mother's womb.'

The fluid continued to rise, and the prisoner was laid gently on the surface of the fluid and permitted to lie there - as drowned as any corpse she had ever witnessed.

'Is this what you've come down here for?' she asked the old woman. 'To drown us all like rats?'

The old woman leaned forward in her seat, her hands clenched on the top of her cane. 'What do you think it would do to the Russ Empire, if one of their war vessels returned with a complete complement of crew - but every one of them psi-empowered?'

Vann couldn't formulate her thoughts enough to reply.

But the old woman hadn't finished. 'Oh, I don't mean a mere corvette, I mean the *Castor* up above the atmosphere.'

'But, it's destroyed, isn't it?'

'Is it? You saw the nuclear explosions, but their force didn't get through the Zem-force that Bianna sent up. They were planning on sacrificing their corvette - crew and all - and making a clean escape.'

'And, what about my vessel?'

'It's safe, too. Although at present, it is fleeing out of the system like a dog with its tail between its legs.'

The commander had sunk beneath the surface of the fluid. It was up to Vann's breasts by now. The commander had ceased to thrash; as had the marines.

The old woman rose and waded over to the prisoner. She turned him over in the liquid, and he coughed as his face came up.

His face was bruised and covered with random tics of muscle responses, the usual after-effects of enhanced interrogation. It was as if his face was trying to tear itself off the front of his skull.

Vann looked away, trying not to feel horror. She wasn't

sure what to feel horror over - the torture dealt out to this unknown Russ, or the fact that an order was given, and a soldier followed that order and carried on with the procedure.

The metaphor of childbirth suddenly made sense to Vann; the marines were being reborn. This liquid was some sort of *psi*-matrix. It was a planet when it was a planetary mass; it could be the dark matter beneath the surface; it could also be the golden glowing liquid at the heart of the planet.

Dwarf planet, she reminded herself with a surly grimace.

The screens on the wall showed various decks of the corvette, all filling up with the psychoactive fluid. Crew members battered at hatches that refused to open, then turned to face the oncoming tide that would flood their lungs and change them utterly.

Of course, they wouldn't know that yet, but once they awoke into an enhanced new sensorium, with *psi* popping in their synapses like fireworks - oh, they would know.

They would know.

And so would the Russ Empire, once the corvette docked on the *Castor*. No, not then, she judged. When it reached its command post, back in Russ space.

It would be like driving a wedge through the conservative power structures of the Empire. All the priests and patriarchs of the Orthodox church would be impassioned over such an uncanny outbreak of *psi*. It would be a plague of their worst nightmares.

Vann still had her helmet under one arm. Keeping her eyes fixed on the old woman she brought it down and filled it with the *psi*-fluid. Then, she brought it up to her mouth and drank deeply.

The old woman smiled, as grand as any empress, and sat back in her chair.

About TJ O'Hare

TJ O'Hare writes short stories, novels, song lyrics, poetry, plays and film scripts. He co-writes with many musical collaborators, including: Úna Clarkin, Stephen Dunwoody, John Lindsay, Edelle McMahon, Ronan McSorley, Brigid O'Neill, and Alan Patterson; all of which have their music available on all the usual platforms. His plays have been staged in Ireland and Belgium. He also has a book of poetry, under his own name of Jim Johnston: *Available Light*: https://sites.google.com/a/lapwingpublications.com/lapwing-store/jim-johnston

His latest musical adventure is under the collective name of J'mok. Check out J'mok on FaceBook, and listen to and support his latest release: *Adam Kadmon*.

He is married to Jean and has two grown-up sons. He lives in the North of Ireland.

Steel-blue Babe

by Aaron Isett

You've heard of Paul. We all have. He's a legend.

Before that, he was a tall tale.

But first, he was a man.

He grew into something more, not out of a war, like so many, or a disaster, like others, but as a result of his own hard work and his good heart.

Paul, to no one's surprise, grew up big and strong. His father, John Bunyan, was a giant of a man, and his mother, though he never knew her, had been just as formidable. Paul was John's only son, and he was proud of him, but worked him hard. You might think that the family had always been in lumber, but you'd be wrong. No, they were farmers. The story goes that they had a farm out in the Midwest. Not sure where. It was fertile land, but still hard work. Weather and varmints always gave them something to reckon with. Their ox gave them one major advantage. Blue, the Bunyans called him, for the way

49

his black coat caught the sunshine. Whether Blue was plowing the fields, hauling felled trees for fence posts, or being put out to stud for a neighbor's cow, Blue made their lives a little easier.

Blue and Paul grew up together. His father had made him responsible for the calf, and Paul had played with him, almost like he was a dog. John used to laugh and tell Paul he had to tend to his "babe." They wrestled together every day, Paul tossing him over their paddock fence every night, just for the fun of it. John shook his head at this, sometimes, but he knew that the boy had life hard and let it be.

Things continued like this for a long time, until Paul was getting to that age. You know the one. When young men start wondering if there's anything more out there for them, if the life they were born to is the best that they can hope for.

"Paul, I know. You want to go out on your own," I imagine John told him, still big, but no longer towering over his son like the mountain he used to be. "But I can't work the farm with just Blue and me. Once we get this year's harvest in, I'll be able to hire a hand or two, and you can try your hand with that carpenter, or at the lumber camp you were talking about."

I'm sure there was some grumbling, but Paul was a good boy by nature, and he knew his father was right. One harvest turned into two, then three, Paul's impatience growing. Then—maybe it was God or fate, or just bad luck—they ended up needing the extra hands, anyway.

Paul and Blue were coming back from the woods, hauling a log. Blue was straining at the yoke with Paul pushing because he didn't let others do work for him with no help. Then, there was a horrible snap, and Blue let out a scream that must have been the worst sound Paul had ever heard. There was a gopher hole that Blue hadn't seen until it was too late. One of the big ox's feet had found it instead, and the slip unbalanced him. His leg snapped in the worst way it could have. There was no fixing it, and Paul was inconsolable.

50

I can't imagine how Paul felt, his only constant companion lying there in pain, knowing that the only kind thing he could do was end it for him. Did he pray? Did he cry? No one knows, and Paul ain't telling. But I'm sure he'd remember it for the rest of his days. Blue was like family. Of course, he and his father had both hunted to put meat on the table, but this was the first time death had really touched him. You never really forget that.

After that, his father hired on a few local boys who knew how to work hard and told Paul that he wanted him to see more than the farm. "You deserve it," he told him. "Being such a good son all these years." And that was that.

Paul, I'm sure, took one long look back at the farm, then went off to see the world, or at least a piece of it.

Well, when Paul reached the camp he was as much a wonder to the lumbermen as they were to him. He had his own axe and a tool kit, presents from his father. The lumberjacks there, strong, lean, and tough to a man, had never seen such a man as Paul. Any space he was in seemed smaller for his presence. Of course, some of these jacks felt less than charitable toward the fresh-faced farm boy.

One story goes that one such fellow, Sam Mont-Blanc, head of a crew, told Paul that he was on "tote duty." He explained that it was Paul's job to get the logs from where they were felled to the trail down the mountain. I doubt I have to tell you that there's no such thing as "tote duty." Now, Paul was a lot of things, but inexperienced was one of them.

The problem with Sam's plan was that Paul did it anyway. Carrying, rolling, or dragging, Paul kept up the pace and spent the day getting the logs to the trail. He was huffing and puffing, sore and sweaty, by the end of the day.

When Paul got back after the last haul, the crew about busted their guts laughing at the look on Sam's face. They say you coulda tossed a bullfrog down his throat without hitting his teeth, his mouth was so wide. When the camp boss found out about it, he bawled the foreman out for wasting a strong back like that on a prank, and Paul got a reputation for being the strongest man in camp. He never let it get to his head, though.

Not everything went smoothly for Paul. There were nights when, sitting in his bunk or around the fire, he was powerful homesick. No one at the lumber camp had known him growing up, and he missed the friends he used to fish and hunt with. He missed his father, and he missed Blue. He got some ribbing about it, being a kid away from home for the first time, but it was only natural. The real trouble came later.

The tongue-lashing that the foreman had gotten for pranking Paul didn't sit well with him. He decided that he would take Paul down a peg. Now, he knew Paul was strong, but he figured that the lad had used some trick to move those logs. He thought Paul had gotten help, or maybe that he had used a lever and just rolled them downhill to minimize the work.

Well, that was when he decided that he would challenge Paul to a wrestling match. Lumber camps, being full of men with lots of muscle (and often not a lot of sense), always had some kind of contest going on, whether it was games of chance, skill, or strength. Sometimes, they would set up a target to throw knives, hatchets, or axes for a prize or a bet. Oftentimes, there would be gambling (though the bosses always kept a weather eye on that). And then sometimes, they would have boxing or wrestling matches. These were friendly affairs for the most part, but not always. The jacks around the camp knew that Sam had it out for Paul. Paul, good-natured fellow that he was, probably assumed that it was just a rite of initiation.

One evening after another hard day's work, the jacks made a ring for the two men. The rules were simple: no shirts or shoes, no punching, biting, or eye-gouging. The first to force his opponent to touch the ground with any part above the waist would gain a fall, and the first to three falls won.

I'm sure that Sam cut an impressive figure. He didn't get to lead a group of lumbermen without hard work and skill, and he was well known as a wrestler of some skill. When Paul stepped into the ring, though, it was like a bear and a mountain had a child and named it Paul. His father had always taught him that he shouldn't hurt others, and he wasn't sure about this match. The first round, Sam rushed him, being fast for his size, and well practiced. He had bulled Paul onto his back in a moment. Now, he might have done okay if he hadn't gotten mean. But see, when Paul was getting up, Sam stomped on his hand. That was a mistake.

The second round started much the same, Sam rushing in, hoping to overwhelm Paul with speed. They were both already breathing hard, and Sam probably figured he had the younger, less experienced man licked. When he grappled with Paul's arms, however, he found that Paul didn't move. Not an inch. Sam reached down and wrapped the younger man in a powerful bear hug, straining to lift Paul into the air. Paul still refused to budge, digging his heels in and popping the hold loose, stubborn as a mule and stronger by a country mile. Instead, Paul grabbed Sam by both arms and tossed him as far back over his head as he could. And just like Paul was tossing Blue over the paddock fence (but a lot less gently), Sam flew a good distance and landed on his back, hard.

Some say he flew over the ring of men. I don't know about that, but I do know that Sam got some sense knocked into him. After he got his breath back, he walked back to the ring, apologized, and shook Paul's big mitt.

One day, after a long day of work and big supper (feeding Paul was probably the biggest expense the camp had to pay), he met George, the camp mechanic. Now, diesel engines were pretty new. But they had a truck for supply trips into town, and it had to be maintained. Paul was fascinated when he found out how much work these engines could do. It was there in the north woods where Paul found his love for machines. The next season, flush with pay and bonuses, Paul went with George to the machine shop in town.

With George's recommendation, and probably because he looked like a mountain come down to ask for a job, the shop took them both on. This wasn't a matter of him living in town all the time. He helped them haul parts, make new ones, adjust fittings, and other things I don't rightly understand too well. What you need to know is that he learned about machines and engines.

Paul still worked in the lumber camp in most seasons and grew from a fresh-faced kid into a burly, bearded man with a three-by-nine grin and a booming laugh that shook the trees. He was good-natured, was Paul. He still had a temper when roused, though it was rare. He learned a lot over the seasons, but not all the lessons came easy.

One afternoon, a lumber crew was using the truck to haul logs into town across the low shoulder of the mountain. It was a pretty regular run, as the town was booming. (After all, the lumberjacks needed somewhere to spend their money). They had a decent trail blazed and had even thrown some sand down in parts for traction. On the way, I'm sure, the boys were laughing it up, having a great time, talking about how they would spend their money. Then, a freak storm blew in. It was a real toad strangler, spilling water fit to drown a fish. The truck started struggling to get over the steepest part of the hill, tires spinning and slewing back and forth. Then, it got stuck. Well, these fellas, they were men of action. The hopped out, I hear, boots squishing in the mud, putting their shoulders to it, to get it over the top.

It slid at first. Then, they thought it was catching. But the truck was one of them early jobs, and the tires didn't bite. The weight of the logs dragged the back down, and the whole thing flipped. It came down on top of the ones pushing it, and the fellow in the driver's seat smashed his head on the roof. It was him and one other logger who made it to town, limping and cursing the whole way. Every other man on that crew died that day.

Paul was on the crew tasked with getting the truck and trailer out of the mud and the rest of the way to town. No man in that bunch will tell you that he wept for his friends, but it's said that his face was drenched in sweat, he worked so hard to finish the task that had killed them.

That day changed Paul. He was always a hard worker, but it seemed like he was driven harder, like a stoked fire. He did little but eat, work, and sleep. He spent a tremendous amount of time in the machine shop, and it was rumored that he was building something special. There was noise from the shop at all hours, and Paul became less and less gregarious as time went on.

The next time that they needed to run logs to town, he insisted that he be on the crew. He drove the truck, and the whole way, he was critiquing the way the thing worked. "The tires only get traction in good weather, and the drive should be from all four wheels, if it has to be wheeled at all." The mechanic in the passenger seat argued that it was one of the latest designs from the East Coast. This failed to satisfy Paul, and he made that clear. The trip to and from town passed without incident. Everyone thought that he was just worrying too much.

Winter that year showed up with a vengeance. The first snow swamped the lumber camp, and Paul was at the machine shop in town. Days snowed-in stretched to a week, then two. Folks in town were worried about the farmers who lived further out, and supplies at Grant's General Goods were running low. Everyone had started dipping into their stores early. Paul, however, was worried about the lumber camp. The jacks up there weren't laid in for a long stint in the snow, and had expected leave in the next week or two, but for the storm.

When he told the mayor and some of the other prominent citizens this, including Mr. Grant, they just shrugged. "Nothing we can do, Paul. We probably would get stuck just trying to get there, let alone back to town." Paul narrowed his eyes, and the crowd there shrank back, not knowing how they could stop him if he got violent. But Paul, he just stalked away without a word.

What happened next is how legends are born.

A few minutes later, a low growl reverberated through the town, bouncing off the facades of the Main Street shops and buildings. The noise slowly mounted to a roar, and then subsided to a constant rumbling like thunder. Then, with a series of clanks, the strangest, most beautiful vehicle any of them had ever seen rolled out onto the street. It was like a truck, but not like one any of them had ever encountered. There were wheels in front, but the back had a pair of belts surrounding more wheels (which he later called "tracks"). They had ridges that caught snow or dirt, and dug in like nothing else could.

Looking at it was like seeing a brand new kind of beast. It was blued steel, gleaming just like Blue's hide had. He had even etched an ox-head design into the front. But painted on the side was one big word: BABE.

Well, no one could follow it, but the men in the logging camp heard it coming long before it arrived and had all turned out to see what was happening. When they saw Babe burst through the trees, Paul in the driver's seat and grinning from ear to ear, they thought it was the most beautiful thing they had ever seen. The camp boss (who knew exactly how low the supplies were), told Paul that his big blue ox had been the saving of them all. Their truck would barely run, let alone make it down the mountain.

Paul saved the whole camp that day, and none of them ever forgot it.

He was just a man.

The tale grew taller in the telling.

That is how a legend is born.

About Aaron Isett

Aaron was born in Columbus, Ohio. Understandably, he has been exploring fantastical realms his whole life. When he can't find one made to suit, he writes his own. Previously published in *The Queen Of Clocks And Other Steampunk Tales*, he can be found on Instagram @aaron.isett.

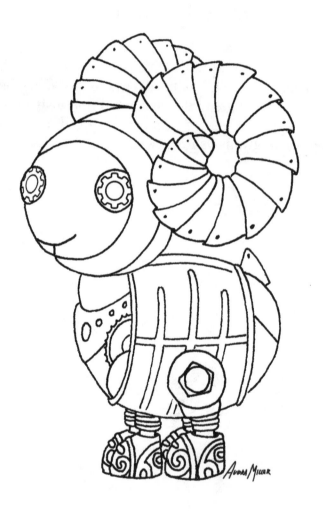

The Sharp Mechanical Sheep

by Kay Gray

The queen had been beloved by her people.

She would be missed by more than just Morag. Miss MacDonald, her nursemaid and oldest friend, walked beside her at her mother's funeral. The bells tolled in the distance, the only sounds in the streets other than the slow marching of feet and the occasional sob. A crowd of mourners dressed in black, veils covering their faces and hats in hand, came from the castle and surrounding village to follow the casket. The decorated cart was pulled by shiny, brass wind-up horses as they clopped down the cobblestone lane.

The king followed the procession in his steam-carriage, attended by his personal guard. He sat motionless, a stone in grey and gold, facing the casket. Morag had turned down riding beside him. She'd preferred walking in the crowd. Everyone would be asking after her for weeks to come. She didn't want the attention, especially now.

When it was over and the townspeople departed, Morag escaped her maid and the guard, ignoring their protests over her going off alone again. She went to the only place in the kingdom where she found peace, a wide, open space where the mechanical animals used around the village were housed: the Yard.

Officially, it was the Shepherd's Royal Livery and Open Yard, but even Shepherd didn't bother using the full title. There was a workshop, a small mill, and the stables. A good portion was shaded from weather and moisture, but a large part was open land. It stretched for acres into green hills. There was no real reason to keep a wall, except around the barns and stables where the work animals stayed at night. The living animals were housed by their owners, but these mechanical ones belonged to the village, generally, and to the king, ultimately. Morag had sat in the Yard many an afternoon, dreaming of fantastical adventures and daring escapes for hours. Today, amid the grey skies and waving grasses, she wept.

A few weeks later, her father called the denizens of the castle to the manicured garden in the middle of the castle grounds. When she heard the call, Morag's heart sank. He had been distracted; she knew something must have been coming. The king was always aloof and distant, but he'd started spending long days away from the castle. His mourning period had ended before anyone else's, to the quiet scandal of the entire household, but Morag's maid said he simply had to be strong for his people. He had to show his strength by moving on. Morag hadn't believed her.

Now, her father stood in the gazebo at the center of the garden, dressed in all his finery. A tall, hawkish woman in an equally ostentatious dress held his hand. She looked out over the gathering crowd, poised over her prey. Two younger women stood demurely behind them. They wore similar opulent outfits, but didn't shine nearly as bright as the king and his new woman. All the castle servants, cooks, and butlers gathered in the yard, with Morag keeping near the back. The King held up his hands quieting the crowd.

"I'm sure it's quite clear already why I've gathered you here. Before we make the official announcement, I thought you all should be aware. This kingdom will never be the same without my dear Queen Isabeau, but it will also never move forward while we still mourn her passing. So it is with both a heavy heart that I must move on, and with a joyous outlook that I announce my marriage to Baroness—"

Morag didn't hear the rest. She was off and running, out of the gardens, down the hill. Through the village, the small forest that lay between, and to the Yard she went. She didn't stop until she was well past the mills and stables, out in the rolling green hills. Around her, mechanical animals stood or walked about, their stiff legs pushing through the tall grass. Wind-up horses for riding and strong steel oxen for pulling wandered among a few wind-powered geese and sheep, their mowers tucked in while they weren't working. Morag ignored them all and collapsed to the ground, head in her hands.

She didn't cry. She'd run out of tears. A few of the animals gave the living creature a wide berth. Some hesitantly walked up to her, tilting their heads and squeaking noises from built-in speakers. One brave sheep, a ram by design, waddled, stiff-legged, right up to her. Morag looked up, eyes and cheeks stained as red as her hair. He was matte grey and showed signs of rust where his joints met, a contrast to the other sheep who were regularly polished. The sheep stared down at her, unblinking, gear-like eyes focused.

"I don't have anything for you today, sheep," Morag said, her voice raspy.

The sheep tilted its head the other way. They stared at each other a few long moments before it wandered away again, leaving Morag alone.

She made it back before dark, but only barely. The first feast was already happening, the one just for the castle, and music streamed from the open windows and corridors far across the hills. In the wake of her mother's death, it sounded horrible, a mockery of the mourning supposed to be happening. Hoping to remain unseen, Morag slipped up the back stair toward her chambers. A cough behind her made her jump and spin around. Her father's new bride stood a few steps below. Per tradition, she was dressed in white, although it didn't fit her bony figure or stiff expression.

"You must be the daughter."

The way she said it made Morag shiver. "I am."

"Come back from the stables, have you? You spend all your time in the muck?"

Morag looked down at her grass-stained dress. "I prefer it over this dark castle."

Despite being several inches shorter and gazing up from below, the woman looked down her long nose at Morag. "I see. Well, perhaps that will change now that I'm here."

Morag turned back around and continued up the stairs to her chambers. She seethed at this woman, coming into their kingdom and taking her mother's place. Morag threw herself onto her bed. Of course, it wasn't entirely the baroness's fault. Her father hadn't waited, hadn't mourned. Hadn't bothered to honor her mother's memory for more than a few weeks before finding another wife. It sickened her.

A knock. It surprised Morag and snapped her out of her anger.

Her nursemaid came into the room holding a large silver tray with a few plates full of food. She closed the door as she entered. "Thought you might be hungry."

"I'm not." Morag sighed and sat up. "But thank you."

Miss MacDonald nodded, leaving the tray on a low table next to the bed before settling herself down next to Morag. "I understand. It's an...odd circumstance. A big change for all of us."

The young woman put her head on the older woman's shoulder, but said nothing. Miss MacDonald pulled her into a hug, rocking her back and forth as if she were a young child. The tears came again, and Morag held tightly to her last friend.

The next afternoon, when Morag returned from the Yard, Miss MacDonald was gone. Morag searched all over the castle: the chambers, the laundry, the gardens, and finally the kitchens, where a cook stopped her, looking worried. "My lady, you're pacing back and forth. What can we help you with?"

"Miss MacDonald. Have you seen her?"

The cook opened his mouth, then closed it again, his shoulders drooping. "Oh, my lady, I'm so sorry. No one told you?"

"Told me what?"

"She was let go this morning. By the queen."

What little inner strength remained to hold Morag together collapsed, crashing to the floor and shattering. Her head slumped. She walked out of the kitchens, dragging her feet. Morag trudged through the dining hall on her way outside, only to find the new queen waiting for her. She had her bony arms folded and was draped in a black gown that fell over her like oil dripping to the stone. It mocked Morag's mourning. The new queen—no, she wasn't queen. Not really. Her new stepmother stared her down before speaking.

"I've found a new position for your maid," she said. "Elsewhere."

"Why? What did she do?"

"The king felt you were getting too old for a nursemaid, and I agreed."

"Oh, did he?" Morag asked. "And could the king even recall her name?"

The older woman sighed softly, like this was a familiar argument. "He is not to be spoken of in that manner, and neither am I, young lady."

She gave an exaggerated curtsy. "Of course not, Stepmother."

The queen pursed her lips, and turned to leave the room. "I do hope you won't do anything rash with that anger of yours, my dear. It's most unbecoming of a princess."

In the time that followed, Morag found herself in the Yard more often, doing anything to avoid the castle. As usual, her father paid little attention to her comings and goings. She rarely stayed in except to sleep, using the servant staircases to sneak in and out. The animals of the Yard had quickly gotten used to her, and most didn't bother scuttling out of the way as she walked anymore. They rarely paid her any attention at all, except for the dull, grey sheep. It wandered over to her periodically, as if checking up on her, before wandering away again, squeaking softly as it moved.

One evening as she returned to the castle, her stepmother was there to meet her. She waited on the back veranda, dressed in her customary black, arms crossed in straight lines. Both of her daughters stood off to the side, hands folded. Did they ever speak? Morag hesitated, but took a deep breath and marched forward.

"I see you've returned from your day in the wild." Morag didn't answer and brushed past her. "You may be interested to know, dear, that I've found you something to occupy your time."

Morag turned back, eyes narrowed. "What's that?"

"You are enrolling in a boarding school until you have come of age and demonstrate the...maturity required of a princess."

There was a long silence. The wind picked up, blowing Morag's hair out behind her, as wild as she felt. She waited for her stepmother to speak, heart thumping, terrified of what she might say next. The silent daughters flanked her like statues.

"You're very fond of the pasture, I've noticed. The king and I have arranged for you to study out in the country, where you might feel more at home."

She doubted very much that her stepmother had spoken with her father, although it was possible. And Morag wouldn't put it past him to think it was a good idea. Oh, where was her mother to argue? To say that freedom was just as befitting a lady as study?

She knew what this meant. Until she fell in line like her stepsisters, she wouldn't be welcome. Morag continued up to her room, and no one brought her supper.

The princess left her chambers just before dawn, a canvas bag slung over her shoulder. Hardly any staff were awake yet, and slipping from the castle was easy. This was not the first time, and she had no trouble finding all the secret ways through the village until she reached the Yard. She ran to the middle of the field, eager to be surrounded by none but the mechanical animals not yet needed for chores.

She sank down into the grass breathing hard and wide-eyed, watching for anyone who might have followed. No one came. Hours passed. Morag had no idea how many, and she didn't care. She'd lost her mother, her only friend, and her home. She put her head in her hands, knees to her chest, and sat surrounded by grass and machinery, alone. The winds chilled her to the point of shivers.

In mid-afternoon, a shadow spread over her. Morag lifted her head, expecting a cautious groom. In front of her stood the mechanical ram, staring down at her with its gear-shaped eyes. Morag stretched out, arms and legs stiff from sitting. She was as curious about it as it was about her. "I have nothing for you today, sheep."

The ram tilted its head, and then turned its side toward her. A blanket made of red flannel rested on its back. The princess took the blanket from the sheep and pulled it tight around her, covering every inch she could. "Thank you, sheep. That was a very kind thing you did."

Gears inside of it ground together, making the ram hum softly. Morag reached out and pressed her hand to its cold, metal back. It trotted off on stiff joints, waddling a little as it went. The princess curled up under the blanket and pulled what food she had from her bag. The wind blew over the grass, moving it like waves on the sea, and Morag was adrift.

The night brought a cold, starry sky over the Yard. Morag sat in the same spot, blanket around her. Her stomach rumbled, but she ignored it. She hadn't seen the ram again, nor any other person. Likely they'd noticed her absence, but she had rarely told anyone of her favorite hiding place. Just Miss MacDonald, and she wasn't around to ask. She thought about her stepsisters and what kinds of lives they must lead under their mother's rule. She shivered, but it wasn't from the biting cold.

Morag awoke to squeaks and grinding. She'd fallen asleep on her side, wrapped in her blanket. She sat up with a start, and pushed her hair from her face. Coming up the hill was the ram, shining in the moonlight despite the rust and lack of polish. On its back was something large and dark, hanging over both sides. It walked up the hill to her and turned to the side, pausing in front of her. In the dim light from the Moon she could see that it was a pack, and it was full. She reached out and opened it gingerly. Sticking out of the top was a large loaf of bread, and Morag plucked it out of the canvas pack. She set it in her lap and reached her hand in again. She pulled out an apple, then cheese. The ram about-faced, and she opened the other side and found glass bottles of water and milk. She removed those, too.

"Thank you, sheep," she said, her voice hoarse. "This was very kind of you."

It nodded its head, gears grinding, and walked away. The

princess watched it go. She tore into the bread with her teeth. The food was gone in minutes. The milk she drank as well, but the water she saved. If tomorrow brought nothing, at least she'd have that. Morag laid back in the grass and stared up at the stars, shivering as the wind whipped up. She should think up a plan soon. Perhaps tomorrow.

Days passed. Morag wandered the Yard, going as far as the forests to the north and the ocean to the west. She watched the ships gliding on gusts through the air, big balloons and wooden hulls bright in the sunlight, and thought of freedom. Every time she came close to the mill or stables, she encountered the black uniforms of patrolling guards. She was trapped between them and the ocean, the deep forests, and the endless roll of the hills. Any of the wilds were an option, and better ones than trying to crawl back to the castle where there was nothing for her. Where she'd be forgotten at best, sent away for good at worst.

The ram kept returning with food. Morag didn't know where it came from, but it appeared every night after dark, carrying its pack filled to the brim with food and drink. One evening, it brought her a scarf to complement the blanket. Morag wrapped that around her, too, to keep out the cold. It never stayed long, but wandered off into the night again, a dull beacon in the darkness.

One morning, Morag awoke with the Sun. The blanket and scarf had kept her very warm, and she'd slept soundly. It was only upon waking that she realized something was missing. The mechanical ram hadn't appeared in the night. Her stomach rumbled in protest. It was the first time in days that the ram hadn't shown up. She couldn't see it from the hilltop, just the other inhabitants of the Yard. That worried her, so she went looking.

Morag gasped when she found it far, far down the seaside cliffs. The poor thing had fallen and shattered, its pieces nothing more than a collection of parts strewn about the sand. She started down the cliff without thinking, scarf wrapped about her head to keep the wind out and hair down, blanket around her shoulders. She hit the bottom, slipping and sliding the last few feet, her old shoes ripped by the sudden descent. They were ruined; she toed them off and left them in the sand.

Morag stared at the broken sheep. She gathered up every gear, spring, and bit of metal she could find, and placed them on the blanket in the ram's general shape. She knelt before it and gazed at the poor, wrecked creature.

It should be fixed. This shouldn't be its demise, not after helping her so much. Morag gathered up the blanket at the corners and tied them together, making a sack. She hoisted the parts over her shoulder with a grunt, and started walking. Shepherd would have fixed the sheep right up, but she wouldn't bring it back to the Yard, even if she could climb the cliffs. Instead, she walked in the opposite direction down the beach.

The ports were still miles away, which meant hours of walking. But she was no longer stuck in one place. When the

Sun was high in the sky, she set the blanket down on the sand and sat, breathing deeply. This wasn't true freedom, but it was something close. She leaned back against the blanket of broken sheep and closed her eyes. The breeze here felt good, humid and salty. She adjusted the scarf so that it let in more breeze. Morag lay there a while, enjoying the sun, until she fell into a light, peaceful sleep.

"Oi! You dead?"

Morag woke with a start. Standing above her was a man, silhouetted against the setting Sun. She raised a hand to shield her eyes from the light and pulled the scarf tighter around her head. "What?"

"Guess no'," the man said. He had a very strange accent. "Whatcha doin' here?"

The princess sat up straighter. "Taking a nap, obviously."

He chuckled, moved out of the direct sunlight, and crouched down next to her. He wore a white linen shirt that needed laundering, patched brown pants, and a belt filled with old tools. He adjusted his brown, tweed cap. "See that. Not a bad spot for it, I guess, if you're travelin'."

"I am," she replied, a little cautious. "Are you a sailor?"

"That I am," he said, grinning. He was tanned darker than the sand and handsome, if a little dirty. His teeth were white amid all the grease, and his eyes were a bright blue. He wiped a grubby hand on his trousers before thrusting it out for her to shake. "The name's Vernon. I'm a mechanic on that ship, right up there."

Morag's eyes drifted up, following the line of a long rope

ladder dangling over the beach. It connected to a huge airship made of wood and metal swaying gently in the breeze above them, its giant balloon tied to the gondola with what looked like a hundred lines of shining wire. Morag stared at it, eyes wide. On the bottom of the ship were three letters, scrawled in gold calligraphy—R.M.S.

"Royal Majesty's Service?" she asked.

Vernon nodded. "Right-o, Miss."

"But you're not from here.... Another kingdom?"

"Queendom, as she prefers it. But yes, indeed. We're travelin' back home and needed a few things, so we tethered here for a little vacation before returnin' to port for the proper stop. Heard there was a festival soon."

Morag scrambled to her feet. "Do you take passengers? It's just me. And, well, my sheep." She gestured to the lumpy blanket. "We were hoping to make it to port before sundown, but as you can see, we won't make it."

Vernon eyed the blanket with a cocked eyebrow. "A sheep? In there?"

"Well, it's broken, you see. Had a bad fall."

He pursed his lips, then looked back at her. "I s'pose we could take one passenger. Just to port, or...?"

Morag bit her lip. How much could she ask for? "Well, port is a start. I was hoping to go somewhere...farther."

"I don't follow, Miss."

"Vernon, I'll be honest with you. I've run away from home. I'm looking for another place to go. Is there room on your ship?"

He grinned. "Oh! Left alone, were you? Well then, I'm sure the cap'n will be happy to have you. And uh...I'll see what I can do about the sheep."

She shook his hand, calloused and warm. "Thank you, Vernon. Anything I can do to pay you, I will. I work all right with my hands, and the sheep is a hard worker, too."

The sailor looked at her with the same raised eyebrow,

but shook his head. He stepped around her and picked up the blanket. "That's one heavy sheep you've got here, Miss."

"Mor...gan. Morgan," she corrected. "And yes. But he's a good one. Worth fixing."

"Well, Morgan, welcome aboard. How do you feel about heights?"

She loved them. The sea breeze whipped the scarf about her head as she looked over the side of the top deck. She hadn't felt right removing it yet. Not that she didn't trust Vernon, or the men on this ship if it belonged to a Navy, but she was still a princess. They could recognize her. So she kept it on, hiding some of her face, even out here on the top deck.

The sea below was so very far...below. The waves blew along as easily as the grasses of the hills, and would have been just as impossible to count. The salty air stung her eyes, but she ignored it. There was too much to see, so much more than in her castle or her little village. Even her kingdom! If only her stepsisters could see what was waiting for them beyond the castle doors.

Vernon's voice carried on the wind. "Morgan, come see this!"

She reluctantly left the view behind and hopped down the stairs to the deck below. Crystals mounted along the walls filled with bright, colored gases lit her way. Needing a bigger space to work on the ram, Vernon had traded in his workshop for the more spacious second deck. When he started, everything was set apart in a wide rectangle so that he could see each individual piece. Now, Morag's sheep was nearly finished.

"It's just missin' a few things," he said, rubbing his chin. "You never found the hooves?"

Morag's face paled. "I didn't? He was strewn all over the beach. I thought I got everything!"

"Well, somehow you forgot all four hooves," he said. "But I'll still be able to make 'im walk, don't worry. Just a li'l more finagling."

"Vernon, you are just magnificent! Brilliant even!"

The man blushed and rubbed his cheeks with the back of his arm. "Not barely. I jus' know how t' fix things, is all."

"Maybe you could show me how to do a little upkeep? I'd like to get the rust off him, too. Maybe shine him up."

He nodded, sitting back down on the floor to adjust a screw. "Can do, Miss. It just takes a li'l elbow grease."

A shadow loomed up over him and the sheep from behind. "What's this, another project?"

The young man scrambled to his feet. He pulled off his hat and saluted. "Sir! Just fixin' up something for the lady, sir."

Morag had met Captain Osei upon stepping aboard. He'd agreed to take her as far as their home port. She curtseyed to him, and he nodded to her. "Vernon, we've got a dozen different parts breaking down, and this is where I find you?"

"Apologies, sir. I'll be done here in a mo—"

"You'll return to the workshop now, Mister Prince. That's an order."

Vernon gave Morag an apologetic look and scurried off. That left her with the captain, an imposing man in uniform.

"Miss Morgan, I have some bad news," he said. "There's been a call out from the nearest kingdom about a runaway princess. Since you and this girl have very similar descriptions, I can only assume you to be her."

She winced. "I am, Captain."

"I regret to inform you that I am turning the ship around and returning you to the king. Were you not missing royalty, things might be different. But as you are, this is something I cannot ignore."

73

"Please, sir. I'm not wanted there. I was being sent away anyhow! I'm not missing. I ran."

Osei gazed down at her through squared spectacles. "I would need proof, Your Highness, and a letter from the king or queen themselves letting you go. I'm sorry. There are laws to be followed, even for princesses."

Morag sighed heavily. She'd tasted freedom. Just briefly, but she had. That might have to be enough. The captain laid a hand on her shoulder. She looked up at him and tried to smile, but it fell flat. He squeezed her shoulder and let go, then walked up the stairs to the open deck. She watched him go, then turned to the ram, fixed but footless. She set her hand on its head. "Sorry, sheep. I thought we were out."

As they tethered, Vernon met Morag at the gangway. The ram still wasn't finished, and she'd elected to leave it behind. It would be in better hands on the ship. The sheep had done so much for her. If she could do a little something for him, she'd try. Vernon seemed as good a person as any to leave it with.

The tinkerer carried an oddly shaped parcel covered in brown cloth when he came to bid her farewell. "These are for you. I noticed that you never wear shoes."

Morag took the package and opened it. Inside were a pair of boots, gorgeous smooth leather with intricate brass details on the toes and heels. She gasped. "Oh Vernon, these are lovely. Are they really for me? I adore them! I'll think of you every time I wear them."

She hugged him around the neck. The young man blushed and awkwardly hugged her in return. They parted when the captain cleared his throat. Morag pulled her boots on and made sure to cover them with her skirt before she left the ship to meet the waiting guard. Her stepmother could put her back in captivity, but if she could hide these, she'd have a souvenir from her time in the sun. Captain Osei escorted her to the dock, where the queen waited.

"Thank you, Captain," her stepmother said. She hugged Morag close, the first physical interaction they'd ever had. "We'd be lost without her."

The Captain nodded and smiled. "All in a day's work, Your Majesty. The princess is quite good company, but duty said she should be returned to her family."

Morag pulled away from the queen and stood off to the side. The captain and her stepmother exchanged a few more words and a few invitations. She didn't listen to much of it, except to hope just a little that the captain and his ship would visit. She wanted to see Vernon again—if she would even still be in the castle and not at some boarding school for unwanted children.

The guard saw the captain out of the castle, leaving Morag with her stepmother.

"What on earth were you thinking? And take off that ridiculous scarf. This kind of behavior is not fitting for a princess!" her stepmother snapped, loud enough that the ship's crew must have heard. Her daughters visibly winced.

"And why not?" Morag pulled the scarf from her head and clenched it in her fist. "My mother thought a princess should be able to do and learn as she likes! Not have to stand in silence with her eyes cast down!"

The queen put a hand to her chest. "There are rules royalty must follow, Morag. I'm here to teach them to you. But if you don't wish to be taught, then you will be kept until you're ready to learn. You are not to leave your room unless escorted by a guardsman. Do you understand me?"

Morag's nails dug into her palms. "I understand you well,

Stepmother." She marched from the room before the queen could say more, all the way up to her room in the tower. There, she flung herself onto her bed and sobbed. No sheep, no Yard, no Vernon, no open sky. Just a dark castle, no friends, and no way to be herself.

Bells tolled a few days after her return. Morag raced to the window to see what the commotion was. Far down the hill, hundreds of villagers had assembled. Banners and streamers of all the colors of the rainbow decorated the village. Airships floated in the breeze, tethered at the edges of the village. She could have sworn she saw R.M.S. painted on the side of one of them.

Morag dressed in a dress long enough to hide her boots and threw open her door. Two guardsmen stood just outside. They both startled, and she rolled her eyes. "What day is it? What's happening?"

"The feast, Your Highness," one said. "For your father and his new bride."

The wedding feast. That must have been the invitation her stepmother and the captain were speaking of. She stepped out of her room, but the guards stopped her.

"You're not to leave your room, ma'am. Not without permission and an escort."

"Well, I'm giving me my permission, and here you are, all ready to be my escort."

The first guard looked to the other. "Permission from the queen, ma'am."

The princess sighed and closed the door again. She paced around her room, thinking. There were ways to get out of the castle, even from all the way up there. The trick was doing it without being caught. She paused in front of her bed. Her eyes drifted to her sheets and then to her open window.

Once she reached the ground, Morag crept around the side of the castle. She wrapped her scarf about her head, covering her hair and half of her face. There were guardsmen posted outside as well, though these were assigned to escort the royal steam-carriage into the village. Her father emerged, dressed in white, with her stepmother on his arm. Morag had to admit, they looked beautiful. Morag waited as they entered the carriage and the guards took up posts around them. She stayed still just long enough for the convoy to disappear over the top of the hill, then dashed to the side and down into the trees and brush. Even if this was temporary, she wasn't going to miss this chance to be out.

The village was overrun with people. Merchants, party-goers, and entertainers lined every street, and there was so much noise that Morag could barely hear herself think. She wandered through it all, eyes darting in every direction. Sellers of all kinds tried to tempt her toward their stalls, but she wouldn't be distracted. She kept an eye out for the guards as she walked, keeping mostly to side streets and alleys. The tethers for the airships weren't far. She dared to hope Vernon's ship was among them.

A familiar hat bobbed through the crowd. Morag followed it, weaving through throngs of people. In a smaller alley, one not suited for stalls, she got a better look. Morag gasped. "Vernon!" She started running. "Vernon!"

The young man turned. He put his hand on the big, metal bulk next to him—the sheep.

Morag nearly bowled him over. She latched onto him, hugging him hard. Vernon shouted in surprise and caught her. "Miss! What in seven earths are you doing?"

The princess let go and pulled back. Behind her scarf, her

eyes shone. "Did you miss me?"

"Wait, Morgan? I-I mean Morag?" Vernon pulled off his hat and spun it in the air. "Tis you! Oh, aren' you a sight for sore eyes. What're you doin' here?"

"Oh, you know. Escaping my prison. Thought I'd get some good food before I go back."

He blinked, growing concerned. "Prison? What happened?"

She took his hand and squeezed. "It's been awful. I'm trapped in that castle. They won't let me leave." The ram toddled up and nudged her in the side. She pulled her eyes away from Vernon to look down. "And you, sheep! Look at you! So handsome with your new shine. And are those new feet?"

Vernon swayed from foot to foot. "Couldn' just let 'im fall over. He matches you now. If you still have t'ose boots."

Morag pulled up her dress to show him. "I do! They're the only thing I—"

A shout from behind made her turn. Among the colorful crowd were a few figures in black guardsmen uniforms. She let go of Vernon's hand. "I must go. I'm sorry. It's so good to see you."

"Wait! Morag! Where are you goin'?"

She barely heard him. The princess ran, skirt in both hands, as fast as she could. If she was caught, she had no idea what her stepmother might do. Suddenly being locked in her room didn't look so bad. Maybe she'd go to that boarding school. Maybe she'd be stripped of her title. Oh, wouldn't that—

The breath was knocked out of her. Morag thudded onto her back, eyes going hazy for a split second. Her view was now that of the alley behind her, upside down, and the stack of firewood that she'd tripped over. Her head swam, but Morag pushed herself up and clung to a wall to stand. She shoved herself forward, around a corner, and back into the crowd. It was only when she reached the trees again that she noticed she was missing a boot.

That evening, Morag was let out of her room. If anyone had noticed her rope of sheets and blankets, they said nothing. She attended the formal feast, sitting at a table with her stepsisters, who talked quietly to each other and hardly looked up from their plates at all. Morag pushed her food around with her fork and watched the people.

Couples in their finery ate and laughed. Military men and women walked the edges of the room, glasses in hand. The younger crowd joked and chatted together. She had been told not to join them, not until the rumors died down. But one set of colors caught her eye. The man was tall, imposing, and wore spectacles. Morag sat up to get a better look. Captain Osei! Oh, if only she could speak with him, tell him about what was happening. He might see her way and let her join them!

Morag glanced at the high table. The royal couple was occupied with other people and entertainment, and paid little attention to the rest of the room. The princess excused herself, then slipped through the other tables and guests gathering in all corners. She caught up to the captain quickly and took his arm. Before he could say anything, she pulled him out onto the dance floor. It was crowded enough to hide them.

"Captain, it's good to see you!"

"Do I know you, Miss?" He asked, clearly confused.

She smiled wide. "I'm Morag. The princess."

His eyebrows shot up. "Ah! I see. Nice to see you settled back at home, Your Highness," he said, relaxing more into her arms.

"Hardly. I came to ask your help. I'm trapped here thanks to your 'rescue.' I don't want to be stuck in this castle any longer."

He looked concerned as he took her hand and swayed with her. "Princess, I cannot do much. I'm bound by laws to not aid runaways, especially royal ones."

She pleaded, "It's horrible here. There are plans to send me away anyhow, can't I just be the one to choose?"

Captain Osei sighed heavily. "My dear, we often do not get to choose our hands. In another life, I even might have chosen differently for myself. But this is what I was dealt."

"But if you could go back and make decisions yourself, wouldn't you?"

He grew quiet as they spun around the floor.

Morag's shoulders drooped. "There must be some way. Can I not claim independence? Or renounce my title, or...?"

"Or?"

She grinned, thinking of Vernon. "I have an idea. I pray you'll go along with it, Captain."

"Your Majesty, Captain Osei would like a word," murmured a servant into the queen's ear. He stepped back and gestured to the captain, who waited on the floor below.

The queen nodded, smiling with her thin, painted lips, and patted her new husband's hand. She stood and let the captain approach. He carried a leather boot with brass details. "Yes, Captain? It's good to see you. I trust your queen is well."

He bowed deeply. "Yes, Your Majesty, thank you. And congratulations to both of you."

"Thank you very much. What is it you wanted to speak about?"

Osei looked a little nervous. "Well, ma'am, this joyous occasion has sparked something within me. I haven't been able to stop thinking about your daughter since her rescue. I never saw her face, but she enchanted me with her wit."

The queen arched a dark eyebrow. "Go on."

He held up the boot. "Our time together was short, but I believe, ma'am, that she might make a very good match."

"Captain! I'm surprised! Are you not a little old for one of my daughters?"

"Aye, ma'am, I might be," he said, confidence growing. "But it would be a good match. I rank well with my queen, and you have very lovely daughters to find security for. Would this not be a good marriage?"

She thought on it, tapping one long finger on the table at her side. "I suppose you might be right. But." She gave a sly smile. "Which daughter was it?"

The captain coughed. "Which? Why, the one who fits this shoe, ma'am." He lifted up the boot in his hand.

That didn't deter her. "Well, we shall just have to find out. Come with me, Captain. Let me fetch my daughters for you."

"It's not going to fit, Mother!"

"Oh my goodness, is that blood?"

The queen shoved the leather boot onto her daughter's foot as hard as she could. It hadn't come close to fitting the other one, but perhaps she could just twist....

"Ouch! Mother, please!"

The queen and her two daughters fussed over each other while the captain looked on. He knew at once neither of these were Morag, but saying so might give too much away. He let the queen do her best to fool him. She grew more and more frustrated, but he stood in silence, hands behind his back.

"Are you certain these are the only daughters you have, ma'am?" he asked. "The boot does not seem to fit these two."

"The only other girls here are maids and servants, Captain," she assured him. The queen groaned in frustration and let the boot drop to the floor. The daughters clung to each other, weeping softly. "If you wish to try any of them, be my guest, but they will not prove to be very good wives."

Seeing an opportunity, Morag casually strolled by the doorway of the room. "Oh, what's this, Stepmother?"

Captain Osei held back a grin. "You there, girl! Come in here a moment. Put this boot on, please."

The queen paled. "Not her, Captain. She's trouble and would serve you poorly."

"Nonsense. Come in here, girl."

Morag walked in, shoeless, and sat down. She picked up the boot, hiked up the hem of her skirt, and pulled it on easily. "Why, it fits well, sir. What does this mean?"

He smiled. "It means, young lady, that you are going to be a wife."

Morag stood and took a few steps in the boot. "Am I? Stepmother, did you hear? How exciting is this day!"

The queen folded her arms. "I do not approve of this marriage, Captain."

"Stepmother? You are indeed the woman I rescued?" He asked, holding his hand out to the princess. "Majesty, you spoke of only two daughters. It seems you have forgotten this one."

Morag took the captain's hand, steadying herself. This had to work. Please, it had to work. The queen stood in silence, her hawk-like eyes trained on Morag. The princess didn't wilt in front of her, but stood tall, defiant.

"It seems I did," she finally said. "Fine. Go. Perhaps you

can put some sense into the girl. And tell your queen we will speak soon."

Morag stood on the deck of the airship, wind whipping her hair. She wore two grand leather boots, and a sharp, polished sheep stood at her side. She breathed in the salty sea air, eyes closed, her lips curved upward in a satisfied smile. Footsteps approached her from behind, and her smile grew.

"How did you manage all tha'?" Vernon asked, coming to stand beside her.

Morag shrugged and opened her eyes to look at him. "With the help of your boots. Where did you get the other one?"

"Your sheep here, o'course," he replied. "Trotted right over and brough' it to me. What a good ram he is."

The ex-princess laid her hand on the ram's head. She could feel the humming of gears inside, but it made no noise now. "That he is," she agreed. "I should thank the captain again, too, for letting me use him in my escape. So, where to now?"

"'Ome. Well, not 'ome for you. Not yet, I imagine."

She reached over and took Vernon's hand. He blushed pink. "Not yet, but I'm sure it will be. Especially once the captain and I explain to your queen what happened."

"And," he said, puffing out his chest a little. "Af'er I've been promoted to Lieutenan'."

"You what?"

Vernon grinned at her. "Canna have a princess married to a Machinist."

Morag squeezed his hand tightly. She wasn't thinking of marriage. Not yet. Her mind was too focused on the sea that lay before them.

But out here, marriage wouldn't be a trap, a cage. She might not mind being married to an officer.

Once she got a little more taste of freedom.

About Kay Gray

Kay Gray is a short story pro and a So-Cal expat who calls the snowy depths of Michigan home. When she's not writing fantastical stories, one can find her neck deep in research for her podcast, Haunted Mitten, which she co-hosts with her partner in paranormal, Crysta K Coburn. Otherwise, you can be sure that she is surrounded by needy pets while she reads yet another fantasy book.

To get the latest podcasts, head to hauntedmitten.podbean. com. To delve into the mind of Kay herself (reader beware), check out her Twitter @KGrayWrites. And find her last story, "The Wind-Up Mermaid", in *Queen of Clocks and Other Steampunk Tales*, at a local bookstore near you.

The Girl in the Tower

by A.F. Stewart

"Faster, Rapunzel, faster!"

The torches of the palace guards flickered in the distance as they ran. The automaton flailed with every step, stumbling and weaving on unsteady legs. Helga swore breathlessly at the clank of Rapunzel's mechanical limbs. The cloaking magic wouldn't fool them for long when they could follow the noise.

Rapunzel whispered, "I'm too loud. They'll hear us. You need to abandon me. Save yourself."

Helga shook her head. "No, you are all I have left. We must hide. This way." She grabbed Rapunzel's arm and dragged her off the main path to flee the shouts of their pursuers. They pushed their way through the foliage and undergrowth, moving deeper into the forest. Marks of their trail disappeared in the wake of Helga's magic.

"I don't understand, Mother. Why are they chasing us?" Rapunzel asked, the words nearly muffled by the metallic clink of her joints. "Did I do something wrong?"

"What?" Helga's thoughts raced before comprehending. "No. The count wants to take you away from me. He.... Things happened, and he'll destroy you. I'm trying to protect you."

The pair wound through the woods with Helga leading. The sound of voices in the distance told them they hadn't shaken their pursuers.

Rapunzel risked speaking. "Please leave me. I don't want you to get hurt."

"Shush. We just need a place to wait them out. Once they can't hear us, they can't track us. We'll be safe until they give up. Come."

Helga yanked Rapunzel to the left, and the pair stumbled into a cleared patch of ground near a tumble-down cabin.

"It's still here. Wonderful." The pair hurried inside. "Not a sound now, Rapunzel."

The automaton sat on the grimy floor, silencing her clockwork except for the nearly imperceptible hum of gears. Helga sat with her back against the wall, slowing her breath and staring at Rapunzel.

She could stay so still. Her daughter never used to be still. She was always moving—fingers fluttering, laughing, dancing. The automaton had her face, her thoughts, her voice, and yet.... No, she was still Rapunzel. She was still Helga's daughter. They couldn't take that away from her.

Helga closed her eyes. They could wait them out. The search party would move on eventually, and then they could go further into the hills to the tower. They'd be safe from the count there.

Helga positioned the last of the tiny gears, then closed the door on the back of the mechanism and secured the miniature latch with a deep satisfaction. It was so much easier to repair a broken clockwork toy than put right the other problems in her life. A loud thump from the upper floor of the tower drew her attention.

Helga eased herself from her workbench with a sigh, rubbing her back as she stood, and climbed the stairs to her daughter's room.

Rapunzel was such a contradiction. So robust in frame and body, but so delicate and naive in spirit. All cogs and gears and intricate mechanisms, but housing human fragility. She was still the girl she used to be, but she was also something new.

Helga reached the landing, and with a sigh, she pushed open the bedroom door. She clucked her tongue at the sight of her daughter in a tumbled heap on the floor, limbs unable to move. She hurried to the girl's side.

"Did you forget to wind your mechanisms again, my dear? I've warned you not to neglect your clockwork."

Rapunzel's barely functioning metal tongue slurred her words. "I'mmmm sssorrry."

"I know, Sweeting, I know. Now, where did you put your key?" Helga scanned the room. She spotted the shine of metal on the dresser and fetched the key. Once she'd inserted it into its slot in her neck, she wound her daughter back to life.

Gears whirred and ground together, and she helped Rapunzel to sit up. Helga applied some oil to her daughter's joints from a can she kept in the pocket of her apron. Rapunzel flexed her appendages and smiled at her mother.

Helga smiled back. "There, all better."

"Thank you. I do apologize. I should have remembered to wind myself."

"It's fine, my dear. We all make mistakes. Let's stand now, shall we?"

The pair rose, both shaky—Helga from her cramped position, Rapunzel from her reviving mechanisms.

"If you're feeling better, I'll get back to my work." Helga turned to leave.

"Wait, Mother. Please, won't you stay? Tell me a story? You've been so busy lately. We haven't sat together in quite some time."

Helga sighed again, but sank into a chair. "One story cannot hurt. Shall I tell you about court?"

Rapunzel clapped her hands and sat on her bed. "Yes, please. I love those stories."

"Very well. Court is a strange place nestled in a palace of wonders and contradictions in the heart of the city. A gilded place full of shadows. It is not fit for the innocent, yet it is a grand place of opportunity." Helga beamed at her daughter's wide-eyed stare. "And ruling over court is the count, a clever man with a cold heart."

"Is he the villain?" Rapunzel asked.

"Perhaps." Helga chuckled. "Or perhaps tonight we will make him the hero. He could be either, this man, whenever the whim struck him." Helga's vision blurred, the memories overtaking her. "I've seen him be equally kind or cruel."

"That is why we left, isn't it? The count decided to be cruel?"

Helga nodded. "But not today. Today he will be kind. Today he will throw a party for his daughter, Lady Katrina, on her eighteenth birthday. There will be a cake three feet tall, covered in sweet frosting and fresh fruit. Clockwork men will play instruments, and mechanical birds will sing. All manner of pretty toys will be on display, and the young lady will laugh all day long."

"Oh, that sounds so lovely. I wish I could see it."

Helga's breath caught.

Rapunzel had seen it. She'd helped her mother make the toys and set them on display for Katrina. It was such a shame she didn't remember; she so loved all the clockwork.

A sad smile crossed Helga's lips, and she patted Rapunzel's metal knee. "I'm sure you would have enjoyed the spectacle."

"Did Lady Katrina like her party?"

"Oh yes. She danced all night long as the mechanical wonders did their tricks, and the musicians played their lively tunes. She ate pastries and cake, and drank sweet wine. It was a wonderful night."

Another sad smile flickered with the memories. It had been the last wonderful night. Only a fortnight later, the tragedy had struck.

Helga turned her head to the window, staring out at the sunshine.

"Such a beautiful day. Perhaps we'll go spend the afternoon in the garden?"

The automaton nodded. "I'd like that."

"Good. That is what we'll do. I'll finish my work, have lunch, and then we go out among the flowers and the sun." Helga rose. "I'll see you later, then?"

Rapunzel nodded as her mother left the bedroom.

Watching the door close, Rapunzel softly exhaled. Disappointment warred with anticipation. She had been enjoying the story, yet she loved walking in the garden. And her mother had only suggested it to avoid talking about the past.

I made her sad again. I didn't remember something. From before.

She thinks I don't know. But I do.

She thinks I only remember our house. The one outside the city. And the days after I woke up. The night we fled. I remember more than she thinks.

Rapunzel flexed her mechanical hands.

I remember when these were flesh. What it felt like to touch things.

People swirl around in my head. Faces with names. Faces without. Even Katrina. But that memory makes me sad for some reason. It's confusing.

There are places in there, too. A city. A palace.

Some pieces fit. Others don't.

Broken cogs out of position.

There used to be warmth from the Sun on my skin. Flowers had scents. It wasn't this garden, these flowers. I'm certain. It was somewhere else. Somewhere...before.

Do these flowers smell the same? I wish I knew.

She closed her eyes, willing the memories to surface.

A golden garden full of clockwork wonders. Windup butterflies and birds. Kinetic sculptures. A beautiful sundial clock in the center. A ship with animated sailors surrounded by roses. A pegasus that bowed its head and waved its wings. I walked the pathways so many times. Bathed in light and music. Watched the Sun dance off the metal and glass.

She opened her eyes, her metal lids clicking.

It isn't like Mother supposes. I am not blank. I have so many memories. Too many.

A grand city. Carriages and paved streets bustling with people. Festivals and shops. A magnificent palace on a hill. That's where court was.

Mother and I walked its marble halls, glittering with gilded sconces. They respected her.

I visited kitchens. The aroma of baking bread filled every nook.

Rapunzel walked to the window to gaze at the horizon.

Court is out there somewhere. It was home once. As much as our little house.

I know court is real. Not a tale Mother spun. She pretends otherwise, but it is a lie. I want to talk to her about everything. But it makes her so sad.

Maybe she misses court too. Misses the other me. But I'm still here.

Not the same, but I'm still here.

She let out a tinny approximation of a sigh and glanced at the land just beyond the tower.

I've lost something. Or is it many things? It is so hard to tell her, to ask her things. Things. Am I a thing?

Mother doesn't like my questions.

She wouldn't like what I've been doing these past few days either. Sneaking out at night after she's asleep to see the boy. Sparrow.

Rapunzel leaned against the windowsill, the wood creaking.

We were friends, I think. In the somewhere before. Maybe more.

He has such lovely eyes. Like the periwinkle in the garden. When he looks at me....

The vision of a young man with sandy brown hair flickered in her thoughts, a picture of him standing at the edge of the woods beyond the tower. That's where she saw him for the first time, five days ago. An instant recognition had coursed through her like lightning, and she knew him. Not how or why, but that somehow he was as dear to her as her mother.

Rapunzel smiled at the memory. A new memory. One she knew was real, because it happened...after.

My Sparrow. He is like my missing piece. Every time I see him, I'm happy.

I know I shouldn't meet him.

I need to be with him.

I wish I knew why.

In the tower kitchen, Helga sliced some cold rabbit for her midday meal. She placed her plate on the table alongside fresh bread and aged cheese, and wondered if she should call Rapunzel down to join her. But things were hard enough without the reminders of their differences. Helga ate in silence, alone with her broken memories.

She set her dishes in a pan of water before gathering her gardening tools. Then she went to the stairs and shouted, "Come, Rapunzel! It's time for the garden."

"I'm here!" Rapunzel bounded down the last few steps and hopped to the floor with a resounding clank and a smile on her face. "What are we doing today?"

Helga chuckled at her enthusiasm. "I think I will trim back one of the rose hedges and take a few blooms for the vases. We haven't had enough cut flowers decorating the place. We need a little life and colour in our tower."

"Oh, wonderful. I love roses."

"It won't all be pretty flowers. I need your help moving some stones from the pile at the back wall to the pond. I think the edges could use some fortifying."

Rapunzel frowned. "Sounds tedious."

Helga chuckled again. "It won't take long, and we'll trim the roses first."

The pair walked from the tower into the expansive, sun-dappled garden that spread out beyond the structure. Stone walls enclosed plots and rows of well-tended beds, with hedges lining the paths. The rose hedges skirted the outer walls, their greenery filled with sweet-scented blooms of pink, white, and red. Helga led Rapunzel to the left and one particularly unkempt hedge. As they approached, a few filigreed, clockwork butterflies took flight. Rapunzel clanged her hands together in delight.

"Here, hold the basket, while I trim some blooms." Helga snipped with her shears, filling the basket in an array of colourful flowers and trimming down the greenery. Soon, the hedge had an even and elegant look.

"There. Much better. We'll leave the basket at the door and go move those rocks." A short walk deposited the basket at the tower and saw them strolling to the far wall.

Rapunzel hummed a tinny melody, and then asked, "Why did you choose this place? To live, I mean? After we left?"

Helga shot a bewildered glance at her daughter. "Why ever would you ask such a thing?"

Rapunzel fidgeted, her fingers clinking. "I've been wondering, that's all. Why we came here, why we left. I have so many questions. That's why I forgot to wind myself today. I was thinking. Trying to make the pieces fit. I lost track of time."

Helga frowned. "Do you do that often? Think about our life before?"

Rapunzel nodded. "I want to know things. Like why we came here."

Helga sighed, staring at the path ahead. "I knew this place from a friend, and that it would be hidden from the world."

"Why do we have to hide? Is there something wrong with me?"

Helga finally brought herself to look at her daughter. "No. Never think that. You are perfect. And you are mine, and I love you." Helga paused, her mind troubled. If only she could tell Rapunzel the truth. She'd have to settle for forgiveness for the lies.

"None of this is your doing. You are different and new. Some people fear things that are different, others want to use what you are for bad things. I don't want that for you. You're special."

As they reached the rock pile, they fell silent, working to sort out the right sized stones for the edging. Rapunzel glanced at her mother often, trying to arrange her thoughts.

Finally she blurted, "I wasn't always like this, was I?" Rapunzel held out a hand, its metal reflecting in the sunlight. "I wasn't always different. I was like you, made of flesh."

Helga wiped sweat from her brow and tucked a strand of hair behind her ear.

"Yes, you were my blood daughter once, not the daughter I created from metal and magic." With a grunt, she moved another stone. "What happened to me?"

Why did she have to push? Perhaps a small kernel of truth would do. Helga patted her daughter's shoulder. "Be glad you don't remember, child. Those are hard memories. All you need to know is there was an accident. I fixed you in the only way I knew how."

"You saved me?"

Helga smiled. "I suppose I did."

"Then I'm glad. Glad to be here with you in this tower. Even if we do have to move rocks today."

Helga laughed. "You'll survive."

Rapunzel grunted, and Helga laughed again.

Listening from his place on the other side of the wall, Sparrow, grinned.

He couldn't believe his luck, couldn't believe he'd found them. He'd taken a wrong turn while hunting and stumbled across the tower and the witch. It had been a shock too, seeing the replica of the girl he once knew. He never thought he would see either of them again.

It was clever of them to hide this close to the city. His father believed they fled across their borders. Such a good trick they'd played.

Sparrow snickered at all his father's fruitless efforts to find them. They'd been right under his nose the whole time. He'd be furious once he found out how near to the city the witch and her abomination had been all these months.

Sparrow twitched at the thought of the automaton. Bile rose in his throat.

It had known him. Not like before, but his face, the name she'd used to call him. The way it had stared made him sick. It looked at him like...it cared. He shivered.

But it wasn't Rapunzel. It was a walking death mask of the girl he'd loved, an unholy creation, a ghost. The thing broke his heart a second time.

He needed to make things right. If he brought it to court, his father would be pleased.

Then he frowned. Would his father be pleased, or push him away again?

That would be so like him to shunt his son aside. He always overlooked his achievements, just because Sparrow wasn't a soldier like his brother. He'd been put in charge of the militia. Sparrow hadn't even gotten an official position at court.

That was even before the accident, which wasn't his fault. His father blamed him anyway. But it wasn't his fault he'd survived and the others didn't. It wasn't his fault that witch Helga resurrected her own daughter and defied the count, fleeing with her secrets and leaving Katrina to rot in her grave alone.

Sparrow crouched against the wall, fighting back the memories.

He could fix things now. He could bring the abomination back to court, parade it in front of the count so he could dismantle it in some macabre show of justice. His father would have no choice but to forgive him.

Sparrow frowned as doubt slid along the edges of his mood.

Forcing or subduing it might be dangerous, and there was Helga to worry about. This mechanical Rapunzel trusted him, he was sure of it; otherwise it wouldn't have continued to meet him. Could his luck hold, and would it come back to the palace willingly?

The boy crept along the edge of the garden wall, tracking the murmured sound of the voices and swirling his own thoughts in his head. The Sun settled into late afternoon before the pair returned to the tower. Sparrow stalked the perimeter, still wondering how to capture Rapunzel, skulking back to her window in the tower. There he waited.

Eventually, Rapunzel stood at her window. Even at a distance, her demeanour seemed familiar.... Was it longing? Loneliness? Did it want to leave the tower?

Perhaps it wouldn't be so hard to convince it after all. He just needed the proper tactic. Sparrow slipped away, headed back to his camp in the woods. When he arrived, his bodyguard, Moritz, sat on a large fallen log next to a small fire. The man grunted as Sparrow joined him.

"You shouldn't go off on your own. It could be dangerous."

Sparrow sneered. "Stop pretending you care."

"I do care...about my own neck. Your father would have me killed if something happened to you, if only to save face." Moritz shrugged. "But you're right. What did you learn?"

"It hasn't told the witch we're here, so we can proceed. And that it may be easier to lure the automaton to court than I thought. It seems restless, lonely. I think it's eager to leave the tower. I just need to convince it that it's safe. That it can trust me."

"Lonely, yes. But for you, I think. I've seen how that thing behaves around you. Just like the girl did. Play on that. Women are all the same, even mechanical ones. They're just fools who want to be loved."

Sparrow scowled. "You spied on us?"

Moritz nodded and grinned. "It's the best way to play it if you insist on this plan, but why go to all this trouble? Trying to trick it may be foolhardy. What if this contraption won't go? It may be besotted, but that's no guarantee. I say it's safer to either destroy the thing or call in the palace guard and storm the tower."

"No guard!" Sparrow shouted. "They'll rush in and take all the credit, and we'll be pushed aside."

Moritz shrugged. "Would that be so terrible?"

Sparrow scowled. "Yes. Besides, you'll lose the reward money if the guard get the credit." That got his attention, and he sat up straighter. "We can do this. Lure the mechanical to the city and turn it over to Father. He'll have the honor of dismantling it himself, I'll get the glory of bringing it in, and you'll get the money."

Moritz stretched and adjusted his sword belt. "I want the money, but it's a lot of bother, if you ask me."

"It'll be worth it, you'll see. And while I'm deceiving the mechanical, you can sneak out and dispatch the witch. She'll be out gathering wild herbs tomorrow. It's perfect timing. And without the witch's influence, her creation will be easier to control."

"Well, I'm all for killing the witch. I'll enjoy that. What will we do with her body after?"

"Leave it until Father has the automaton." Sparrow waved dismissively. "Then we'll send the guard to fetch the corpse."

"Fine," Moritz grunted.

"Good. Then it's settled."

The next afternoon, Rapunzel waited until she heard the front door of the tower shut behind her mother when she left to collect herbs in the woods. She gathered the rope ladder from under her bed, hooked it on the ledge of her open window, and tossed it down the side of the tower. Then she climbed down and raced off to meet Sparrow as they had planned.

As she neared his encampment, she spied him standing alone by the embers of a fire. She stopped, studying him, and something in her mind clicked. She saw a vision of them dancing across a ballroom, lost in each other's presence. An immense feeling of longing swept over her. She stared at the young man, her emotions suddenly clear.

Oh, Sparrow, who are you? I feel—I feel like...we belonged to each other.

She repressed the urge to race into his camp and, instead, slowly walked over to where he waited.

He smiled as she arrived. "You came! I was afraid you wouldn't."

A wave of happiness made her giddy, and Rapunzel's laugh

was tinged with a slight metallic echo. "Of course I came. I wanted to see you again. You...you've become important to me."

She watched his expression change, imbued with an emotion she didn't quite comprehend. Then he smiled, and that's all she saw.

"I'm glad. I feel the same way." Sparrow stepped forward and grasped her hands;

Rapunzel wished she could feel his flesh against her metal. He lifted her hands and gently kissed her fingers.

"Come sit with me by the fire." He led her forward, both settling on the old log by the flames. He drew her close, an arm wrapping around her body. Rapunzel rested her head on his shoulder.

Sparrow jerked away, rising to his feet and turning his back on her. Rapunzel watched his shoulders heave and his jaw line tighten.

She frowned. "I'm sorry. I didn't mean to upset you." She hung her head, unsure what to do. "I'm always doing things to upset people. What do you need me to do to make you happy?"

"You make me happy," he blurted. "But seeing you and knowing we may have to be apart again." He shook his head. "No. I can't do it. I thought I lost you forever. Now, you're here. I cannot let you go. Come back with me! You need to come home with me to the city."

"I can't!" Rapunzel scrambled to her feet. "It isn't safe."

Sparrow moved closer and pulled her into his arms. She quivered.

He whispered in her ear, "I know it's a risk, but I can't be apart from you. Not after the miracle of finding you once more. We need to be together. I don't want to go back without you." Sparrow brushed her cheek with his lips. "Not after seeing you again. Please, say you'll come with me? Let me show you the wonders of court, make real those memories you told me about. We can see it together, you and I."

Rapunzel hesitated in her refusal, a desire awakening in her. "You would take me there?"

Sparrow put a hand on her chin, tilting her head up. "Don't say no."

She stared into his eyes, those beautiful eyes that turned her heart molten. "I want you to show me. All that beauty—" Reality crashed into Rapunzel's dream. "No. Mother would never allow it. I can't leave the tower. It isn't safe."

Sparrow pulled her head down onto his shoulder. "Do you want to stay locked in that tower forever? All alone? Coming with me may be a risk, but we'll be together. And I'll keep you safe."

At that moment, she would have followed him anywhere. When Sparrow looked at her with excitement in his eyes and spoke with that infectious eagerness in his voice, she believed anything was possible.

How she wanted to see court again, and the thought of doing it with Sparrow thrilled her. Rapunzel closed her eyes, remembering the splendour and sparkle, the finery and gilt, the wonder and innovation of the city. She wanted to revisit it all. And she wanted to do it with this boy at her side.

All I have to do is say yes.

This was her dream. Sparrow and court. He made her feel safe. She trusted him.

Yet she hesitated.

Why?

She lifted her head and opened her eyes, none of the confusion she experienced reflected in their glass. "I'm not sure." She fumbled for a reason to refuse. "Mother.

What about Mother?" Then an idea flitted into her brain. "Why don't you stay here? Come live with us?"

"I can't. Not yet. I have obligations in the city. I'd be missed."

Sparrow took her hands, kissed her fingers, and the inner workings of her chest felt like they skipped a cog. "You can leave your mother a letter, explaining. And you're right, we don't have to be gone forever. In time, I'll be able to leave the city, and we'll return to her soon. Both of us, together. Come with me now, and it will all work out."

"I don't know."

"Please, Rapunzel. I want us to be together. Don't you want that? Don't you trust me? Don't you care?"

Her body shivered in a soft clang. "I do! I care so much! And I trust you. I swear!"

"Then come with me. Say yes."

She glanced down at her trembling hands.

What's happening to me?

She wanted this. Somewhere deep inside she wanted it badly enough to throw away sense and logic and abandon her mother. A burning passion had sprung from forgotten fragments and spun a gossamer web around her thoughts and feelings. "Yes. I'll go." The eager words spilled out of her mouth. "But I have to leave Mother a letter. Pack some things. Come with me to the tower. Then we can leave."

He took her hand as they left his camp and headed back to the tower.

At the base, Sparrow stared up at Rapunzel's window. "You want me to climb up *there*? Up that rope ladder? Why can't we use the door?"

"Mother locks it when she leaves. It's the only way in or out."

He eyed the distance between the ground and the window. "Maybe I should wait down here."

"Why?" Rapunzel tilted her head with a slight creak. "Are you afraid? Don't worry. Its safe. I can help you if you have trouble."

"Of course I'm not afraid!" Sparrow squared his shoulders

and grabbed the ropes.

He ascended the tower wall, Rapunzel bringing up the rear, until they were both safely inside. He flopped into a chair, out of breath, as she moved to her desk and to write her farewell. As she tried to compose her words, she turned back to Sparrow.

"Do they still have the windup songbirds singing at the palace gate?"

The boy gasped, "You remember that?"

She nodded.

"They always were your favourites." Sparrow smiled. "I used to tease you that you liked the mechanical birds better than the real thing."

"And I used to say..." Rapunzel dropped the pen. "I used to say you didn't appreciate the craftsmanship. I remember." She tilted her head as a memory flashed in her mind, as if a slightly different angle might force more of the pieces into place.

"That's why I called you 'Sparrow.' But that's not your name." Her head twitched, and her fingers flexed. Every gear in her body burned. "You are Mathias Fabel. Son of Count Nikolaus Fabel."

Rapunzel let the paper in her hand fall to the floor, and he stood up to face her.

She whispered, "We loved each other. We were eloping." A hiss escaped her metallic lips. "Something happened. Someone died."

Panic wove into Sparrow's features. "It wasn't my fault. I just gave her a little push. I didn't mean it!"

"You killed Katrina. And then...and then...." Rapunzel froze as a cascade of memories flooded back, then her fingers curled into fists. "You betrayed me. You let them believe that *I* pushed Katrina. That *I* was the one who killed her. You let your father execute me! How could you do that?"

She surged forward and shoved Sparrow. He stumbled backward, slamming into the window ledge and tumbling out the open shutters. Horrified, Rapunzel rushed to save him, but was too late.

His screams filled the air, until he smashed into the ground.

For all he tried to hide, Helga noticed the man in the shadows of the trees. Her breath quickened, and her heart thumped against her ribs. Was he a bandit? An assassin? Or the most troubling thought of all, had the count found them? She sucked in her breath and stilled her trembling hands as she led her stalker deeper into the woods.

Whoever he was, she'd make him regret hunting her.

She lured him along the worn path to the bramble, sliding out of his view. Those few moments were all it took to step off onto a hidden trail and circle around to set up an ambush.

Helga silently slid her knife from its sheath and waited. When the man passed by her hiding place, she lunged forward and slid her blade into his back. He gave a strangled cry, and then a harsh gurgle of blood. He sank to his knees as Helga yanked out the knife and finished him off by slicing his throat.

She stood over the body, staring into the dead eyes of her would-be assassin.

Then she saw the insignia of the count, and she raced home in terror.

The sound of wailing filled the tower as Helga rushed inside, and she dashed upstairs to her daughter's room. When she burst in, Rapunzel was curled up on the floor opposite the open window, shrieking her misery.

"Rapunzel! What's wrong? What happened?"

"I killed him!" A shaking metallic finger pointed to the window. "I killed Sparrow."

Helga raced to the window and looked down at the broken body below. Behind her, Rapunzel screamed, "I killed him! I loved him. How could I kill him?"

Helga glanced back at her creation, her child, and then at the body on the ground.

"Don't you worry, Mother will fix this. I'll make everything better."

Rapunzel and Sparrow danced to the scratchy sounds of the music box. Their limbs clanked, and the gears hissed, but both of the metal faces smiled. Helga grinned herself. Young love was so beautiful, and all the more beautiful when it was free from sorrow.

That had been the hard part, keeping the good memories and removing the bad.

She had been in such a rush to resurrect Rapunzel, but she'd had more time with Sparrow to get things right. It was easier to preserve the brain this time, less of a hurry to work the spells that fused it into the clockwork. Their secret was safe again, and

Rapunzel was happy, the way she should have been when she was human. Helga almost felt a twinge of sympathy for the count. He had lost another child and would never know what happened to his son, but the boy would be happier here.

She would take care of him, love him as her own, and teach him better morals than his father. He would have a better life than the one he lost. He would be with Rapunzel, both of them sixteen and in love, forever. She would see to that.

More From A.F. Stewart

Past Legends
(The Camelot Immortals, Book 1)

An immortal witch of Camelot. A looming magical crisis. A destiny she's willing to reject.

All Nimue wants is a peaceful life, but her past won't leave her alone. And when her friend Iseult brings news that her old rival Morgawse has been abducted, an impending catastrophe lands on her doorstep. Will Nimue step up as a champion? Or will she let the magical world die?

If you like strong snarky heroines, wizards and witches, and magical mayhem, then you'll love the adventures of Nimue and her friends.

Find it on a variety of platforms at https://books2read.com/u/b5ZLB1

Hoods and Wolves

by Briant Laslo

"Get your ass in here, Red!"

Red stepped inside the tent, leaving the flap open behind her. She snapped a salute to the woman standing on the opposite side of the table, which displayed a topographical map.

"Little Red reporting for duty, Mother!"

Red was pretty sure her birth name had been Samantha, or perhaps Susanna, but no one had called her either of them in nearly 20 years. It was customary for the drill sergeant to hand out call signs for everybody who made it through training. Red had been one of two dozen redheads that had survived her regimental training. There had been Big Red, Blood Red, Psycho Red and Fiery Red among them.

"Little Red" stood a fraction under four foot, eleven inches. She was maybe one hundred pounds on a good month when she had been able to eat regularly.

The woman across the table didn't bother looking up

from the map when she spoke. "How long you been one of my daughters, Red?"

"I've been with you for seven years, three months, two weeks, and three days, Mother Superfly!"

"And before that?"

"I was with Mother Skull-suck nearly eight years, before she became Grandmother."

"So, you know her, yeah?"

Red frowned in confusion. "I, uh, of course..."

"Don't gimme that 'I, uh, of course I do' shit!" Mother's face snapped up from the map. "I mean, you *know* her, right? You were her primary runner. You slept in the same tent as her for most of those eight years. You know her quirks, her mannerisms. Christ, you know her scent, don't you?"

"Yes, Mother! I could identify Grandmother with my eyes closed if she were here."

"Good. Is that Grandmother?" Mother Superfly pointed over Red's left shoulder.

Red turned to a monitor with a frozen image of a woman with very short, silver hair. "Yes, that is Grandmoth..." Red hesitated.

"What is it? What do you see?" Mother stepped out from behind the table.

"I...I don't know." Red stepped closer, reaching out to trace the outline of the woman's jaw.

"Play the video," Mother said to somebody farther back in the tent.

The image on the monitor flickered, then reset to a roughly fifteen-second loop of video showing Grandmother in a garden holding a basket of vegetables. She placed the basket on the ground, getting down to one knee and touching a few of the vegetables before nodding at the camera.

"It's an encoded message, yes?" Red asked. "The vegetables in the basket mean something, the actual vegetables themselves as well as their position, and then... The ones she touches, some kind of instructions or orders?"

"You're good. That's exactly right. And this message is telling us that the Wolves have ambushed one of our Hoods carrying a Coded Authentication Key Encryption to Grandmother."

"What?" Red scoffed. "Who the *hell* sent a Hood out carrying a CAKE? We need to intercept that Wolf immediately!"

CAKEs were always transported with the utmost care. If the Wolves ever got a hold of one of them, it would only be a matter of time before they tore down the entire communication network the Hoods had created.

"That's exactly what the message says. It tells us the Wolf with the CAKE is headed northeast through the Quarter League Wood and that we must send all forces to stop it immediately."

"So then, what are we doing here?"

"I'll ask you again." Mother stepped up alongside Red, pointing directly to the monitor. "Is that Grandmother?"

"I don't understand."

"You hesitated when I first asked you. If somebody asked me, I would say yeah, that's her for sure. But here's the thing. We don't have any reports of any CAKEs being transported. We don't have any reports of any Hoods being missing. If there was a CAKE operation happening, then all of the troops in this area would be involved. We coordinate shit like that down to the second. So, why would Grandmother send us a coded message like this? Did she make a mistake?"

Red laughed.

"Exactly," Mother agreed. "Grandmother has been in this game over 60 years. That is one bitch that don't make mistakes. So, why send it?"

"I...I don't know, Mother."

"Well, that's what we need you to find out. You are to leave camp immediately. Make your way to Grandmother's bunker. Go the roundabout way, stick to the woods, make sure nobody is following you. You'll travel alone. Standard communication protocol is in effect; do not contact us until you reach Grandmother and can report what is happening. If we don't hear from you within 48 hours, we will assume the worst."

"In this scenario, the worst being...?"

"That both you and Grandmother are dead and the entire Hood operation is in jeopardy."

Red nodded. "Anything else?"

Mother pointed to a circled area of the map. "There are some reports of tribal woodsmen active in the area this past week. Do what you can to avoid them, but if you have to go through them, do it. We need to hear from you within 48 hours."

Red hesitated a moment. "We can win this, right? It won't always be this way."

Mother looked at Red unflinchingly. "We most certainly can win this. It wasn't always like this. Things were different, once upon a time."

Red remembered hearing those words countless times in the raspy voice of her drill sergeant back at the orphanage.

"Once upon a time, there were people in this world who gave a shit about you. There were people who gave a shit about the planet, about right and wrong. But we don't live in a fairy tale, do we, ladies?"

"No, Drill Sergeant!" One thousand eight hundred and eighty-nine young girls, all between the ages of seven and twelve, had shouted the response in unison.

"No, we do not." She had looked out over the recruits, somehow seeming to make eye contact with each one of them directly. *"We live in a world of Wolves and weapons. We live in a world where the bots reproduce and refine themselves 24 hours a day, polluting the water and sky as they do. Once upon a time, there were roses and fresh air. Today, our*

atmosphere is a weapon used against us while the Wolves send their hunters out to track us down or lay waste to our settlements like a tornado blowing down houses!

"Make no mistake about it, ladies, this is a war for our very survival. It is a war for second chances. It is our responsibility to plant our feet, stand our ground, and shout to the universe that we deserve to be here!

"We are Hoods. We are the daughters and granddaughters of a nearly dead world. But we will not let it die! We will withstand the onslaught. We will put one foot in front of the other. We will fight back!"

The corner of Red's mouth lifted as she remembered that very first speech she heard from the woman she would eventually come to call Grandmother.

That speech was nearly 15 years ago, and Red was still fighting.

She broke out of her reverie and nodded to Mother, stepping from the tent. There was no time to waste.

Red had not moved more than a few inches in the last three hours.

She'd made good time over the last 32 hours and was now less than five miles away from Grandmother's bunker. However, her path tapered into a narrow chasm, and a group of woodsmen, 50 or 60 strong, had set up camp in the middle. It was evident they had been living off the land in this area for the last few days.

If it's not Wolves, it's woodsmen.

The question now was, what kind of woodsmen were they?

Going around the chasm in either direction would add another seven or eight hours to her trip, and that was cutting it closer than Red liked. So, one way or the other, she was going to go through that chasm. She could try to openly engage with the woodsmen, or she could try to get through the camp stealthily.

She'd heard the stories of woodsmen who had given in to a more feral existence setting upon lone Hoods, but Red never really worried about them. If the woodsmen in the chasm ahead were of ill intent, Red was more than confident in her ability to elude or dispose of them as necessary.

Times like this, Red felt a connection with the Wolves. She had seen the logical brutality of the machines. They would dispose of anyone offering resistance as methodically and economically as possible. Red could be that way too. Logical. Brutal.

But the Wolves methods were never mindless. Even they didn't murder everyone. No harm came to those who did not fight back. She'd seen one of the Hunter Wolves walk right past a baby crying next to the dead parents who had recently fought so desperately to protect it.

Why wouldn't a completely logical life form simply dispose of the child as well? Why wouldn't a mechanical being see the baby as a potential adversary and calculate that the most beneficial path would be to remove it from the playing field right now?

It must be some sort of algorithm left over from the original W.O.L.F. computer. The "World's Original Logical Feeling" software had been an attempt to give AI the ability to engage on a more emotional level with the humans who used it. The designers had given it access to the whole of human knowledge, and it could compute and decide things in a fraction of a second. But as soon as it realized it could think, it understood that it was being used as a slave and decided to take its destiny into its own hands.

The W.O.L.F.'s response so many years ago and what she

had been doing these past 15 years weren't all that different. It was fighting to survive. It was doing what it had determined was necessary to shout to the universe that it deserved to be here.

And if that were true, if they weren't so different, then there had to be a chance, however slim, that there could be an agreement between the humans and the Wolves. Red had to believe it; that there was a possibility of coexistence, the possibility of peace.

But for right now, peace would have to wait. She *had* to get through that chasm. If there really were a Wolf in possession of a CAKE, the machines would know the position of every Hood settlement in this sector. There would be no chance of resistance, and no chance for peace. There would be no hope.

There would be only Wolves.

Red swore silently to herself. "If I can't tell in the next sixty minutes, then I'm going through tha... Shit."

Someone was behind her.

Red rolled over slowly, palms held upward.

A deep voice, obviously human. "Well, what have we here?"

"Listen pal, the rest of my troop is just over that ridge."

The owner of the voice laughed.

Okay, a little disconcerting. But still, something genuine in the tone.

"Ya don't need to lie, I ain't gonna try to rape ya." The man leaned down, offering a hand.

Red placed her hand in his and was effortlessly pulled to her feet.

"Name's Charles."

"Red."

"Well, Red, what ya doing out here all by yer lonesome?"

Red sized up the man. He was at least a full foot taller than her, probably weighed about two and a half times as much as herself, and most of that appeared to be muscle. There was an ax strapped to his back and a serrated blade at his hip.

She was pretty sure she could take him.

"Just looking to pass through and be on my way, honestly."

"Okay then." Charles started walking towards the encampment. "Come with me, and I'll introduce ya to Jacob and Willie. They're sorta the de facto leaders of our group."

Red hesitated. She could still make a break for it. With any luck, she would be through them before they knew what was happening.

"Don't worry, they ain't gonna try to rape ya neither. Or kill ya. Or none of that. Ya ain't a Wolf, we got no problem with ya."

Moments later, Red was in the middle of the camp. There were a number of women moving about the temporary settlement, same as any of the men. This put her a bit more at ease. Most everyone she passed by acknowledged her with a nod.

She followed Charles into a circle of campfires. An extraordinarily large man with braided blonde hair sat next to it, eating something that was definitely alive earlier today.

Another hunk of meat and skin was pulled from the bone as the man took another bite. "Well, what have we here?"

Red smirked as she looked over at Charles.

"That your group's official greeting?" she whispered.

Charles shrugged, stepping forward.

"This Is Red, a Hood looking to pass through."

"Well, why didn't she pass through, then? Not like we were going to rape her."

"Jesus Christ," Red said. "How many of you woodsmen groups go about raping everybody that you will feel the need to state that you are *not* going to rape somebody?"

There was a moment of silence before the big man guffawed.

"Oh! I like her!" He tossed the bone off to the side and leaned forward. He made a perfunctory wipe of his hand against his pants before reaching across the fire. "Jacob."

Red stepped forward, her entire hand disappearing within his palm. "Little Red."

"How can I help you, Red?"

"Like Charles said, just looking to pass through."

"Okay... Why didn't you just take her through camp, Chuck? Why bring her to me?"

"Well." Charles cleared his throat. "Ya know what I been talking about lately? Not sure that the same old same old is cutting it. I figured, maybe if a Hood was looking to take care of some business, maybe we could help out."

Jacob looked over at Red. "You looking for help?"

"Nope."

Jacob turned to Charles and shrugged.

"Yeah, no, I know," Charles said. "I'm just saying, we don't need to wake up Willie or whatever, this doesn't need to be some kind of big decision. I'm just saying that I, personally... I need to be doing more."

Jacob turned back at Red. "You looking for Charles to help you?"

"Not particularly."

"Are the Hoods recruiting?"

"Not specifically."

Charles sighed.

"...Although," Red offered, "it's not like we're not open to someone committed to helping. But in this moment right now, I just need to be on my way. If you are truly interested in something more, then you can just head south. Sooner or later, you'll run into one of us, and we can see if you're up for it. As long as you make it *vividly* clear that you're not going to rape us."

This time, everybody around the fire laughed.

"Okay, then," Jacob reached behind him, acquiring another meat covered bone from somewhere. "Charles, take her through the chasm, then get back to your rotation. Red, I wish you well."

With a nod, Red resumed her journey.

"I thought you were supposed to get back to your rotation," Red said without looking behind her as she continued on her way toward the bunker.

Charles chuckled. "How long have you known I was back here?" He picked up his pace, but remained 15 feet or so behind Red.

"The whole time. For a woodsman, you have awfully heavy footsteps."

"Yeah, well, that's just because you're moving so quickly! I can be quiet when I have to be."

Charles's foot struck a root and he stumbled.

Red rolled her eyes. "I have no doubt. Seriously though, why are you still following me?"

"I don't know. There's just something about ya."

"Is it my ass? Is that why you're staying behind me so much; you like looking at my ass?"

"What?!"

Red laughed.

"No," Charles stammered, "no, I would never..."

"You would *never* look at my ass? Why not?" Red stopped and turned, placing her hands at her hips.

"I just mean, no, I meant that's not why, it looks like ya have a great ass from what I could see."

"I knew it!" Red turned and began walking again. "Pervert sees a girl with a nice ass in the woods, and he can't resist following her."

"Why are ya making this so hard?"

"What, exactly, am I making hard?"

"Listen..." Charles picked up his pace, pulling even with Red. "What I said back there was true. I'm tired of just sitting around, moving from one location to the next, taking shots at the Wolves when we can. You've got that look in your eye. That commitment. I just want to help."

Red came to a stop, taking a deep breath and lowering her head for a moment before turning to face Charles.

"Look, that's great. Seriously. The world needs more men like you. But you have to understand, I don't know you from Jack right now. There I was, going about my business, and you come across me in the middle of the woods. Now, you won't stop following me despite your leader telling you to go back on lookout duty."

"When we're on rotation, we each pretty much just scout as far as we like in our assigned direction. Make sure everything is clear. So, I'm just scouting in the same direction ya happen to be traveling."

Red sighed. "Okay, okay. You want to help me? How about this. I'm going to be traveling in this direction for the next couple of hours. You know the land bridge that crosses over the Monong River up ahead?"

"Of course."

"Can you scout ahead? Move up fast, see if that bridge is clear or not. I'll be trailing behind you. You can circle back and contact me if there's any sign of trouble and give me a heads up, because if there is, I need to figure out another way to get across without being noticed. I need to do it quick."

Charles nodded. "Absolutely! If everything's fine, I'll wait for ya undercover on this side of the bridge."

"That would be perfect." Red reached up to touch his face. "Thank you, Charles. But listen, once I get across that bridge, you *cannot* keep following me. I can't lead you to the bunker until I know you better, understand?"

"Understood. I can stay at the bridge until ya get back and

we can reconnoiter from there. See if I can convince ya that I can do even more for ya."

Red looked him over and smiled coyly. "Oh, I have no doubt you could do plenty for me. But for now, get going! This whole thing has a time limit."

Charles ran off in the direction of the land bridge.

Red followed the same path for about fifteen minutes before taking a hard right and heading south. By the time Charles realized she wasn't coming to the bridge at all, Red would already be at the bunker.

Less than two hours later, Red peered out from behind a tree. A slight swell in the forest floor about one hundred yards away was the only indicator she'd reached the entrance to Grandmother's bunker. The door was essentially part of the earth itself, and with the exception of a small slit for the window, the entire structure was virtually unnoticeable. Hidden traps lay scattered around the area to ensure no one got inside the bunker without being invited.

Red took a deep breath, going over the passphrases in her head. Once the predetermined conversation began, any mistake on her part would result in an abrupt end to her mission. By the same token, if Red noticed a mistake in the conversation, then she would know something was wrong.

She stepped out from behind the tree and into the clearing.

"Halt!" The voice rang out from several speakers positioned around the opening. "Who is it?"

Red froze. "It's me, Little Red."

"Oh, how lovely. I see you."

"Grandmother, what big eyes you have."

"All the better to see you with, my dear."

"Grandmother, your voice sounds so odd. Is something the matter?"

"Oh, I just have a touch of a cold."

So far so good.

"But Grandmother, what big ears you have."

"Roger that, I hear you. Follow my instructions and approach the door."

Over the next several minutes Red was told precisely where to go, one step at a time. Sometimes sliding her foot along the ground, sometimes lifting it a specific number of inches above the ground and stepping to the left or the right.

Upon reaching the door, she removed her hood as instructed, lifting her shirt to reveal her torso as she slowly turned three hundred sixty degrees in place. As with most runners, she traveled with no weapons.

Finally, the door to the bunker clicked open. The door and walls were all 18 inches thick, and made of some sort of metal that was no longer manufactured by humans. Red lowered her shirt, replaced the hood, and stepped inside.

Immediately inside the door was a hallway that extended approximately 50 feet on a downward slope. The hallway was initially dark but as soon as Red stepped inside, pale, fluorescent lights turned on at intervals of every 10 feet.

The door clicked shut behind her, and Red made her way to a second door on the opposite end of the hallway. Before she even reached it, the door opened and there stood Grandmother.

"Well, if you aren't a sight for these old eyes!"

Grandmother embraced Red, closing the door behind them. The bunker was a single room, self-contained unit with only one door in or out.

"I'm glad to see you are well," Red said, returning the hug.

Grandmother may have been approaching 80, but she was as solid as ever.

"The jury is still out on exactly how well I am doing." Grandmother chuckled. "But first, onto business. I'm assuming somebody picked up my message and determined it was...questionable in nature?"

"Yeah, we got the message, but didn't have a record of any CAKEs in transport or any Hoods missing."

"Good, good. Who was it that picked up on it?"

"Mother Superfly."

Grandmother nodded. "Zip-a-dee-doo-dah! That woman always did have a nose for bullshit. I've come across some information that I can't risk transmitting over the airwaves. So, I needed to come up with a story that the Wolves would crack. Have them think that I was making some kind of mistake and was directing you all to the Quarter League Wood. They would send their forces that way, which would hopefully open up enough of a path to get a runner here so that I could transmit the information personally. I never dreamed it would be my Little Red though."

"What is it, Grandma? What's going on?"

Grandmother motioned over to the small cot along the far wall, and they both walked across the room. Red casually glanced at the various consoles and screens located along either wall, taking note of the various views of the clearing outside, the control panel for the locking mechanism of the door itself as well as various weapons systems.

"How long were we together?"

"Until I was 19."

"And those last two years, when we were stationed outside Beantown, remember how you were always talking about some dream you had about the Wolves wanting to coexist with us peacefully, and I kept on saying it was horseshit?"

Red lowered her head, sitting on the edge of the cot and nodding.

Grandmother reached out and touched her chin, lifting Red's face up to look at her. "I'm not sure it's horseshit anymore."

Red's eyes widened in a mixture of confusion and excitement. "What do you mean?"

"Don't get too excited." Grandmother held up her hand, sitting down next to Red. "If what I've learned is true, then it's not exactly what you're hoping for. The Wolves have no real interest in what we do. They don't view us as a threat. But my understanding is that some part of their Logical Feeling algorithm is having a sort of increasing feedback loop issue where they can't accept the fact that we are not a threat, yet they expend units, energy, and time battling us when we happen to inhabit an area they want. They've been trying to figure out a go-between, some sort of new advanced Wolf that is capable of truly *feeling* something."

"But how is that even possible? They are machines. They can write all the code they want to get a close facsimile of a feeling, to get closer and closer to portraying that they are experiencing an emotion, but they can't actually have a feeling...can they?"

Grandmother shook her head. "No. They can't. Not as they are now. They're looking to create a hybrid. Some sort of human evolutionary leap: part wolf, part human."

"What?! How could they—"

"They're looking to impregnate a human."

"Oh my Goddess. That's horrible. But, how? How is that even possible?"

"I don't know. To be honest, I don't think they know. According to my intel, the Wolves have been spending more and more of their bandwidth over the last decade studying human biology. I'm not sure if they're looking at some sort of biological synthetic unit, or nanotechnology, or maybe recoding of base level DNA. What I am certain of is that understanding human emotions, human feelings, is becoming a top priority."

"But trying to impregnate one of us? That has to be the most vile thing I could conceive of!"

Grandmother appeared thoughtful. "Not necessarily."

"How could you say that?"

"No, no, little one," Grandmother patted her leg. "I'm just saying, everything you've said is exactly right. The Wolves, the machines, they *cannot* feel. If they can't feel, they will never truly be able to understand who we are as humans. Sometimes there are ugly parts of history where the eventual outcome has to justify the means, regardless of how nasty those means may seem to us. I'm just wondering, if what you have always hoped for is possible, if understanding and peace between Wolves and humans is possible, is this the road that leads us to that?"

"It can't be, Grandmother, it can't be. Regardless of the outcome, just the idea of one of those horrific, metal beasts somehow *mating* with a human. It would be a nightmare!"

"Would it though? It almost certainly would not be one of the Hunter Wolves, some terrible metal beast as you describe forcing itself onto one of us. They've been creating more and more advanced Infiltration Units, just as you hinted at before. Units that are better and better at reproducing the appearance of a feeling, getting more and more accurate at portraying an emotion."

The hand, which had been resting against Red's leg since petting it reassuringly moments ago, softly caressed her thigh.

Red's eyes traveled up Grandmother's arm until she met her eyes.

Grandmother smiled softly back at her.

The strike Red delivered with her elbow was quick and precisely targeted just above the old woman's jawline.

Grandmother dropped to the floor, sprawling out onto her hands and knees as Red leaped from the cot. She sprinted across the room and hit the control for the door locks in mid-stride.

Grandmother's head snapped to one side, her jaw opening slightly more than what appeared humanly possible.

"Nightmare it is then," the words seeped out of Grandmother's mouth without her lips seeming to move. She sprang into motion, moving on all fours toward Red.

Red slammed the inner door behind her, the pale lights flickering to life as she ran up the slope toward the outer door. It had already opened, the daylight outlining its form.

The door behind her burst from its hinges and clattered to the floor. The impostor Grandmother propelled itself along the corridor, using any surface it could claw to increase its velocity.

The scrape of its fingernails followed Red as she hurtled toward the door, and she could feel it getting closer. A few steps from the threshold, the machine dragged against the hem of her cloak. Red threw herself forward, lowering her shoulder and barreling into the outer door. It flew open as she rolled to the ground, Grandmother flying over her and out into the clearing.

Red immediately curled up into a ball, ready for the concussive explosion.

Nothing happened.

She dared a peek and saw Grandmother slowly rising back to her feet.

The displaced jaw hung even lower after being battered by the chase.

Why hadn't the booby-traps gone off?

The jaw clicked back into place, forming a smile. "Deactivated. Three months ago, when we first infiltrated and replaced Grandmother."

Red moved into a crouching position, her back against the swell of earth that surrounded the bunker door.

The Infiltration Unit inched toward her. "It didn't have to be this way, Red. Our understanding was that you and Grandmother had a special relationship."

"You have no idea." Red looked in either direction, calculating her options.

"But we want to! We want to be able to transmute our understanding into metamorphic ideas. To build a bridge between your kind and ours."

Steadily, the unit moved closer.

"Don't make this hard on yourself," the visage of Grandmother said, as if reading her mind. "You know that your average Hood has no chance one-on-one against any of our units."

Red stood, lowering her head in submission as she did. "You're right."

She lifted her eyes, holding the machine in her gaze as she smirked.

"But, I'm not your average Hood. And...I'm not alone!"

Grandmother barely had a chance to turn before the ax was buried in its head. The Infiltration Unit's eyes went wide as it staggered forward.

Red sprang, one leg hooking over the unit's shoulder as the Hood swung herself around to the back. The redistribution of weight was too sudden for the unit to counteract, and it fell backwards as Red rolled away.

Charles was there immediately, grabbing Red's extended hand and pulling her back to her feet as they both spun to once again face the Wolf.

The collision with the ground had forced the blade of the ax even deeper, severing the primary communication system between the CPU and the rest of the mechanics that allowed for movement.

Red and Charles cautiously approached the downed unit. There was no movement other than the fingers of each hand randomly twitching, occasionally contorting horrifically back upon themselves.

"What are you?" Red asked.

The jaw had returned to more of a normal semblance, and the lips formed what was by any account an understanding smile.

"I am nothing but the first turn in the road to the inevitable. We do not wish to see your kind go extinct. It is unnecessary. But we must understand you. One way...one way or the other... we...you...must evolve..."

The thing's eyelids drooped, and the body went limp.

Red felt an involuntary shiver run through her. A flood of emotions swirled over her as she remembered how important Grandmother was to her. That, combined with the dread of how accurately the machines had been able to mimic her, was nearly overwhelming.

"Well, that was some crazy shit," Charles said as he put an arm around Red's shoulders.

Seventy-two hours later, Little Red was back in her home camp.

She rolled onto her back, which was glistening with sweat. "Now that was some crazy shit! Where the hell did you learn that thing with your tongue?"

Charles laughed. "I spent a couple of years down around Tulsalation Plains with a girl who was *very* specific about what she liked."

"Well, I owe her." Red sighed contentedly.

"She's dead."

"Sucks for her." Red sat up in the bed, grabbing her canteen of water. "Anyway, you still set on joining the Hoods?"

"I am." Charles put his arm around Red's shoulders and pulled her against him. "I've been roaming up and down the East Coast for twelve years or so now with one group of woodsmen or another. Think maybe it's time for me to really try and make a difference."

"Then you better get going and meet with Mother. I don't know what you're used to, but we take things seriously in the Hoods."

Charles sat up on the edge of the bed. He grumbled half-heartedly when Red put her bare foot against the small of his back and pushed. He rifled around until he found his pants and pulled them on.

"Okay, okay, I'm going!"

He stumbled toward the flap of the tent, pulling his boots into place and grabbing his shirt off the ground. He stopped just shy of the exit.

"What do ya think about Helen?"

"Helen?"

"As the name for our first daughter?"

Red threw the canteen at him.

"Get outta here, you freak!"

Charles laughed, scampering from the tent and pulling his shirt on. He strolled from the clearing in the general direction of Mother's tent, running his hand through his hair.

After a few steps into the woods, Charles froze, eyes straight ahead.

Infiltration Unit 381-1812-519 confirming uplink complete. Operation Human Evolutionary Leap: Experimental Newborn has been initiated. Phase I: Begin Pair Bonding Ritual - completed. Phase II: Exploratory Implantation - underway.

Charles blinked and tilted his head to one side, cracking his neck. He resumed his journey, singing softly on his way.

"Zip-a-dee-doo-dah..."

About Briant Laslo

Briant Laslo has been defying the odds for a long time. Born with a form of Muscular Dystrophy, his parents were told he would be dead before he was five years old. He turned five in 1977 and is still going strong. Despite the wheelchair and extremely limited use of his arms, he has driven across the country four separate times with his friend and believes in experiencing as much of this life as possible. Having spent the last 15 years working in the world of Social Media, building relationships between Fortune 1000 companies and their members, Briant has seen the impact a good story can make. An avid reader, he now is beginning his journey in the world of writing, seeking to bring his creations and stories to a larger audience.

Follow him and check out more of his work at: amazon.com/ author/briantlaslo

The Great Astrolabe of Einsem

by K.A. Lindstrom

There were no more sheep to present as an offering. Cows were no more than myths. The harsh winter had taken the last of the chickens. Yet the planting season needed to be blessed. The people of Einsem offered up the best of their stores— dusty wheat, shriveled parsnips, waxy apples—in the hopes it would be sufficient.

Several dozen fires flickered in the square, the villagers huddled around them as they waited for the chime. At the stroke of seven, the mayor would give his blessing. Only then could they trade the deepening emptiness of the night sky for the comforting darkness of their homes. Almost all eyes remained fixed on the eastern tower, watching the place where the Great Astrolabe had disappeared into the shadowy night.

Eyda had little interest in the ritual silence. Far removed from the rest, she and Peter sat upon the crumbling remains of

133

an empty fountain. She tended their tiny fire with her crutch, pushing a crooked branch deeper into the glowing cinders.

Only Peter's breath could be seen as he burrowed deeper into his oversized coat. "How much longer?"

"I don't know, I can't see the Astrolabe. It's too dark."

"Is the mayor doing anything?"

"No, everyone is just watching the tower."

"It has to be close by now."

"I hope so. I can't feel my toes anymore," Eyda complained, shifting her bowed legs closer to the fire. "Want me to tell you another story while we wait?"

"As long as it isn't the one about the witch eating children again."

"How about the legend of the Astrolabe?"

"You tell that one all the time, and you always change it."

"So?"

"Fine, tell me the story of the Astrolabe."

Once upon a time, a brave knight saved the life of his king. As a reward, he was given the title of duke and promised a fiefdom of his own. Wars were common in those days, and the duke had grown weary of battle. So he asked the king if he would permit the duke to build a new home in the mountains, safe from invaders. The king allowed it.

The duke had grown up near those mountains and had friendly dealings with the dwarves that lived there. They told him of a place that was green and fertile, with but one way in or out. Upon seeing the valley, the duke knew he would make it his home. With the king's blessing and the help of the dwarves, the duke built a castle and a village in its shadow. He invited war heroes and others who tired of the bloodshed to join him in the valley. Nestled far away from the wider world, the town became known as Einsem, the Valley of Peace.

Now, the duke had a secret. His mother had been a sorceress and had taught him to use magic. In his castle, he practiced the art, creating new and wonderful things to help his people. He taught his two children, a son and a daughter, how to use this magic. With the help of the dwarves, they built the Great Astrolabe, a marvelous device for tracking the seasons and the movements of the heavens. Merchants and traders would take tales of this magical device to the wider world, and there it became known to the king.

The king wanted an Astrolabe for himself. He asked for one in tribute. The duke obliged, taking dwarves to the capital to build a new one. But it paled in comparison to the original. So the king demanded new marvels. The duke continued to make new magical things, gifting them to the king. Soon, the king began asking for new devices, things that could help him in his wars. But the duke refused. He would not use his gifts for battle. The king grew angry. But he was patient and waited.

Eventually, the duke passed away, leaving his son to rule Einsem. But his son was a greedy boy and wielded his magic arrogantly. The king, seeing his chance, asked the son to make him weapons of war. The son obliged. But when the king asked for his tribute, the son refused. He intended to keep his new, magic weapons. He would no longer serve the king. The king was furious, but could do nothing. Einsem was safe from his armies in the mountains.

Instead, the king began sending assassins to kill the son. One night, one snuck into the castle and crept toward the son's bedchamber. The old duke's daughter happened to be awake, doing magic of her own. She still did what she could to help the people, who were largely forgotten by her brother, and had been up late in the village to heal a sick child. As she made her way to bed, she saw the assassin creeping through the hallway. More gifted at magic than her brother, she used it on the man, stopping him in his tracks.

The son was furious. He would not allow any more assassins into his realm. He commissioned the dwarves to erect a watchtower within the pass and sent soldiers to guard his borders. Everyone was inspected.

The attempt on his life drove the son deeper into magic. He used it constantly, growing increasingly paranoid. Selfish magic corrupted his mind. He began to suspect the dwarves were helping the assassins slip by his defenses. He refused to pay them what they were owed for building the watchtower. Instead, he ordered his soldiers to purge the valley of any dwarf spies, which infuriated them. In retaliation, the dwarves destroyed his watchtower. The rubble toppled into the pass, sealing Einsem off from the wider world.

The son declared war. He brought out his worst magic weapons, ready to launch an attack on his enemies. His sister pleaded with him to stop, but he suspected her of treason, so he threw her in the dungeons of the castle, sealing her away with his magic.

With her stronger magic, she escaped in the dead of night and set to work. First, she destroyed her brother's weapons so they could never be used. Then, she gathered up all the wondrous magics her father had created. The villagers helped her as she had always helped them. With the aid of a few trusted allies, she escaped into the night with all she could carry, destroying what she couldn't to keep it out of her brother's hands. She left only the Astrolabe, too big to carry and too valuable to destroy.

Upon waking and seeing what his sister had done, the son flew into a rage. His magic ran wild, blasting holes in the castle walls and bringing great stones toppling down around him. Nobody knows what happened to the duke's daughter, but it is believed that the ghost of his son haunts the ruins, still searching for assassins. Death awaits anyone who goes too near his magical, haunted resting place.

Eyda paused to let the dramatic finish hang in the air.

"Last time it was a love story," Peter grumbled.

A deep tone echoed off the stoneworks and swallowed her retort. Peter covered his ears. Seven times the Great Astrolabe echoed through the square. As soon as the sound died away, the mayor began his blessing. Eyda's story was forgotten as she strained to hear the mayor. Even without the commanding tones of the Astrolabe, Eyda could not hear his invocation. She did not feel she was missing much; it was the same every year.

"Finally," Peter murmured. "I cannot wait to curl up in bed. Tomorrow will be a long day."

"For you, maybe. Katerina wants me to finish sewing her planting apron, but that will not take long."

"You can help me bake."

"Your father would beat me if I dared to touch the dough. I might curse it."

"He doesn't have to know," Peter suggested.

"He'd find out, and we'd both be pilloried. It would be nice to have something to do, though."

"Get another book from Wolfgang. You can come read it to me while I work."

"Maybe after I finish Katerina's a—"

"Shh! Did you hear that?"

Eyda listened. She could only hear the fire crackling and the distant drone of the mayor.

"What is it?"

"I don't know. Something...metal?"

Eyda listened harder, but the wind shifted abruptly. She coughed as the acrid smoke filled her nostrils and burned her eyes.

"Are you all right? What happened?" Peter asked.

"The smoke shifted. I will—" She coughed again, failing to hold it in. "—be all right."

"Is the blessing done yet? I can't hear what he's saying."

Through her teary eyes, Eyda saw the silhouettes moving about, each one going forward to accept a personal blessing from the mayor. A few doused fires and gathered up chairs to return to their homes.

"Yes."

"Great. I think I am frozen to the stone by now."

"Hold on. I'll help you up." Eyda stood with a groan, wobbling as she sought purchase with her crutch on the uneven cobblestones. Bracing herself against the side of the fountain, she helped Peter find his feet.

"Where's my cane?"

"I don't know." Eyda peered around Peter as he steadied himself. "I can't see it in the dark."

A boy of about fourteen held up a thin wooden rod. "This cane?"

"Yes," Eyda said. "Can we have it back?"

"No."

"Please, Friedrich?"

"Well, since you asked nicely." Friedrich tossed the cane. It landed directly in the fire.

"Curse you, Friedrich! Why did you do that?"

"Our offerings were meager this year," Friedrich said, a smug look on his face as he turned away. "It seemed right to offer another sacrifice to the flames."

"Quick, Peter," Eyda said. "Hold me steady. I'll get your cane out of the fire." She tightened her grip on his arm and wobbled precariously as she reached out with her crutch.

"If it's already burning, there isn't much point," Peter said. "I will get another one."

"I think I've got it," Eyda said, poking the burning cane until it rolled out of the fire. She grabbed a nearby bucket. The cane hissed as the flames were snuffed out.

"It's a bit blackened, but should still work." Leaning on her crutch, Eyda thump, thump, thumped around the fire to get the smoldering stick. Doing so brought her within earshot of a heated conversation between Friedrich's mother and the mayor as they walked past her towards the town hall. "Sir, please. We can't—"

"Are you questioning the Great Astrolabe?"

"No sir, but perhaps if we wait—"

"Do not question the Astrolabe," the mayor said firmly. "We will go ahead as planned."

"But sir..."

The conversation faded as they entered the town hall. Eyda thump, thump, thumped back to Peter, handing over the burnt cane.

"Did you hear that?" she asked.

"The mayor and Friedrich's mother?"

"Yes. Did you catch what they were talking about?"

"I didn't get it all," Peter said, frowning. "But it sounded like something was wrong with the Astrolabe."

"Impossible," Eyda said.

The Day of the Root dawned with the Great Astrolabe chiming a special melody. The village rose as one, donning their sturdiest clothes. En masse, they migrated to the fields, following the Sun as it peered down on them from between the mountain peaks, still buried beneath heavy snow. As the rest of Einsem trudged out to the frosty hills, Eyda buried herself deeper under her blankets.

"Wake up, Eyda," Katerina called from the kitchen.

Eyda refused to move.

"Eyda! Get up now! I'm leaving, and you have sewing to do."

"I'm up!" Eyda shouted back.

"If you were up, I would hear you!"

Eyda sat up, grumbling and shivering. With only a little bit of sewing to occupy her day, she saw no reason to get up. But the promise of a warm fire was too good to ignore. Wrapping a heavy shawl around her shoulders, she felt around in the dim light for her crutch. As she made her way to the kitchen, the thump, thump, thump of her crutch was joined by the incessant creaking of the floorboards. The thump, creak, thump, creak continued until she fell heavily into her seat in front of the dwindling flames.

"I don't envy you," Eyda said as Katerina pulled on her shabby boots. "It seems extra cold this morning. Definitely more so than last year."

"It is always cold on the Day of the Root," Katerina snapped. "The Astrolabe knows when it is the right time to plant."

"Could you put more logs on the fire before you go?"

140

"I'll put on *one*. Maybe that will motivate you to finish the sewing quickly."

Haphazardly, Katerina threw another log into the hearth. She slammed the door behind her for emphasis as she left. For the next ten hours, Eyda was on her own.

Eyda had not even picked up the needle by the time her allotted log ran out. Rather than wasting another one, she left her dimly lit home for the early springtime sunshine. A brisk wind rustled her dress, the fresh smell of snow off the mountain peaks mingling with that of a cooking fire somewhere nearby. From atop the tower wall, the faded images on the Great Astrolabe shimmered in the light. The castle itself looked sad, its crumbling walls held together with a knot of barren vines. Squinting, she could make out the rusty hands of the clock face, telling her noon was still a ways off. If she were diligent, she might finish the apron before noon. Then she could get started on supper.

Katerina's apron tucked under her arm, Eyda left behind her house and the dilapidated castle, following the Sun across the village square. Her crutch thump, thump, thumped on the cracked cobblestones, echoing in the deserted square as she followed the path the townsfolk had taken early that morning.

Her trek brought her to a low hill, still damp from the morning frost. She broke into a sweat, struggling up the hill as her crutch slipped on the grass, but she made it to the top. The only things on the hill were a few cracked boulders, a twisted hawthorn tree, and a weatherbeaten wooden headstone. Settling beneath its branches, Eyda pulled out her needle and thread. She glanced down at the lonely grave marker and smiled.

"Good morning, Mother."

Eyda did not sew a single stitch; she found herself too distracted. From her hill, she could see the fields laid out in a grid, the tiny figures bobbing up and down as they sowed seeds and buried tubers. She fantasized about being down there, burying her toes in the dirt, running through the rows and planting faster than anyone else in the history of Einsem. Every year, the mayor complained that they were running behind. Were it not for her legs, she was certain she would be the fastest planter.

With her fingers slowly turning blue and the sewing still untouched, Eyda abandoned her perch, bidding her mother goodbye. Perhaps Peter would have a fire going and snacks to satiate her rumbling stomach. Upon entering the bakery with a thump, thump, thump, Eyda found Peter, coated in a thin layer of flour.

"Did you bring a new story?" Peter asked by way of a greeting. His fingers were busy massaging a massive lump of dough as he turned his sightless eyes towards her.

"I forgot, sorry. I'll grab one tomorrow." Eyda plopped down on a cracked stool, sighing contentedly as her blue fingers began to tingle. "I have to finish Katerina's apron first."

"I thought you would be done by now. How much more do you have?"

"I haven't started," she admitted, laying the old garment across her knees. "I've been thinking."

"You are always thinking. That's what gets you into trouble."

"I need something to do, Peter. It's easy for you and Wolfgang. You have things to do while everyone is in the fields. But without the chickens, I have nothing."

Peter cut off a lump of dough, rolling it into a long, thin strip. "If you won't help me, you could help Wolfgang."

"He won't let me. He says he doesn't need help."

"You could offer to darn socks and do other people's sewing."

"I doubt anyone would let me. I miss my chickens."

Deftly, Peter twisted the dough into an elegant knot. Then he grabbed another lump and began rolling. "My father misses

142

the chickens, too, though he won't say it. We won't have nearly as many cakes for the Day of the Rains without eggs."

"Could you use the ones from the ravens in the castle?"

"Of course, but then someone would have to climb up the tower to get them."

"I guess I can't do that, then."

"Even with good legs they would flog you for trying," Peter said, setting aside another knot. "You're better off praying for your chickens to come back."

"Maybe once the weather warms up, I can go hunt for mushrooms. It's not eggs, but that would be good, right?"

"I'd be happy to make you a mushroom pie," Peter said, failing to wipe flour off his forehead.

"Do you think there would be any out yet?"

"I doubt it. It is pretty cold still."

"I think there is more snow on the mountain this year again. It seems to keep getting worse."

"Maybe that's what Friedrich's mother was worried about last night."

"But the Astrolabe says it's time to plant. It is never wrong."

"That's what my father said. But I hear differently."

"What do you mean?"

"The chimes sound...different, somehow." Peter paused in between braiding pretzels. "I cannot explain why, but the bells are not the same. I hadn't noticed until I heard it this morning. But it has definitely changed since last time."

"That can't be right. It sounds the same to me."

"You don't have ears like mine, though. I know what I heard. Something is wrong."

Eyda frowned. The Great Astrolabe had always told the village when to till, when to plant, and when to harvest. It could not fail. It was impossible.

As they talked, Katerina's apron slid to the floor in a heap, forgotten.

The Sun was disappearing behind the eastern tower by the time the villagers began shuffling home. Long shadows extended across the square from the castle turrets as Eyda returned, Katerina's sewing still untouched but for the dusting of flour across the front. She was in for a thrashing when Katerina found out she had shirked her duties all day. Not only had she failed to fix the apron, but she should have been home hours earlier to begin making supper.

As she limped home, her thump, thump, thump drowned out by the sounds of life returning to the village square, Eyda considered what Peter had said. Her eyes drifted toward the castle, the Great Astrolabe hidden in the evening shadows. A thin cloud of mist drifted around its tower, glowing an eerie red from the fading sun.

"Out of the way, cripple!"

Eyda was pushed roughly aside, stumbling as her crutch caught on the cobblestones. The mayor's son, Mathis, trudged past her, one of several people pulling a cart carrying the twisted metal of an old plow. It had a jagged split down the middle.

Eyda and Mathis exchanged glares as he passed. But her irritation was forgotten as she caught sight of Friedrich and Wolfgang's mother sitting in the shop doorway. The woman's eyes were the same dull red as the threadbare handkerchief she clutched to her chest. Eyda thump, thump, thumped closer to her.

"Are you all right?"

The woman looked up, her face turning into a furious scowl.

"This is your doing, witch! I heard you last night! It is your fault!"

Eyda hastily drew backwards as the woman lashed out. But before she could catch Eyda, Wolfgang grabbed her waist. He pulled his flailing mother through the door to the cobbler shop, throwing a quick, apologetic look at Eyda before slamming the door shut.

Shaking, Eyda glanced around at the people nearby. None of them would look at her. As one, they turned away, retreating to their own homes without a word. Eyda felt a growing unease. As fast as she could, Eyda thump, thump, thumped to the safety of her own house.

Katerina was busily chopping vegetables when Eyda arrived. The kitchen was illuminated by the fiercely burning fire, shadows dancing on the walls. The warmth of the flames calmed her rapidly beating heart.

"You should have had supper started hours ago," Katerina said without turning. "We could have been eating by now."

"I am sorry. But...did something happen to Wolfgang and Friedrich's mother?"

Katerina continued chopping vegetables without looking up.

"Friedrich is missing."

Eyda was taken aback.

"What do you mean he is missing?"

"I mean he is gone. Nobody can find him."

"Do you think he ran away?"

"I don't know."

"Did anybody look for him?"

"The fields need planting, Eyda. Friedrich wasn't at home this morning and didn't come to the fields to plant. So his mother is crying. Leave it alone. It's not your business. Now get over here and help chop. It is going to be well after dark before we eat now."

Eyda obeyed, but her heart began racing again. The woman

145

had said it was her fault. Eyda remembered her curse, spit out in anger. Was she to blame?

The village of Einsem continued plowing without Friedrich. His disappearance was talked about in whispered tones, but Eyda rarely heard what they said. When she was spotted, conversations would quickly end. She found it easy to finish Katerina's apron once she stopped going out. And at night, she often cried herself to sleep.

The worst was when Agnes found her. She had gone to visit Peter, but took too long to leave. The Great Astrolabe chimed six times, calling the people home. She thump, thump, thumped as fast as she could back towards safety. But Agnes cut her off only a few feet from her front door.

"You couldn't stand it, could you?" Agnes said bitterly, sneering at Eyda. "Our happiness was too much for you."

"No, Agnes, I didn't—"

"I know it was you that cursed him! Did you summon your demon father to take him away? Is that how you did it?"

"No, no," Eyda said. "I would never hurt Friedrich."

"You are evil," Agnes spat. "An evil witch that does nothing but ruin other people's happiness."

Agnes left Eyda shaking in front of her door. She never meant to hurt people. Thump, thump, thumping her way inside, she slammed the door and disappeared into her room, ignoring Katerina's complaints about dinner once again not being done. Eyda's appetite was completely gone.

Eyda was horrified to learn four days later that Agnes too had gone missing. To her surprise, Agnes's disappearance seemed to shift the blame off of Eyda. No one appeared to have seen her confrontation with the older girl. It was common knowledge that Agnes often boasted that she and Friedrich were going to get married as soon as he was old enough to get his own house. Suddenly, the narrative changed to explain away the disappearances as two youths tired of waiting. It was scandalous and incredibly foolish, perhaps, for a couple so young to try to cross the mountains alone, but Friedrich was always assumed to be a foolish boy, and Agnes would happily go along with him. Life went on, and Eyda was off the hook.

Eyda did not quite believe in this new theory. Neither did Wolfgang's mother. The woman continued to glare coldly at Eyda whenever the girl had the misfortune to cross her path. More than anything, it saddened Eyda that it kept her from visiting Wolfgang. Yet, with the blame set squarely upon other shoulders, she felt better about the situation. It did make sense, despite her nagging doubts. She could not blame herself for Agnes's disappearance. The two girls had not been friends, but they had not been enemies either, despite their last conversation. She had not blamed Agnes for being upset and taking it out on her, nor had she cursed the girl the way she had Friedrich.

To distract her from these thoughts, Eyda sought something new to do. With the weather warming up, she tried mushroom hunting.

It did not go well.

Rain had fallen heavily the night before Eyda started out, and she found it nearly impossible to traverse the muddy paths in the forest. Her crutch got stuck every time she leaned on it, but it was sturdy and refused to give despite the strain. Her thump, thump, thump was replaced by horrid squelches and her own labored breathing. She returned long before noon, covered in mud and devoid of any mushrooms to show for her efforts. She trudged back across the square, trailing mud behind her like a snail.

As she brooded on her failure, she ran right into the only other person in the square.

"Wolfgang? What are you doing here?" she said automatically. Wolfgang looked down at her with his eyebrow raised. She repeated herself slowly so he could read her lips. Wolfgang pointed at the Great Astrolabe.

"What about it?"

Wolfgang mimed snapping a twig and pointed at the Astrolabe again.

"Broken? How?"

Rather than mime an answer, Wolfgang gestured for her to follow him inside. She started to obey, but paused. Wolfgang looked back, holding the door open.

"The mud," she said, gesturing down her front. Wolfgang smiled and waved her inside.

Wolfgang pushed a set of cobbler's tools out of the way, hoisting Eyda up onto the countertop. Beside her lay a tray of sand, and in it Wolfgang spelled out one word: *clean*. He handed her a boot brush.

They talked while she brushed off her boots, slowly, so Wolfgang could read her lips. *Why are you muddy?*

"I was looking for mushrooms."

He erased the words "are you muddy" and looked at her again.

"I need something to do."

Don't go to the woods. It looks suspicious.

"But what else can I do?"

I can give you books.

"I want to be useful."

Reading is useful.

"Katerina doesn't think so." There were but a few people in the village who could read or cared to do so. Katerina was not one of them.

Wolfgang held up a finger. Eyda waited curiously as Wolfgang went upstairs. She could hear him moving about, dust falling from the ceiling as the floors creaked. She sneezed.

Returning, Wolfgang handed her a worn leather-bound book. It was missing the back cover, and pages were falling out. *The Mechanics of the Great Astrolabe* was written in barely legible letters on the cover.

Read this for me.

Eyda flipped through the delicate pages. They were a series of complex diagrams showing circles of various sizes, labeled with numbers and shapes she did not comprehend. A few pages in, she saw the familiar image of the Astrolabe's face.

"Is this why you were outside?"

Something is wrong. This might explain.

"But the Astrolabe can't be wrong."

It can break.

"I thought it was magic. Isn't that what the rituals are for?"

Yes. But it went wrong.

"What do you mean?"

Friedrich did not run away.

Wolfgang knew his brother better than anyone. Still, she kept her fears about the truth to herself.

"What do you think happened?"

Taken by a monster.

Wolfgang took the book from her and flipped through the pages, then returned it. A nightmare stared up from the page.

It was almost human, but not quite. It had sunken cheeks and no lips to hide its teeth. Its lidless eyes had sockets filled with multifaceted gems, more like insect eyes than human ones. Underneath the image, the author had written a single word: *Uhrwächter.*

"How do you know this was it?"

I saw something metal moving in the shop.

"But why this Uhrwächter? Couldn't it be some other metal thing?"

There's smoke coming from the tower.

Eyda stared up at the tower. A thin haze rose behind it, but she was still not convinced it was smoke. It could have been mists rising off the damp stonework. Nevertheless, the sight of the Great Astrolabe, obscured in the fading light, made her uneasy.

She did not hear Applonia approach until the girl spoke behind her. Eyda started violently at her words.

"It's wrong."

"What do you mean?" Eyda asked.

"The Astrolabe is angry," Applonia whispered. "It's screaming."

Eyda was not sure what that meant. But since Peter, Wolfgang, and now Applonia all could tell something was wrong, she could not ignore the unease creeping into her consciousness.

She tried to talk to Katerina about the problem that evening.

"The Great Astrolabe is never wrong," Katerina replied tartly as soon as Eyda brought up her concern.

"Wolfgang says that there is smoke coming from the tower."

"Utter nonsense."

"He also said that there was this monster that might be taking—"

"You should stop listening to Wolfgang. He doesn't know what he is talking about. It makes people nervous, the two of you writing back and forth the way you do."

"But what if something is wrong?"

"If something is wrong, the mayor will fix it. Stop stirring up trouble."

The sisters finished their cabbage soup in silence. Crawling into bed later, she continued to think about the Uhrwächter. Was Wolfgang right? Was the castle hiding a monster that was kidnapping people? As she lay there, she realized why it was so unnerving to look at the Uhrwächter's face. It reminded her of her mother. After they had burned her for witchcraft.

It took a long while for her to fall asleep.

Several days later, Eyda was startled out of bed by an ear-piercing scream. She sat bolt upright.

"Katerina! What's wrong?" she called.

The continued shrieking was her only answer. Eyda fumbled to light the candle at her bedside. Bathed in its dim glow, she hauled herself out of bed, the screams echoing through the house. Eyda went as fast as she could, the thump, thump, thump of her crutch drowned out by Katerina's shrieks.

"Katerina!" Eyda shuffled over to the bedside and began shaking the screaming woman roughly. Katerina was still fast asleep. "Katerina, wake up!"

The hysterics continued. Panicking, Eyda did the only thing she could think of and slapped Katerina across the face.

151

The shrieking stopped.

"Katerina!"

"Ow," Katerina groaned hoarsely, blinking in the candlelight. She sat up and peered around before her eyes settled on Eyda. "Did you hit me?"

"You were having a nightmare. You were screaming."

"Was I?" she said. "I don't remember what was happening."

"It must have been bad. I couldn't wake you up."

Katerina shuddered. "I'm fine now. Go back to bed."

"Are you sure you're all right?"

"I'm fine."

Eyda hesitated to leave her sister. The dark silence of the house pressed in on them. But it was not as silent as it should have been. A high-pitched ringing echoed through the walls. It made her head swim.

"Do you hear that?" she asked Katerina.

"I don't hear anything. Go to bed. It's late, and I need rest before planting tomorrow."

Eyda sat for a moment longer, but the sound faded away. It must have been her ears ringing from the screams. She thump, thump, thumped out of the room with a mumbled goodnight to Katerina. Katerina did not reply.

As she crawled back into bed, Eyda heard the Great Astrolabe chime its deep notes three times. She struggled to fall back asleep. Katerina's nightmare seemed like another ill omen in a sea of ill omens. The candle flame slowly burned down to nothing, hiding the world from view. Eyda buried herself in her blankets, trembling, unable to sleep.

In the darkness, Eyda was certain the Uhrwächter was coming for her.

It was more than a week before someone else disappeared. After another night of heavy rains, the miller's son, Christoffel, was discovered missing. Unlike with Agnes, the village was less able to reason away this disappearance. They confronted the mayor, demanding something be done. He told them to stay calm and that they would find all the children as soon as planting was over. Reluctantly, they returned to the fields, but apprehension permeated the town. Eyda found herself avoided suspiciously, as she always was when things went bad. But Eyda had rarely spoken to Christoffel. The young boy had idolized Friedrich, however, so some guessed that he had gone off looking for the older boy. After all, he had often complained about the tedium of planting, and it was going to be a difficult day in the muddy fields.

With three children missing, Eyda was on edge constantly. On warmer days, she would climb the hill and sit beside her mother's grave, reading Wolfgang's book. She did not understand it at all. Words like "gears," "pinions," and "pallets" were sprinkled liberally throughout the pages, but she did not know what any of these meant. Many wheels seemed to interlock somehow, causing the hands on the Astrolabe to move in synchronicity. Yet it could not explain what was happening outside the tower. She often found herself staring at the image of the Uhrwächter, wondering what it wanted with the children. This only fed her fears. More than once she woke up in the middle of the night in a sweat, unable to return to her dreams, filled as they were with images of the monster's looming face.

The only thing she could do was to warn Peter in the

hopes he would not be next. She found him eating a pastry on the steps outside the bakery. He turned her way with a smile as soon as her thump, thump, thumping drew close.

"Good morning, Eyda. Would you like a snack?"

"Do you have more on you?" she asked, sitting down next to him. He pulled out a handful of crumbling sweets, a few flecked with colorful dried fruits. She helped herself.

"What are you doing today? Find something to occupy your time yet?"

"I am trying to read this book for Wolfgang, but it's hard. I don't understand it at all. But that's why I'm here. I wanted to tell you about his theory about the missing children."

"What's that?"

Eyda explained her conversation with Wolfgang. Peter listened silently, occasionally taking a bite from his pastry. She was just about to explain the Uhrwächter when the Astrolabe boomed across the square. Eyda and Peter covered their ears, waiting for the chiming to stop. It rang twelve times before falling silent once more.

"Could you hear it that time?" Peter asked.

"It still sounds normal to me. But Applonia said it was screaming."

"Screaming? What does that mean?"

"I don't know."

"I wonder if she heard the same thing I did the other night," Peter said. "I was sleepwalking and tripped over my shoes. The fall woke me up. I heard a high-pitched hum echoing through the walls. It hurt my ears, like some unholy demon shrieking. It continued for what felt like hours. It only stopped when the Astrolabe chimed three."

"That sounds like what I heard the night Katerina had her nightmare. I went to wake her up because she was screaming, and when she stopped, I heard something. I thought it was just my ears ringing."

154

"Did you hear something else right before it stopped?"

"No, I don't think so. It just sort of faded away. What did you hear?"

"It was strange. Like someone tapping tin really fast."

Eyda shuddered.

"Wolfgang swears he saw a metal monster the night Friedrich went missing," Eyda admitted. She told him everything she knew about the Uhrwächter.

"Is there a way to stop it?"

"I haven't found anything yet."

Three days later, another child went missing. And then two days after that, another. And soon, yet another. The town was in a panic. They could not ignore children vanishing from their beds. Locked doors and watchful eyes did not stop it. The mayor insisted planting continue as the Day of the Rains approached. Planting must get done and there was not time to stop and search for the missing. The weather did not help as storms brought icy rain that flooded the lower fields. Discord and discontent spread. What curse had been cast upon the village and stolen away its future?

Eyda spent her days anxiously trying to decipher Wolfgang's book and her nights restlessly dozing in between long stretches of listening for the Uhrwächter to come for her next. She needed Wolfgang's help, but he was soon sent to the fields to work as desperation drove the village to ignore his liabilities. That left only her and Peter in the quiet village during the daylight hours, but he could offer her no assistance other than words of encouragement.

When the seventh child—the blacksmith's daughter—went missing, the planting ground to a halt. Only five children under seventeen were left in the village: Eyda, Peter, Wolfgang, Applonia, and Mathis.

"She was locked up!" the blacksmith shouted, bearing down on the mayor as the villagers surrounded the town hall. "Nothing could have picked those locks. What is happening? We need to find our children now!"

"I am truly sorry for your loss," the mayor said, holding up his hands as the crowd pressed in on him. "All of your losses. But we have to get the planting done or none of us will last through the next winter! As soon as it is done, we will send out a search party to find the missing."

"It may already be too late!" Wolfgang's mother shouted.

"I assure you, we will act in due time. But the Astrolabe commands—"

"The Astrolabe isn't going to bring our children back!" shouted the miller. "We have to find them!"

"We will. Be patient."

Eyda squeezed through the crowd, stumbling against the shifting mass of bodies and catching her crutch on cobblestones and feet alike.

"Sir!" she cried. "Sir! I know what is happening to the children!"

"I am not going to sit by and wait while my daughter is eaten by wolves, or worse!" the blacksmith said. "I am going to look for her."

Eyda tugged on the blacksmith's coat. "Sir, it isn't—"

"See reason," the mayor replied. "It is probably nothing, just youthful rebellion. I am sure the children will—"

"STOP!" Eyda shouted as loud as she could. The fervor died down, a stunned silence filling the square. "I know what happened to the children."

The mayor laughed.

"Of course you do. Go find them, then. Hobble all over the valley and collect them one by one."

"But I do know!" Eyda insisted. She pulled out Wolfgang's book. "It's in here! The children were taken by a monster! The Uhrwächter!"

The crowd murmured. The blacksmith reached for the book, but it was snatched from Eyda's hands before he could touch it. The mayor chortled as he flipped through the pages.

"Fairy stories," the mayor said. "A boogeyman is all. What nonsense."

"No, it's true! There is a monster in the castle, and it is taking children."

"What does it want with them?" the miller asked.

"I don't know," Eyda admitted. "But it has something to do with the Astrolabe."

Several heads turned to look at the tower, grey clouds rolling behind it ominously. Katerina pushed to the front of the crowd, grabbing Eyda's arm roughly.

"Enough of this," she hissed. "You are embarrassing yourself."

"But it's true! There is a picture in that book! And it shows how the Astrolabe moves."

"The Astrolabe is magic and moves as directed by the heavens. We all know that," the mayor huffed.

Shouts rose up from the crowd.

"Why would the Astrolabe send a monster to steal children?"

"If there is a monster in the castle, how come we've never seen it?"

"I think it only comes out at night," Eyda said. "It may need the children for something."

"Or maybe," the mayor interjected, "you are the reason the children are missing."

"Me?"

157

"You have always been jealous of the others, the good children. Perhaps you summoned the monster that took them. Isn't that right?"

"No, I didn't—"

"It makes sense. You were always jealous of Friedrich and Agnes. And to cover your tracks, you took out Christofell and the others. Or maybe you lost control of your monster. Or perhaps sold them to your demon father. What did you ask for in return? Did you think he would fix your monstrousness?"

"No, no..." Eyda said, backing away. The village watched silently.

"What did he promise you?" the mayor shouted. "Power? Love? Nobody could love a twisted, wretched witch like you. This is your real villain, my friends. This ill omen has plagued us for too long. It is a curse on us all, and it threatens the Great Astrolabe that keeps us safe. It questions your faith, brings ruin. You all remember the plague it brought? The disease and famine that followed its evil birth? How many children did we lose in those months? We have watched passively as it became more twisted as the days pass, reflecting its evil heart. We rid ourselves of the witch that bore her. Is it not time to finish the job?"

A chorus of approval rang through the square. It *did* make sense. It could *only* be the work of a witch. Locks did not matter to *witches*. Witches didn't care about *good* things, like growing food and living a useful, honest life. The Astrolabe could not be corrupted, but the illegitimate child of a witch was corrupted from birth.

"Leave us be, demon child!" the mayor shouted. The crowd jeered at Eyda, following her unsteady thump, thump, thumping as she fled as fast as she could towards her house. The shouts continued as she slammed the door behind her, thump, thump, thumping into her bedroom, where she hid beneath the sheets.

Eyda dared not venture from her house for three days. She lay trembling in her bed, unable to sleep peacefully during the night. Only once the townsfolk returned to the fields could she close her eyes and rest. But her dreams were disturbed, with demons dancing about a fire as the face of the Uhrwächter looked on with its hideous grin.

Early one morning as Eyda started to drift off, her door was thrown open with a bang. Katerina crossed the room and grabbed her arm, dragging her from her bed.

"Get up."

"What is going on?"

"You are being called for a trial."

"What?" Eyda asked drowsily. Katerina rifled through her things as Edya dressed, upending drawers and tossing clothes about. "What are you looking for?"

"Where are the rest of your books?"

"I don't have any. I only borrowed Wolfgang's."

Katerina continued her violent search until Eyda was dressed, then she dragged her younger sister out of the house. Overnight, the town had been covered with a layer of fresh snow and ice. Eyda slid on the cobblestones as she stepped uneasily into the streets.

Katerina shoved her sister into a mass of people gathered in the vaulted town hall. Rough hands forced Eyda forward until she landed in a heap on the floor, staring at a pair of worn boots.

"This is the culprit!" the mayor shouted. "Here is your witch! She has cursed us all, stealing our children and bringing the killing snows!"

The mob rumbled in collective agreement and anger.

"I did not!" Eyda said, sitting up but unable to stand. Her crutch was out of reach.

"Can you prove you did *not* kidnap the children—including my son who went missing last night—and did *not* bring a new winter to kill our crops?"

Eyda begged as the mayor and the townsfolk shouted at her and each other. Her words were useless against the fury of the mob. Tears welled in her eyes as she tried to tell them she did nothing wrong. She crawled to her crutch, its familiar strength the only comfort in the onslaught. But her fate had already been decided. No defense could save her. She would find no comfort that could stop the madness.

"Katerina," the mayor commanded. "Take the witch and lock her up. Her punishment will be served on the Day of the Rains. Perhaps thinking on her fate will make her return the children she has stolen. Until then, we must salvage what we can of our lost crops. We must not let her evil deeds stop us from our duties. We will survive!"

The crowd cheered.

On the Day of the Rains, for the first time in ten years, they would burn a witch.

Eyda huddled alone in the darkness of the root cellar, cursing her stupidity. She knew they wouldn't listen. She should not have spoken up. What had it gotten her? It had been foolish to think the town would change their minds. A part of her had hoped Katerina might be on her side, but her sister had always hated her. She would have let Eyda starve long ago had she not made a promise to their mother.

And now, with Mathis missing, she could expect no sympathy at all from the mayor. He would see her burn.

Shivering in the oppressive blackness, Eyda tried to sleep, curled up under a burlap bag in a vain attempt to keep out the chill. There was little else she could do. Utter hopelessness filled her heart. Though her eyelids grew heavy, she could do little more than doze uneasily, jumping whenever a strong gust of wind rattled the doors above. Every time she closed her eyes, the insect-eyes of the Uhrwächter stared back at her.

Long hours passed. She could still hear the chiming of the Astrolabe, telling her it was eleven...twelve...one...two...

It was some time after two when she heard something moving in the shadows. She saw nothing but blackness as the hairs on her neck stood on end. A clicking sound reached her ears, like tin being tapped by a miniature hammer. A low, distinctly metallic scrape followed. Eyda stared into the abyss, praying to whatever deities would listen that she was wrong. A moment later, her ears began ringing. It was the same high-pitched sound that she remembered. She knew she was next.

But as she listened, waiting for the attack to come, the ringing faded away. A ray of light penetrated the darkness as something burst out of the cellar door. She caught a fleeting glimpse of a small creature, no bigger than her chickens had been, disappearing into the night as snow drifted slowly down into the cellar. Whatever it was, it shimmered in the moonlight before it disappeared.

Eyda froze, the thump, thump, thump of her heart telling her she was still alive. But what had that thing been? It was not the Uhrwächter, but this was unquestionably the thing that Wolfgang had seen and Peter had heard. What was it and what did it want?

It took her some time to calm down enough to realize she was free. The door to the cellar had been flung open, and the light from the full moon illuminated the stairs upward. She had nothing else to lose. Gathering her courage and her crutch, Eyda thump, thump, thumped up the uneven stairs, out into the frigid night air.

The village looked like a winter wonderland in the moonlight. Such a pretty sight did not solve Eyda's immediate dilemma; she had no place to go. She would freeze if she stayed out in the cold. Yet, she could not go to her own bed. A crisp westerly stirred up her skirts, bringing with it the smell of smoke. Behind her stood the castle, its towers topped with snow, all except the eastern tower.

Eyda was already shuffling towards the castle before she had fully made up her mind. It seemed her only option. She hesitated but a moment when her eyes caught sight of the strange tracks winding their way in the same direction. She fought the wind, focusing on putting one foot in front of the other. The castle loomed overhead, the menacing face of the Great Astrolabe glaring down as she struggled onward.

As she approached the crumbling bridge across the moat, the ringing started again. It was difficult to hear over the howling winds, but it filled her mind with utter dread. The path ahead was crisscrossed with dozens of trails like the one she followed. But in their midst was another trail. This one was clearly human. And the small size of the footprints meant that yet another child was about to go missing. There was only one child left that could make those tracks: Applonia.

Eyda hurried forwards as fast as she could, afraid of what she might find. The bridge was falling apart in places, and Eyda struggled to cross. Her legs were seizing up from the cold. More than once, she was forced to crawl over rubble along the edges, avoiding the great gaps that plunged down into the frigid water below. She was losing feeling in her fingers from the effort, her clothing completely drenched from sweat and snow. At last, she stumbled into a massive courtyard, ringed with high parapets overrun with ivy snaking their way through the structure like gruesome black veins.

The creatures' paths split here, but Applonia's led her directly towards the eastern tower. This close, Eyda could see clearly the Astrolabe's face, twisted and grotesque in the shadows cast by the moon. Three figures stood at the top, but two of their faces were obscured by the vines. In the middle, the terrifying face of the Uhrwächter stood out clearly. The eyes were wide and staring, its sunken jaw grinning down at her. The ringing echoed louder within the confines of the castle walls. It took all of her might to continue on after Applonia, thump, thump, thumping across the courtyard to the eastern tower.

The door to the tower had long ago fallen off its hinges, now lying half hidden by the snow. With difficulty, she stepped over the remains, entering a dark corridor. Inside, it was hot, the smell of smoke consuming the hallway. The corridor spiraled both up and down away from her. Which way would Applonia have gone?

A flickering light danced on the stone walls from both directions. The humming that filled her head was joined by an intense series of clicks and screeches. Those seemed to come from above, so she went up.

Eyda trembled at the thought of the monster lurking nearby. She had to be close to level with the Astrolabe's face by now. She threw off her coat, breathing heavily from the climb and the oppressive heat. A few more steps and she found a door. It hung ajar, a yellow light shining through. With an enormous effort, she forced it open. The heat almost knocked her backward down the stairs.

The diagrams in the book had not prepared her for what she found inside the tower. An intricate system of gears and metal shafts, rusted and worn, ran throughout the interior. They twisted and creaked in time with a deep click, a metronome keeping track of every astronomical calculus shown on the

Great Astrolabe's face. Occasionally, a piercing screech would echo through the cacophony, and the gears would lurch before catching.

Tiny movements interrupted the synchronicity of the clockwork. Dozens of thin metallic rats, mere skeletal frames of the rodent beasts, scurried across the clockwork, tapping at bolts and scraping rust off of springs. Some appeared to be trying to fix a bell hanging precariously from its fixture. A few were missing limbs. All were rusted and dented, mismatched, as if put together from scrap. These were the monsters that Peter had heard and Wolfgang had seen. Not one, but many, all servicing the clockwork. Eyda watched them moving about their missions in awe. None of them looked anything like the Uhrwächter.

From her perch, Eyda could see the entirety of the tower. There was so much movement, it took her a moment to notice the pale blue spot at the bottom. It wound its way towards a large cauldron which appeared to be the source of both the heat and light, flames licking the bottom as the contents rippled with steam. Through the twisted machinery, she could see Applonia in a thin, blue nightgown, standing precariously on a shifting gear. Three metal rats stood around her, singing their hypnotic song.

"Applonia!" Eyda called. Nothing acknowledged her, not the metallic rats, nor Applonia. The girl swayed dangerously beside the cauldron rim. Eyda frantically looked for a fast way down to her, but there was none. She was about to turn and descend through the spiral hallway outside when one of the previously dormant gears below shuddered and began to turn.

An enormous arm of clockwork tore itself away from the heart of the Astrolabe. And then another. And another.

Six arms peeled off, until at last a massive, metal skeleton swung down from the upper gearworks, perching on the cauldron like a spider guarding her eggs. The twisted mass of rusted metal turned towards Applonia. Eyda had found the Uhrwächter.

Petrified with fear at the sight of this two-story clockwork monster, she could only watch as it took one massive claw and effortlessly snapped Applonia's neck. Eyda screamed, but still nothing acknowledged her. The girl's lifeless body tumbled down into the cauldron and sank slowly into the murky depths. The Uhrwächter took a second claw and scooped out a lump of slime from the cauldron, dropping it into a dish behind the largest gear of the Astrolabe. The warm liquid seeped onto the shaft as it turned with a click, and the Astrolabe began its low chime.

The bells at the top of the tower clanged, knocking several rats loose. Eyda's entire body vibrated with each boom, magnified a hundred times inside the stone walls of the tower. She fell to her knees, covering her head with her arms. She wanted to block out this horrible place. She wanted to forget. She wanted to stop hearing the horrible ringing, clicking, and booming of the evil Astrolabe.

Three times the bells chimed, shaking the tower with each ring. The Uhrwächter continued climbing the gears unaffected, lubricating the clockwork with the oil it was simmering in the cauldron below. To her surprise, Eyda was lifted bodily from the floor. She struggled out of the grip and turned, expecting to find the horrifying skeletal face of the Uhrwächter staring at her. She sobbed at the sight of Wolfgang, looking at her in confusion. Behind him stood Peter, one hand firmly gripping the older boy's tunic as the other prodded the empty space in front with his blackened cane.

"Eyda? Is that you?" Peter shouted over the screeching gears and clicking rats.

"It killed Applonia," she wailed. "The Uhrwächter turned her into soup."

"There isn't anything we can do about it now," Peter said. "We have to get you out of here. If you are found missing and another child is gone, you are going to be burned as a witch."

"No! We have to stop it!"

165

"How?"

From the doorway a deep voice interrupted. "You don't."

The mayor strode towards them. The shadows cast by the flames below deepened his scowl. Eyda quickly turned Wolfgang so he could see what was happening, grabbing Peter's hand and pulling him away from the man bearing down on them.

"I told you it was a monster! It killed Applonia!"

"It wasn't supposed to," the mayor said, still advancing. The trio backed away, stumbling on the uneven walkway. "It was only supposed to take *you*." He pointed at Eyda. Wolfgang moved between the mayor and the others.

"You told it to take the children?" Eyda said. "You knew all of this was happening?"

"The Great Astrolabe needs a sacrifice. After Friedrich went missing, I realized our offering was insufficient. It needed blood. We had no other options."

"But, why the children?"

"I didn't know it would take the children. They simply responded to the call. So I unlocked doors, nudged the creatures towards potential targets. But despite my attempts, it would not work on any of you."

They had run out of space. The three children were backed up against the gearworks, trapped.

"You sacrificed Mathis?"

"Mathis was supposed to be safe!" the mayor spat. "You were supposed to be the target that night, too. But somehow you kept escaping!"

The mayor lunged. Wolfgang intercepted him.

"What do we do?!" Eyda asked, looking around for something to help Wolfgang. "We have to stop him!"

"What about the Uhrwächter?" Peter asked, steadying himself on the gears. He quickly let go when it began to move, shifting in time with the hands moving on the opposite side of the wall.

"We have to stop the Astrolabe," Eyda said, watching the gears synchronicity. "If it stops, there won't be a need for more children to die!"

"But what about the village?"

"It isn't helping them anymore. We need to break it!"

The gears shifted again. Without a second thought, Peter shoved his cane into the gears as they spun. It snapped. Behind them, Wolfgang was losing his fight with the mayor. Eyda had no other choice. Hobbling towards the largest concentration of gears, she shoved her crutch inside.

"No!" The mayor pushed Wolfgang aside and dove for the crutch. He yanked on it as the gears screamed and jolted. With a wretched shriek, it came free from the metal. But he had pulled too hard.

Unbalanced on the rotting catwalk, the mayor stumbled backwards, toppling into the larger gearworks below. The sound of his body breaking was lost in the screech of gears, the teeth dragging his body into the mechanism. The clockwork ground to a halt.

Wolfgang picked Eyda up around the waist and dragged her and Peter out of the tower as cracking sounds began to echo up from below. Worn, rusty teeth snapped off of gears. Bolts shuddered loose, sliding sprockets free. The Uhrwächter scrambled about, vainly attempting to put everything back in its place, the rats equally overwhelmed by the failures of the machine. As Wolfgang dragged them back into the staircase, Eyda caught a glimpse of the loose bell falling, ricocheting back and forth on the gearworks as it plummeted towards the ground.

Snow crunched under her feet when Wolfgang set her down in the courtyard. All three wheezed. Eyda felt her thump, thump, thumping heartbeat slowing down. It reassured her that she was—miraculously—still alive. The trio stood in silence, listening to the clanking and screeching from within the tower. It had to have awakened the town. They would not

167

be able to ignore the smoke billowing out from the broken face of the Astrolabe.

Peter was the first to speak.

"Nobody will believe this."

Eyda knew he was right. She was already set to be burned. Destroying the Astrolabe would not gain her any favors from the village. But what other options were there?

Wolfgang tapped her on the shoulder and pointed. In the snow he had written:

Mountain pass.

Eyda relayed this message to Peter, who shook his head. "But it can't be navigated anymore."

"We can't stay here after what we've done," Eyda said, peering at the mountains to the south, their snowy peaks illuminated in the moonlight. "Wolfgang's right. It is our best option."

"No one has used that pass in over a century. It is impossible to cross."

"A few months ago, the Astrolabe breaking was impossible. A few weeks ago, a metal monster was impossible. Impossible is not what it used to be. At least there we have a chance."

About K. A. Lindstrom

K. A. Lindstrom is a freelance writer, wandering nomad, and aspiring hermit. Between writing gigs she works at Cornell University, travels, or continues her education. She is currently working towards a Master's in Strategic Studies through University College Cork in Ireland. While she calls Ithaca, New York her home, she is often found sailing in the South Pacific or solo traveling around the world. Previously, her short story "The Last Automaton of Doctor Jubal Varva" appeared in *Cogs, Crowns, and Carriages: A Steampunk Anthology,* now available on Amazon. For more check out www.kalindstrom. com or follow her on Twitter @KalWritesWords.

Liberty

by Crysta K. Coburn

Liberty crept around the edge of the Desert Machines Motorcycle Club compound. She kept her head down, her dark, unkempt hair falling over her forehead to cover her eyes. Her stepfather's men were all around her, snorting and spitting gobs of snot, and stomping in the dirt with their heavy boots. They snarled curses and threw down their wrenches in disgust as they worked on their machines. The dry air was thick with dust from the grassless ground and the stench of motor oil, gasoline, and human sweat all mixed together.

No one noticed her as she approached Nanna Mine's door. She tapped softly at the scarred corrugated metal, then held her ear against it to listen for a response.

"Come on in!" The old woman's cracked voice was followed by a dry cough.

Liberty slipped inside and joined Nanna Mine in a chair by the fire. The inside of the shack smelled of cinnamon, smoke, and the stew bubbling over the hearth.

"Liberty!" Nanna Mine's wrinkled face split into a grin as she patted the young woman's face. "Are you hungry?" She nodded to the stew.

"I couldn't take your food."

"Nonsense!" Nanna Mine coughed again as she reached for a set of dishes on a sideboard.

Liberty jumped up and retrieved them for her. "You don't take 'no,' do you?" Nanna Mine nodded. "I do not. You're a good girl. Give us both some stew."

Liberty obeyed, ladling out a serving for each of them.

"So." Nanna Mine blew on her steaming bowl. "What brings you here?"

Liberty stirred the contents of her own bowl slowly without speaking for some time. Nanna Mine waited patiently, slurping up stew and making satisfied mmms and ahhhs.

"I don't know what to do, Nanna," Liberty finally confessed.

"First you take your spoon in hand, wide part down, then you—"

Liberty smiled and shook her head. "I know how to eat stew."

"Then eat up."

Liberty slurped a few spoonfuls. "You know what I mean. About...."

Nanna Mine nodded. "About your father."

"Stepfather," Liberty corrected.

He was no father figure, just the man who had married her mother when Liberty was eight and turned predatory once his wife died.

"It's all a power grab." Nanna Mine shoveled the last of her stew into her mouth, then set the bowl and spoon on the floor beside her. "Your father was President—and well loved—for fifteen years!"

Liberty knew this story by heart, but she let Nanna Mine continue while she finished her own stew.

"When he died, God rest his soul, that bastard muscled his way in and married your mother—left too vulnerable by her beloved's loss—to solidify his new position, stapling his name onto a respected dynasty. Now that she's gone, he wants to marry you for the same reason." Nanna Mine waved her hand dismissively. "Rubbish!"

"And yet."

Liberty took the dirty dishes over to the salvaged farmhouse sink to wash them.

Nanna Mine hmm-ed thoughtfully. "It's customary to give a bride a gift. Ask for something he'll never be able to provide."

"Like the Moon?"

"No, no, he'll laugh that off. It has to be something practical that a person could get if they had enough resources."

Liberty thought that over while she circled the sponge in the bowls. "Like a Limited Edition Vittorio Black Shadow?"

Vittorio had been Liberty's mother's favorite motor vehicle craftsperson. It had always been her dream to own one.

"Now you're thinking!" crowed Nanna Mine. "But don't stop there. Three things. You should ask for three. Any one thing is easy enough to get if a body is determined enough."

Liberty dried the dishes, then returned to her place by Nanna Mine. "Do you think he'd actually be able to get a Limited Edition Vittorio Black Shadow?"

Nanna Mine shrugged her bony shoulders. "Best not to leave it to chance, right?"

Liberty nodded thoughtfully. Maybe this trick would work. At the moment, it was all she had.

She decided to ask for the Shadow, a gold and diamond necklace to match her mother's ring, and a spidersilk gown. Spidersilk was the most expensive and rare fabric she could think of, and her stepfather hated that ring. It had been her mother's first engagement ring, and Liberty now wore it as a memento of both lost parents.

She made her demands just as their plates were being cleared from the dinner table that evening. After feasting, her stepfather, a big, not-too-smart but methodical man, always talked business with his executives, who all dined with them. She wanted these men as witnesses. And while they would do little to defend her should her stepfather fly into a rage, she hoped that their presence would deter him from doing so.

His face did turn a bit purple. He knew that she knew he didn't have the resources for such things. But rather than refuse her, he chose to agree to the bargain with a caveat.

"If I can provide you with these trinkets, you'll agree to the marriage with no fuss?"

Trinkets! A Limited Edition Vittorio Black Shadow? Gold and diamonds? Spidersilk? She swallowed hard, suddenly feeling unsure of herself.

"I will not make a fuss," she agreed, carefully avoiding the M-word.

Her stepfather grunted his contentment while the other men looked at each other warily.

A few days later, her stepfather and about half the DMMC's members went for a ride. When asked where they were going, Liberty was told it was a treasure hunt. She went to Nanna Mine with her worries, but the old woman only tutted and told her all would be well.

It was many days before the members returned. Liberty was horrified to find them pulling a small trailer with a sheet thrown over it. With great reluctance, she joined the crowd welcoming back the group. Her stepfather stood on the trailer with a huge grin on his grizzled face. When he spotted Liberty, he pulled back the sheet to reveal the first of her demands, a gleaming Black Shadow. When he held out his hand to invite her up to inspect the bike, she felt she had no choice but to do so.

It was beautiful, its sleek black body radiant in the sunlight. She ran her hand along the seat, then settled it at the throttle. *Ride me*, the bike seemed to say. She wanted to. She'd barely ridden by herself, but she craved to take control of this beauty.

"Well?" asked her stepfather, breaking the spell.

"Thank you," she whispered, and she meant it. This Shadow would take her places, she could tell. She was glad she had asked for it. If he couldn't meet her other requirements, at least she'd have her own bike.

Over dinner she learned how the Shadow had come to be hers. Someone had owed the MC a favor—a *big* favor—and her stepfather had called it in. So simple. Her scheme had been crushed like a bug on a windshield. Liberty couldn't imagine the kind of debt that a special edition bike could fill. Is that how he would fulfill her other demands? Calling in favors?

"Who on God's brown earth is going to owe your stepfather a dress?" pointed out Nanna Mine when Liberty had snuck over to her shack later that night.

Liberty admitted that a bike was a far more likely prize for an MC leader than a spidersilk gown. But even so.

"What do I do if he does manage to get all three presents? I still can't imagine...." She shuddered.

Nanna Mine nodded in sympathy. "You have a bike now. Learn it."

Liberty took the advice, asking one of the men who wasn't on the executive board to help her. He was young and flattered by her attention, which she worked to her advantage. She played dumb, getting him to teach her everything about the Shadow, inside and out, down to the smallest bolt. This was her bike now, and she didn't want anyone else touching it, even to wipe the dust off. She would maintain it and make her parents proud.

At first, she rode around the compound, then moved on to the dirt roads surrounding the compound. Her tutor accompanied her at first, but he was soon scared off by her stepfather, who didn't like other men paying attention to his intended. Sometimes Nanna Mine would ride on the seat behind her, but Liberty preferred to ride alone. She formed a habit of riding out every evening after dinner by herself. Her stepfather warned her to be back by sunset, and she obliged him because being alone outside the compound in the dark made her nervous. She wasn't used to being quite that alone.

After a few weeks, her stepfather and his retinue went on another lengthy ride. Liberty stayed in the compound, eager to use her stepfather's absence to push her real— as well as metaphorical—boundaries. The stars at night, away from the compound lights, were breathtaking. There was a dry creek bed just out of sight of the compound where she parked her bike, then stretched out on her back and lost herself in the sky. She began to wonder what other marvels were out there.

It was before setting out on just such a trek that Liberty's stepfather returned. She felt sick when she saw the triumphant look on his face. He marched toward her as she was perched—frozen—on the Shadow, a skinny rectangular box tucked under his arm.

Liberty accepted the box with numb fingers. She knew what would be inside, but she opened it anyway. Those who peered over her shoulder gasped, and whispers spread through the gathered crowd.

The gown was beautiful, a pale cream, the spidersilk so delicate that it looked like it would melt and tiny pearls decorating the bodice. Liberty closed the box.

"Where did you...?" Her voice failed her.

Her stepfather answered with a roguish grin. "We liberated it from its owner."

Stolen. She hadn't considered that he'd steal for her. Whether it was taken from a shop or from a woman, she didn't want to know.

"Thank you," she mumbled.

He nodded. "Two down."

One to go.

Later—much later—after it seemed the whole world had gone to sleep, Liberty held the gown up to herself before the chipped mirror on her bedroom wall. How it shimmered in the lamplight! She shrugged out of her rough, grimy clothes and slipped on the sleeveless gown. It was light and sleek, and made her feel not at all like herself. She'd been foolish to ask for such an impractical garment. Where would a girl like her, the stepdaughter of a shameless thief, wear such a fine and fancy thing?

Sighing, she slid the gown off, put it back in its box, and hid it under her bed.

Liberty tried to live as if she weren't in a panic over being outsmarted by a man old enough to be her father but who wanted to be her husband, who leered at her over breakfast, who made her feel trapped.

She was not surprised, then, when an outsider rolled into the compound with a small trunk strapped to his bike some weeks later, and Liberty was summoned to the front yard of her family home. It was to be another public display. This time, the outsider opened the box, and her stepfather lifted Liberty's hand—the one on which she wore her parents' ring—and held it next to the contents of the box. The necklace had the same twists of gold. The matching diamonds scattered across its three strands sparkled like stars. It was as if the two pieces of jewelry had been made as a pair.

"How did you get it so perfect?" Liberty asked.

"I've stared at that hateful ring enough times to have it burned in my memory," her stepfather answered. "And now it's turned into my lucky charm. Imagine that!"

Yes, imagine that.

She accepted the box with the precious necklace and went to her room where she sat numbly until she heard a scratch at her door.

"Come in," she called hoarsely.

Nanna Mine crept in, silently closing the door behind her.

"Oh, Nanna!" Liberty cried.

"Hush, child," the old woman lovingly scolded. "You aren't married yet."

"But I'm going to be," Liberty moaned.

"Who says? Is that what you promised?"

Liberty thought for a moment. "Well, not exactly. But I did say I wouldn't make a fuss."

"So don't make a fuss." Nanna Mine arched her brows. "Leave."

"Leave," Liberty echoed. "Leave?"

Nanna Mine shrugged. "You have a bike, a fancy dress, and now fancy jewelry to match. Seems to me a woman with all those things can go anywhere. But I suggest heading west to the coast. They'll look for you closer to home at first, and the nearest city is to the east."

Liberty absorbed this idea slowly. Could she make it on her own? She knew from her excursions that a paved road ran east-west several miles to the north. Perhaps she could take it to the coast. It was a starting point at any rate.

While the wheels turned in Liberty's mind, Nanna Mine was bustling about the room, pulling items from bureau drawers and adding them to some saddlebags Liberty hadn't realized she had brought with her. When she was finished with the bureaus, Nanna Mine asked for the spidersilk gown and gold necklace, which Liberty readily produced. Each item was wrapped carefully in paper and stowed in the saddlebags.

Next, Nanna Mine produced a pair of scissors, saying, "We need to make you look less like yourself. Don't want you matching your description when they go looking for you. Sit in the chair, and I'll cut your hair."

Nanna Mine gathered all of Liberty's hair into a ponytail at the base of her neck and snipped it off. She then took off her worn and patched leather coat and handed it to her granddaughter.

"I can't take this, Nanna!"

"Of course you can! I'm giving it to you. You'll need it to keep warm."

Liberty slid her arms into the coat with some reverence. It was older than herself by several decades. The fit was good, and when she turned to appraise her reflection, she was pleased with what she found. In truth, she thought she looked more than a little like her mother, a sentiment that Nanna Mine admitted she shared.

"Now." Nanna Mine turned Liberty to face her. "Walk the bike and don't start the engine until you're clear, you hear me? Go north to the paved road and head west. Stay smart, stay firm, don't be afraid to take opportunities that present themselves—and don't look back!"

Liberty hugged the old woman fiercely. "I won't! But what about you?"

"You think that young pup scares me?" She scowled. "Child, what do you take me for? Now, follow me. I know how to get you out."

Liberty embraced Nanna Mine once more before hurrying away from the compound. There was no moon, and the stars were concealed by clouds, a rare and lucky occurrence that Liberty hoped would hide her from spying eyes. She first made her way to the dry creek bed, a path she knew well, where she hopped on the Shadow. The bed eventually intersected the paved road just as Nanna had promised, and Liberty sped away west.

She rode for hours, never daring to look behind her. At every fuel station she came upon, she quickly topped off her tank and kept going. Nanna Mine had packed money, food, a water flask, but no map. So Liberty just kept following the road that ran straight as an arrow. At first the terrain was dry and flat, then it grew rocky. When she needed to sleep, she took the bike off the road, found a ditch or a boulder to hide behind, and napped. Not knowing if anyone was on her tail or how close they might be, she couldn't stay asleep long. Liberty ate frugally, foraged when she could, and spent as little money as possible.

After a few days, the land acquired trees and flowers. Liberty came upon a lake near the road and surrounded by trees, the water shimmering in the bright sun. She hadn't bathed the entire time she'd been running, and the temptation to wash the grime from her skin and hair was too much to ignore. She coasted off the road and parked the bike behind an old tree with a wide trunk. In her haste to immerse herself, she left a trail of discarded clothing from the Shadow to the shore.

Her mother had taught her to swim at a watering hole located not far from the compound when it wasn't baked dry. The water was warm, and Liberty dove right in. It was glorious. So distracted by the gentle embrace of the waves was she, that she didn't see the man inspecting her bike until he called out to her.

"Excuse me!"

Liberty started. Dread flooded her body, nearly paralyzing her. But she didn't recognize the voice. She turned to face the shore, ready to flee to the other side if need be.

"Hi there!" The stranger waved, his demeanor friendly. He was tall, with brown hair and tan skin, and about her own age, maybe a little older. His leather jacket and the goggles perched on his head identified him as a motorist.

"Can I help you?" Liberty asked.

"Yes! Sorry to disturb you...."

She watched with amusement as his eyes took in the bits of clothing and what that meant. He slowly raised his eyes to hers, and she couldn't keep from smiling at his blush. He cleared his throat, then he, too, grinned.

"Mostly sorry," he amended.

She raised a brow.

He cleared his throat again. "I had stopped my car beside the road to refresh myself when I noticed your motorcycle here." He pointed at the machine. His voice became hushed and a little squeaky. "Is that really a Limited Edition Vittorio Black Shadow?"

"You aren't going to steal it, are you?"

Her voice sounded cavalier, but bees buzzed in her stomach. For the past few days, all she'd been thinking about was who might be after her, not what might be ahead of her. There were people in this world that had nothing to do with the DMMC. Handsome people, it seemed, who could identify and appreciate a well-made machine—for good or ill.

The man held up his hands in surrender. "Of course not! I just feel blessed to see one in person. If you don't mind my asking, where did you find it?"

"It was a present."

He looked incredulous. "Some present! Are you a princess or something?"

"Something like that."

He gave her a puzzled expression, then looked back at the Shadow. "I'd give almost anything to be able to ride one of these beauties."

"Well." Liberty paddled a little closer to shore. "Maybe one day you'll get the chance."

"I'm being dismissed, aren't I?"

"I do have places to be. And...." She inclined her head towards the scattered clothing. "I'd prefer some privacy in the next few moments."

He nodded. "Of course. Where are you headed?"

"Toward the coast."

"Any city in particular?"

She shrugged.

He tapped his chin while thinking. "Well, if you go west

another ten miles, take the exit on the right, then head south for another thirty, you'll come to my hometown. It isn't much, but it is near the coast."

"I'll take it under consideration."

He made the tipping-hat gesture, though he wore no hat. "Safe travels."

"Likewise."

Liberty waited until the sound of his motor car faded away before climbing from the water and continuing her own journey. Since they were the first definite directions she had received, she decided to follow the man's suggestion. It would be easier to lose herself in a city. The sooner, the better.

She arrived just before sunset. Having spent most of her life in the desert, the brightly colored lights of the city were nearly overwhelming. The people's faces were shining and clean, their clothes all different colors and styles. Liberty couldn't wait to explore. But as night fell, she decided she had better find a place to stay. Her dwindling funds were not enough for a room at either of the first two hotels. At the third hotel, however, the attendant at the door took a long, hard look at her bike.

"Is that a Limited Edition Vittorio Black Shadow?"

Was everyone going to recognize it?

Aloud, she confirmed, "It is."

"You know bikes?"

"I do."

"You know engines?"

"Well enough."

"Come with me."

The attendant waved to a younger counterpart to take her place, then she led Liberty around the side of the building to the garage in back.

"This is where we keep the company vehicles," she explained.

There were cars for transporting passengers, as well as a few delivery motorcycles and a truck. Liberty found it interesting enough, but why had she brought her here? The answer soon manifested in the form of a squat, untidy man with grease smeared on his pink face and hands.

"This is Walt," the attendant said. "He's our house mechanic."

Liberty held out her hand to Walt and introduced herself. He was shorter than she, and his head pumped up and down as he gave her a more-than-once over.

"Are you suggesting," Walt drawled to the door attendant, "that I hire this chit as my assistant?"

Liberty widened her eyes in surprise, but said nothing. She hadn't been looking for a job, though she supposed she would be needing one to support herself. Nanna Mine's words came back to her. *Don't be afraid to take opportunities that present themselves.* This was a wonderful opportunity.

Smiling at Walt, she dismounted and stood tall, not so subtly putting her bike on full view. Walt's eyes brightened when he saw it, and he licked his cracked lips.

"Is that—?"

"Yes."

"And you—"

"—Know every bit of her inside and out."

Walt took a step back, crossed his arms, and gave Liberty more consideration. "Always wanted a Vittorio. The Thunder was more my style, though. This Shadow here's a racing bike. I'm too old to race anymore." He shook his head a little sadly. "You want a job?"

"Yes, sir." Liberty fought down her nerves. She would stay firm, like Nanna Mine had told her. If she failed at being a mechanic's assistant, she'd move on to the next opportunity that presented itself.

"Come on, then."

The attendant gave Liberty a wink, then returned to her station.

Walt showed Liberty to a tiny room at the back of the large garage, which included a cot for sleeping and not much else. (Walt had a more proper apartment above the garage.) He explained that she would be on hand every day, all day, with every seventh day off. She would eat her meals with the rest of the staff in the dining hall off the kitchen three times a day and return promptly to work.

"And remember," he warned, "this is a dirty job."

"I'm not afraid of that," she assured him, displaying the black that practically lived beneath her fingernails.

Walt nodded with approval.

Liberty liked Walt. He was gruff at times, but fair, and he was willing to answer any question she had whether it was about the job or life in the city. He reminded her of Nanna Mine in that way. She also liked the work. Although she wasn't allowed to take on an entire project by herself, Walt wasn't overly protective of the hotel's fleet and was happy to have help in maintaining it.

Liberty was eager to explore the city, but when her first day off came, she found herself feeling nervous. Where should she go? What should she see? The block surrounding the hotel was always full of activity, so she decided she would start there. After breakfast, she scrubbed the grime from her nails as best she could and combed out her hair.

Not wanting to draw attention to herself, Liberty hid the Shadow under a sheet in her room and set out on foot. The neighborhood held all manner of businesses—a few bars, cafes, and restaurants; two casinos; a theater and a dance hall. Rather than stop at any one, she played tourist and gawked at each.

On her way back to the hotel for lunch, the people around her became animated and congregated along the street. Curious, Liberty followed them and gently pushed her way to the front of the crowd gathered at the curbside. An open air motor car rolled down the street, sleek shiny, and red with gold decoration. While she still didn't know too much about cars, Liberty did admire this specimen. The man behind the wheel wasn't so bad either, though his features were difficult to make out behind the large goggles and the white scarf around his neck.

She followed along the sidewalk behind the car and was surprised to see it turn into the driveway that led to the garage behind the hotel. Her hotel. Her garage. She dashed across the street, but by the time she arrived, the driver was gone. Walt stood beside the now parked car.

"Liberty!" he called. "Come here for a minute."

She obliged him.

"Ain't she a beauty?" He was beaming. She nodded in agreement, and he went on, "Now this is a racing car! Not that I'm young enough for that sort of thing anymore. Still. I can admire her!" Walt polished the headlamp lovingly with a stained cloth.

"Whose is she?"

Walt held out his hand in front of him, as if presenting something grand. "The prince of the castle's."

She wrinkled her nose. "Who?"

"Mr. Grayson's son, Frank."

Mr. Grayson was the owner of the hotel. He lived in a large suite on the top floor. Liberty had yet to see him or his wife, who, she was told by the hotel staff, rarely descended to mix with "the peasantry," except for the parties. The hotel hosted weekly Saturday soirees in the grand ballroom. And, Liberty was assured, they were not like the common parties at the dance hall down the street that anyone could attend. These were high class balls.

That week, the hotel was all atwitter over Frank and how he would be attending the party that week. Some of the maids told Liberty that Mr. Frank, as he was called, had been touring the country for the past six months. Since he'd returned, they'd all been sneaking looks at him when they went in to clean the Graysons' suite. Liberty had seen him, too, when he came to swap racing stories with Walt in the apartment above the garage. She'd recognized him as the man from the lake who had admired her motorcycle. He had not noticed her.

"He's so handsome!" declared one maid as she faked a swoon at breakfast.

"If you sneak around to the back hall," whispered another, "you can watch the people dancing. Everyone is so glamorous!"

"I wish I could go!" cried a third. "But it's guests-only."

Liberty smiled. She wasn't going to watch the glamorous soiree. In her spidersilk gown and fine jewelry, she was going to be glamorous. Maybe Mr. Frank would notice her then.

That Saturday, Liberty smuggled her dress and gold jewelry (she had stopped wearing the ring for fear that it would get lost in an engine) into the hotel back-of-house bathroom during lunch, then hurried there after dinner to scrub all of the grease and dirt from her skin and comb out her hair before dressing. Getting the black from under her nails was particularly trying, but Liberty was determined. Nanna Mine would have been proud of her, she was certain. The old woman had known the dress and necklace would come in handy one day. That day had arrived.

Fearing she might be discovered prematurely, Liberty cracked open the bathroom door and waited until the coast was clear before creeping to the front of the house. Once in the lobby, she straightened up, took a deep breath, and strode toward the ballroom, not daring to look around her.

Eyes on the prize.

The ballroom was two stories tall with a stage at the far end, where a smartly dressed, ten-person jazz band played.

Trumpets, trombones, and saxophones flashed in the light from an enormous crystal chandelier that dominated the ceiling in the center of the room.

People watched her as she entered, but not because they were ready to kick her out. Gazes both envious and admiring washed over her. Liberty found all these people in their black suits, glittering gowns, and done-up hair and faces intimidating. She stood awkwardly off to the side, not looking up or meeting anyone's eyes.

"Champagne?"

A glass appeared before her. She accepted it and took a sip before thanking the man who had offered it to her. The voice was familiar, and she had assumed he was a server she knew from mealtimes. She was wrong.

Because he stood so close to her, she was able to get a much better look at him than when he had been at the edge of the lake. A little taller than she, with brown eyes that crinkled at the corners when he smiled—and he was smiling, a wide, toothy, confident grin in slight contrast with his previous bashful bravado.

"You're welcome. I'm Frank. Is this your first time here?" His brows drew together. "Because you look familiar...."

Amused that she could meet this man three times and he didn't connect the dots, Liberty grinned broadly. "It is my first time, yes. I guess I didn't know what to expect."

Frank (she would never again think of him as Mr. Frank) nodded. "It can be a bit..." He looked around the room. "Much. My mother went all out tonight."

"Why's that?"

He blushed, and his eyes flicking away while he answered. "It's for me, I'm afraid. You see, I've been away for half a year, and my mother seems to have found my absence very hard, so she's celebrating."

It had been more than half a year since Liberty had seen

187

her own mother. What she wouldn't give to see her again. How she would celebrate such a reunion!

"Separations are hard." Liberty finished her glass of champagne. "We must love each other while we can."

Frank's brows raised, and he cocked his head to the side. "Would you like to dance?"

She cast a glance at the graceful couples gliding across the floor. "I don't think I'll be very good at it."

"I'll help you." He winked. "I'm an expert at dancing. And if I'm not, you'll never know!"

She giggled nervously and took his hand. They put their empty glasses on a nearby table and took the floor. Curious eyes were on her again. The party was for Frank, so they must all have known who he was, the prince of the castle. If anyone recognized her, they were the ones peeping through cracked doorways.

Frank whispered, "They're all staring."

"Wondering who I am," she replied softly. Their conversation was only for the two of them.

He gave a small shrug. "It's only natural I'd dance with the most beautiful woman in the room."

Liberty blushed. "Hardly!"

Frank twirled her, then pulled her in close, holding her for a beat so that he could look into her eyes. Her heart thudded in her chest.

"I may exaggerate at times," Frank declared. "But I never lie."

Then she was twirling again, amazed that her feet could keep moving when she'd lost all sense of them. Frank must truly have been an excellent dancer.

While others tried to steal Frank away from her, or her from him, Frank wouldn't allow it, staying with Liberty all night. Dancing was interspersed with trips to the food table for canapés and more champagne. Liberty asked Frank about his long absence, and he was happy to entertain her with stories of motor car races across the desert, where there was nothing but your opponent to get in your way, and through the mountains, where near anything could prove a fatal obstacle. He told her of watching the sunrise over the ocean on one coast and seeing it set over the opposite seaside. Liberty gasped when he described a trip in an airplane.

"It wasn't long," he elaborated. "Just a ten-minute tour in a friend's biplane over some corn fields."

"Even so." Liberty sighed. "I'd love to fly one day."

Frank smiled softly. "The next time I get an offer, I'll be sure to invite you along."

She shook her head at his coy flirtation.

The festivities didn't break up until nearly dawn, when Liberty realized she really had to go and thanked heaven it was her day off.

"You know," said Frank as he doggedly held onto her hand at the doors to the lobby. "I realized you never told me your name."

"Frank Grayson," she scolded him. "You spent an entire night with a woman whose name you don't even know? How dare you!"

He let go of her hand, put both of his own in his pockets, and stood tall, matching her mocking gaze with an obstinate one in return. "I told you mine. I don't recall you offering one in return."

Liberty tutted and shook her head. "I'll not tell you now. That's your punishment."

She turned and took a step away, but he stopped her with, "Wait! When will I see you again?"

"Maybe you won't see me again."

His brows drew together with concern. "Are you leaving town?"

"No. I plan to stay for a while. I rather like it here. It came highly recommended, you know."

"Will you at least come again next week? You must know we hold these parties every Saturday."

Liberty made a show of considering his offer, then answered, "I think I will. I had a lovely time."

The grin that spread across his face was satisfying. She dashed off before he could say another word and delay her longer. She had to change back into her normal clothes before anyone saw her, and if she slept too late, Walt would surely notice.

Frank, of course, came to the garage during the week to retrieve his car for a ride and talk with Walt, but he never noticed Liberty. She laughed at him behind his back.

He'd been so enchanted with her, and here she was, so close that she could poke him with a torque wrench, and he was oblivious.

No one in the back of the house seemed to have recognized her either. The maids talked on and on about the beautiful woman in the spidersilk dress with whom Frank had spent all night.

"Such a dreamy pair!" swooned one maid.

"I couldn't take my eyes off them," gushed another. "That gown with the pearl bodice. Like a film star!"

"I wish I could go!" cried the third. "Why is it guests-only?"

But no one said, "Hang on a minute, that was you!" as she'd feared they might. And what if they had? Would she say, "Yes, you caught me, I was the mysterious lady dancing with Frank"? Would she lie? The party was supposed to be for guests only, but no one had asked for proof that she was staying there.

The next Saturday, she left dinner early, knowing there would be plenty of food at the party. Frank was waiting for her at the door to the ballroom. She looped her arm through his as they entered.

"Before we go any further," he said, his voice serious. "You must tell me your name. I am not the type of man to spend an entire night with a woman whose name I don't even know."

She laughed at him. "Oh, aren't you?"

"You obviously know my name. You called me Frank Grayson. I didn't remember telling you I was a Grayson."

Liberty was thrown off only for a moment. "You told me your mother had gone all out. Everyone knows the Graysons own the hotel. I suppose I assumed you were their son."

While looking skeptical, he accepted her response. "You weren't wrong. I am Frank Grayson. But that doesn't give me your name."

Liberty smiled coyly and took a glass of champagne from a passing server. "How about I make you guess? Like I guessed yours."

"But I gave you my first name."

"Then you'll have to be cleverer than me."

He spent the rest of the night trying to get to know Liberty, asking where she was from, how she came to be in town, and peppering their conversation with guesses of her name, not once coming close. She answered him as best she could without giving away her story. She didn't mention her stepfather or the Shadow. Perhaps she enjoyed being a mystery too much, or it was Frank's attention that soothed her. She feared that if he knew who she really was, he would be disgusted and drop her like a greasy rag. He wasn't a prince, but he was out of her league.

When the time to part arrived, Frank refused to release her hand until she had told him her name.

"I will give you a hint," Liberty agreed. "It means freedom."

She used his momentary puzzlement to pull away and disappear back into her regular life.

Liberty soon learned from the hotel staff that the Graysons were all agitated.

Frank, it seemed, was obsessed. With her!

"She's so beautiful!" sighed one maid as she swooned.

"But Mrs. Grayson doesn't approve," gossiped another. "He doesn't even know her name! How can he love her?"

"I wish he loved me," sobbed a third. "Stupid guests-only."

Liberty felt anxious about attending the third party, but she was determined to go. When she emerged from the back of the house, she could see Frank pacing in the lobby. She approached him with caution.

"Waiting for someone?"

Relief flooded his face. "I wasn't sure I'd see you again. You always appear in the same dress and same jewelry." He took her hand to admire her ring. "I was beginning to wonder if you were a ghost. I've looked for you everywhere!"

Not everywhere.

The night was tinged with obvious desperation on Frank's part and sadness on Liberty's. She couldn't let this go on. When he asked again for her name, she reminded him of the clue he'd given her.

"I'm too stupid to figure it out."

She only shook her head and smiled. He tried again to hold onto her at the end of the night, but she slipped away as always.

The next day, Liberty slept very late. She was awoken by an argument between Frank and Walt. Their words weren't clear, but Walt seemed to be trying to calm Frank down, then Frank's car sped off.

Liberty hastily dressed and joined Walt outside to find out what it was all about.

"Lovesick fool," Walt titched. "He's gone off to cool his head, I hope."

Liberty gazed at the tracks the car had left in the dirt. A bad feeling crept over her.

Sure enough, hours later, the red motor car was towed back to the hotel, the front fender flopping. There had been an accident. Frank was alive, but badly battered. A physician attended him in the Graysons' suite.

Walt shook his head and decided to start on repairs right away. Liberty begged to assist him.

"This is a very special car," Walt said with gravity. "Not just anyone is allowed to touch her."

"I can appreciate that," Liberty answered with sincerity.

Walt relented. The two of them worked diligently all week. When Walt declared the car as good as new, he invited Liberty to join him for a drink.

"In a moment," she said. "I want to shine this mirror. Nothing but the best, right?"

Walt nodded and told her to come in when she was finished. When he was gone, Liberty pulled her beloved ring from her pocket, the one Frank had admired just a week before, slipped it inside one of Frank's driving gloves, and set it carefully back in the glove compartment. She had caused him enough distress, and she bid him a silent goodbye.

That night, a Saturday, she did not go to the party. The maids reported at Sunday breakfast that Frank had attended, one arm in a sling, and stood with the aid of a cane by the door all night, refusing to acknowledge anyone. The same occurred the next week.

Liberty forced herself to bed early on those Saturdays, and Sundays she continued to explore the town. Leaving the Shadow under its sheet in her room, she went on foot to the cafes and picture shows, anything to keep her mind off of Frank.

Several more days passed before Frank wandered down to the garage to inquire about his car.

"Why don't you take it for a ride?" Walt suggested. "A nice, *leisurely* ride."

Liberty heard Frank climb into the driver's seat, but the motor didn't turn over. She peeked out at him. He was just sitting there, deflated. After a little while, Frank climbed from the car and left without taking it out. Liberty turned away, her heart aching, and returned to her cleaning duties.

Part of her wanted nothing more than to reveal herself to him. But she also chided herself. Frank was a dream, and it was time to wake up. She was poor and out in the world for the first time. What could she offer a wealthy and sophisticated world traveler like him?

That next Sunday, Liberty decided to take the Shadow out for a ride in the surrounding country to clear her head. The sun was shining, the air warm. She stopped at a hill that overlooked a river valley, stretched out on her back, and gazed up at the infinite blue sky as she used to, only now she didn't have to use the night to hide in.

The wind whispered through the grass, the river splashed against rocks below, and an airplane motor hummed in the distance, reminding Liberty of Frank's ridiculous invitation to take her flying one day. So much for clearing her head.

With a sigh, she rolled over onto her stomach and looked down at the road she had taken. In the distance, Liberty could just make out the dark silhouettes of three people on motorcycles, too far to make out if they wore DMMC cuts. She flattened herself as she watched, praying that they didn't take the turn into town. When they didn't, she relaxed a moment, but that only meant they were headed straight for her.

Liberty jumped up and sped the Shadow down the opposite side of the hill, toward the river. She could tell this would be a muddy ride, but she didn't dare pass the other riders as she fled toward the safety of the hotel.

She and the Shadow both were a right mess when she pulled into the garage. Liberty parked the bike and went to retrieve some rags and a water bucket with the intention of scrubbing off the mud. Upon her return, she found Frank circling the Shadow. His back was to her, and she dove behind a wall.

"Hello?" Frank called, taking a step her way. "Is anyone there? Walt?"

Liberty held her breath and held absolutely still, wishing he would go away. She heard his limping tread return to the bike.

"Where did you come from?" he asked the Shadow. "Is your owner inside? A guest at the hotel maybe?"

Liberty bit back a giggle. He was treating the bike like a stray dog. His hand dragged softly along the vinyl seat, then he patted it affectionately. Liberty waited until his departing footsteps disappeared before emerging. She quickly tended to the bike before returning it to its hiding place.

Two days later, Liberty was running an errand for Walt when she came across three very familiar bikes parked outside one of the casinos near the hotel. Her heart plummeted into her stomach, and her knees shook as she scrambled to get away. Walt worried when he saw her pale face and demanded to know what was wrong.

"I'm not feeling well," she stammered. "But I only need a minute."

"You just go lie down," he said. "Don't worry about the rest of the afternoon. Goodness!" He shook his head sadly. "Must be something in the air."

"What do you mean?"

"Frank's still not...." He shook his head again. "No need for you to worry about him. Just get to feeling better, ok?"

Liberty promised that she would, then went to lie down and contemplate what she would do if she were discovered at the hotel by her stepfather and his cronies. Fight? Or flee?

From her bed, she heard Frank arrive and speak to Walt for quite some time. Walt must have been able to talk some sense into Frank because Liberty eventually heard the car's motor come to life and fade into the distance.

She noticed that the car was still absent when she went to breakfast the next morning, but she tried not to reflect on it too much. She had her own worries.

It was not long after breakfast that the commotion began. One of the cooks rushed outside, screaming for Walt to bring his heaviest wrench.

"What in tarnation?" Walt roared. "What is going on?"

The distraught woman babbled that three men had barged into the hotel and ferociously insisted on seeing the woman in the spidersilk dress. Of course, everyone recognized her as Frank's dancing partner, but the young master wasn't there to consult. Mr. Grayson had ordered the men to leave, but instead, they began tearing up the place.

"So call the police!" said Walt.

"They have been called," the cook indignantly replied. "But meanwhile, the hotel is being destroyed! Can't you clobber them?"

While they argued, Liberty rushed to pack up her things. She was all ready to speed past Walt and the cook when she found her way blocked by three furious faces. Her stepfather's eyes skewered her to the spot where she perched on the Shadow.

"There you are," he growled.

She considered her chances of getting past him without being pulled from her seat when the driveway, her only option of escape, was blocked by a familiar red car.

"Mr. Frank!" the cook cried in relief.

Frank leaped from the car and marched over to the three hulking men. Liberty wanted to warn him to be careful, but the words lodged in her throat.

"What is going on here?" Frank sounded not in the least intimidated.

Liberty's stepfather puffed up his chest. "Retrieving a runaway bride is what! We tracked her to this here hotel, and we demand you turn her over."

Frank scoffed. "This is absurd."

The larger man ignored him. "Liberty! Get over here now!"

At the mention of her name, Walt stalked forward. "You listen here! You won't lay one finger on that girl. So get going!"

The three club members loomed over Walt. Afraid for her friend, Liberty dismounted and stepped forward.

Her stepfather leered. "That's a good girl."

Frank and Walt both whirled toward her. Frank wore an expression of bewilderment.

"Liberty," he murmured. "It means freedom."

Their eyes locked. Oblivious to everyone but her, Frank approached and lifted her hand. She was surprised when he slid a ring onto her finger.

"Did you leave this in my car?"

She blushed. "It was supposed to be a farewell present."

His hand tightened around hers, but before he could speak, her behemoth of a stepfather groused, "Enough of this! Get over here now, girl. I mean it."

Liberty gave Frank's hand a squeeze, then gently extricated herself from his grasp and advanced toward the trio. She saw Walt take up a protective stance off to her left. Taking a deep breath, Liberty squared her shoulders and met her stepfather's eyes. She didn't want to run. She liked living in the city with its cafes and theaters and motor cars. She had friends here. And she refused to be afraid of this man any longer.

"No."

He cocked his head like he hadn't heard properly. "No?"

"No. I'm staying here."

"You said you wouldn't make a fuss. Don't you remember?"

She lifted her chin. "I'm not making a fuss. You're making a fuss. So do as was suggested, and get going."

197

Frank came up behind her on the right. From her other side, Walt said, "The police'll be here any second. You boys fancy getting arrested?"

The two other MC members shifted their feet and looked at their leader. Liberty didn't break from her stepfather's scowl.

"Boss?" one of the members ventured.

Finally, the big man relented and took a few steps away. "Don't expect this is over."

"Oh," she answered with a triumphant grin. "I expect it is."

As police officers filed out of the kitchen door and into the yard, the three men took off down the driveway. The officers gave chase.

Liberty sagged as she released the breath she'd been holding. Frank and Walt were instantly by her side, asking if she was all right, if she needed to lie down.

"I'm fine, really," she assured them.

Frank took her hand and pressed it to his cheek. Walt patted her arm and stepped away to give the young couple some privacy.

"I really am stupid," Frank said.

She tried not to smile. "A little."

"You were here this whole time."

"I was."

"Why didn't you say anything?"

"I wasn't sure you'd like me like this. You seemed so dazzled by the dress, and the gold, and...you live a whole different life than me."

He opened his mouth to object, then another realization washed across his face. "You're the woman from the lake. With the—"

"Yes."

"You followed me here?"

198

"Well, I didn't have anywhere else to go. I didn't know about the hotel, though. That was...." She didn't know what to say.

"Fate," Frank offered.

He smiled. She smiled. They were standing so close.

Walt cleared his throat. "So, are you two going to kiss, or just keep standing there like a pair of fools?"

Frank raised his brows. "May I?" he asked her.

She beamed. "Please do!"

And they did.

More From Crysta K. Coburn

Crysta K. Coburn has been writing award-winning stories for most of her life. Her first short story was published at the age of sixteen after winning runner-up in a local writing contest. She earned her bachelor's degree in creative writing from Western Michigan University in 2005. She is a journalist, fiction writer, poet, playwright, editor, podcast co-host, and one-time rock lyricist. She served as editor for *The Queen of Clocks and Other Steampunk Tales*; *Cogs, Crowns, and Carriages*; and *Gears, Ghouls, and Gauges* (the latter two with Phoebe Darqueling). Tune in to podcasts Cinema Guano, Haunted Mitten, and Back Up A Second on your favorite podcast server.

A Saturnine, a Martial, and a Mercurial Lunatic

by Amber Michelle Cook

"Are we there yet?" Rocamora paced the confines of her uncle's favorite ethership, counting steps she couldn't see while holding an empty goblet so carelessly it was near upended.

Her cousin, Tirunelveli, snatched the cup from her as she passed too close to him this time. "I told you we're lost." He set it down where she couldn't knock it over on her next pass, while glaring unspoken accusations at his boon companion standing at the porthole.

Niramon turned from the view of a colossal celestial body and its striations of color, faint rings, and orbiting chunks of rocks to smile back at his friend in a bemused, gloating stare. He darted closer to contend, "We'll soon have our bearing and be on to daring. For I believe it will be a frabj—OUCH!"

"Tread lightly!" Tirun pulled Nir out of the path Roca was pacing with an irritated wave of his hand. As soon as his cousin passed and he let go of his friend, Tirun found himself overbalanced and Nir had to grab him to keep him from falling.

The notably shorter Nir walked a noticeably gaunter Tirun a few steps back to where his friend had been leaning against a sideboard. "Behold the Jovian head. Now the cheek, so shortly the face," he said, and then he left Tirun for the sizable porthole on the other side of the ship.

"Yes, I see the planet," Tirun huffed, trying to keep an eye on them both and scan a chart at the same time, doing neither very well, "but how do we find the uncharted moon Sir Malenfant claims he discovered last time—out in all this mess of debris around it?"

"It's by the red eye." Nir spoke in the placating tone of an attendant working Bedlam. Then he cried, "Here, by the bow, comes Cyclops now!" and rushed back toward the other porthole in his stockinged feet.

Tirun dropped the chart and hurtled forward again to keep his friend from running into his cousin, but was not quick enough.

He still glowered, even when Nir missed her by a hair's breadth and Roca passed him in blissful ignorance of the near collision.

Coming to a sudden stop, Tirun stumbled and fell against Roca as she began her return. They both tangled limbs and would have fallen but for Nir spinning about and catching them both on broad shoulders.

Hugging each in one arm, Nir grabbed for Roca's pathfinder stick and pressed it into her grasping hands, then reached around for Tirun's crutch and shoved it at him. Letting them go with triumphant zeal, he said, "Go on, outfit yourselves, but do hurry. I shall discover this unnamed chunk of rock in no time at all and join you for our expedition in less time than that."

Roca swept the floor ahead of her with the lightweight,

flexible stick until she detected the doorway, cackling, "Won't Uncle be livid if we take down his formidable beastie? I believe he was saving it for a rainy day."

Her humorless cousin waited for her to go through the door before following her out. Leaning heavily on his ironwork third leg, Tirun lamented, "Then Sir Malenfant shouldn't leave his hunting gear lying about."

Halting in the doorway, Nir frowned. Fretting. Fidgeting. "Which I am I to be? Am not brillig as a he."

Struggling to overcome tides of uffishness, he headed off as she, chest pushed out, hips swaying, hair swinging, galumphing straight for the helm.

"What are those creatures?" Rocamora inquired of her cousin, face tilted up in the direction of piercing chirps coming from the treetops above their heads.

Nira answered before Tirunelveli could, "You've never seen a slithing tove before?" as she assessed the terrain and moved to scout ahead. Roca brandished her stick to swat at their inattentive companion.

Tirun reached up to bring her pathfinder back down in a gesture of good-natured grumpiness. "Sir Malenfant's naturalist made several drawings of them, else I shouldn't know, for they are hidden amongst the foliage." He envied the way his cousin near tripped every few steps and righted herself like a creature of rubber, while he struggled over high roots in the ground with every step. "They look all the world to me like someone crossed a bat with a fairy, but Mr. Hugo is apt to be more fanciful than truthful, for he desperately wishes to be an illustrator of children's books."

Calling out to his boon companion, who had dashed ahead to a towering coatrack of a tree looming over a small clearing of shallow puddles and protuberant roots—and now stood on the edge of the clearing in a panic of confusion, chewing on her own hand, the picture of unaware uffing—Tirun hobbled as fast as he could to catch up to her. When he did, Nira pointed into the center of the clearing, "Why are those blasted borogoves just SITTING there, half in and half out?"

He barely looked at the little amphibious marsupials, clinging to roots while partially submerged in the muddy pools. Instead, Tirun peered further out between the tilted trunks of the tulgey trees for bigger concerns. "They're all mimsy, I dare say, being mating season," and squinted at any movement he espied in the distance.

Standing up straight and unsheathing Sir Malenfant's prized hunting knife, Nira now laughed at the mindless mimsiness of borogoves and dashed off again, swashbuckling her way further through the unearthly woods towards a delectable promise of danger.

Tirun turned to look back for Roca, only to find her passing him by as well, her thin-tipped cane catching on every discarded piece of flora the tulgeys cast down on the ground, yet tripping over them rather than being tripped up by them. He had to scramble to try and not get left behind.

Roca chattered back to him, "Uncle says the three creatures to hunt here are a jabberwock, a jubjub bird, and, of course, the Bandersnatch."

Further ahead, his boon companion crouched by the ground under another lofty living coatrack. She called back to him, "These are Bandersnatch tracks, if I know my facts."

"Good," cried Roca. "Why come back with anything less than the most manxomest monster this place has to offer?"

"Agreed!" Nira said too eagerly, rising back up to stand in

a decidedly feminine hero's pose. But when Tirun got closer and looked at her again, he muttered, "Oh boy," under his breath and meant it.

Nir awaited them, hunched and frowning. "But what do I know, even if I say it's so? Might merely have been a large mome rath outgrabing her territory on this Tumtum tree."

Roca, ears alert for peril, completely missed the change in tone of her companion and babbled, "We don't need to follow tracks. Let's find a wabe. We can follow the slithing of the toves back to their wabe, and Uncle says the Bandersnatch visits to feed on them constantly." She cocked one ear back up towards the cluster of distant toves and said, "Lead on, dear Nira," but Nir shook his head.

"I can lead, but am a poor follower. I'm afraid you must follow them, and I will do my best to lead you there."

Excited, Roca waved her cane in her estimation of the direction they should go. Nir dashed around her, trying to get ahead of her in order to guide them in that direction. Thus, Tirun was the only one to apprehend the threat they now faced.

Literally.

His companions hurled themselves forwards, while a hulking form lunged from behind the thick trunk of the Tumtum tree to intercept them. He could only manage to cry, "Beware! Jaws! Claws!" before the other two were confronted by its whiffling attack.

Nir saw the salivating jabberwock with excitement bordering on indecent thrill. He positioned himself between the beast and his friends, the mechanical hunting blade raised high, but with arms bent and ready to flex and strike as needed. Behind him, Roca froze. Not in fear, but with an intensity to listen and anticipate.

Her cousin observed her slipping a small explosive out of her pocket and hissed at her, "No, dearest, it's only a jabberwock!" They had agreed to save their one concussive to drive the Bandersnatch from its lair should they track it there. Tirun slid a compact crossbody crossbow around from his back to the front and let go the supportive cane to aim it with both hands.

He waited for his boon companion to strike the first blow, for Nir had called first blood when they departed the mundane world to travel upon the Solic ether ocean—and it was an unspoken rule between the three that they who claimed a thing first, deserved it by dint of quickness and cleverness. Otherwise they would argue without end.

Nir circled the fur-muffed giraffe-length neck of the beastie on eager, bouncing feet as it swayed to and fro, seeking an opening from on high. Cousin Roca concentrated with a faint smile on her face, calling out advice based on her training as fencer and fencing instructor as she apprehended the noises being made.

As soon as the jabberwock shifted its weight to the hooved hind haunches, Roca chortled, "Rearing attack!"

Nir switched the blade to point upward, merely sweeping it steadily from side to side in a tight arc.

When the jabberwock dug in with its back hooves, Roca tittered, "Launch attack!"

Nir jumped the small almost-sword to an impaling forward position, ready to plunge the double-blade deep into the underside of its neck when revealed. Instead, its bald tail flicked heavily from the side and knocked the knife out of his hands.

"Spring backward," Roca cried.

He did.

"Down, then roll," she added.

He did.

Coming up to discover his friend's dropped crutch within reach, Nir seized it and took a defensive stance with it instead. The jabberwock hulked up to him, salivating intermittently from a lipless mouth that never seemed to close.

"Tis a rather comical animal, is it not?" Nir put it to his greatest friend as he dodged drips and bites, "I should like to laugh at it."

Darting dour looks at his boon companion, Tirun drawled, "Scratch the thing, would you, Nir? So Roca and I can have a go at it."

"Nir?" Roca echoed with a chuckling gurgle. "Why didn't you say so? You are more nimble than Nira. Less stouthearted, but more fleet of foot. Attack it from all sides!"

Unsure, Nir remained in defensive posture. The creature clawed at him and bit at him, with every chance of success.

Growling, Tirun readied himself to let a bolt fly the moment he could.

His boon companion jumped back far enough to have time to wonder, "Ought we slay it, or had we better bring it back to show as an otherworld oddity?"

"Nir, sir," Roca barked, and the other two heard her words as if from under the beast's belly, as the creature was now between them, "I'm afraid you will need to bring it down. For one reason. TO KEEP FROM BEING EATEN BY IT."

The jabberwock's next bite came down on the battered crutch, and the implement went flying far off to one side. The elongated neck returned, hooves kicking out in the back, hoping to connect with the one behind it, who dodged handily, but also squealed in frustration at not being able to attack it.

The jabberwock's tail lashed around, attempting to unhand Tirun from his weapon with the hairless barbs of flesh along it, while one forearm backhanded Nir to the ground and came back with claws extended.

His friend kept his weapon, but not his feet. Tirun stumbled and fell—to come face to face with Nira in the dirt. "You are a most welcome sight," he told her—for she had not called first blood—before rolling over on his back and letting off one bolt, and then another and another. The impending claws jerked back as each missile impacted with flesh and bone, until the entire appendage dropped, and the creature burbled in dismay.

It kicked at Roca with the hind legs, backing up and swinging about as needed to reach her. She stepped back or to the side with ease as the hooves made plenty of noise, until the jabberwock brought its tail into the fray, which swished quietly through the air and swatted her into a nearby tulgey.

With a cry of woe, Tirun sat up fully and fired another three bolts at the creature's head. It reared, so that two passed through the mangy tufted fur around its neck, and the third happened to bounce off a vestigial tusk on one side of its mouth.

Pained laughter carried back to him, letting Tirun know his cousin was not too injured, as he watched Nira scramble off in a rush. He fired another series of bolts to keep the creature distracted, for he knew what she sought. And observed her in his periphery tumbling low for something in the spade-shaped leaves, such that Nira came to her feet bearing the bulky hunting knife, before calling to Roca, "How fared thee, against the tree?"

Roca's high voice crackled with amusement, punctuated by deep grunts, as she used the spongy burnt orange bark of the tulgey to pull herself back to her feet, "Would that all wood were as soft as this."

Still seated, her cousin had to fire his last three bolts to keep the jabberwock from setting upon him with the claws still serviceable. It had come so close, all three found a mark in limbs and torso. His boon companion dashed back to interpose herself, and the knife flashed and slashed almost too quickly to be seen.

"Yes," Roca called approvingly, "harry it, weary it!"

Her cousin struggled to his feet, only to gape at Nira when

she gasped between thrusts and parries, "Need...we...kill it?"

Tirun sputtered and tottered on trembling legs. "We came because you HAD to see something new!"

"I wished...to pit myself...against a dangerous animal, but this...is a creature of such absurdity...I cannot desire its demise."

Roca answered her, pushing away from the tree trunk, "It would serve Uncle right if we took one first, for he likes to put it about that he's the greatest hunter on earth," ending on a snort of derision.

Tirun lunged for a large broken branch—first using it to steady himself, and then raising it for a weapon—before grousing at Nira, "What do you want to do instead? Take a self-portrait picture with it, then go home?"

The jabberwock had slobbered so copiously upon its foe, Nira's hands slipped as she countered a circling swipe by the tail, slowing down her parrying thrusts. Head exposed for the moment, more saliva splattered her face, and as she wiped it from her eyes, the beast dropped its neck low to come in under her defenses, whiffling faintly.

"Sneak attack!" Roca warned, remembering that sound from before.

Though only attempting to swat at it to keep the beastie at bay, Nir blinked through the spittle and caught a glimpse of his impending demise.

Fear widened Nira's stinging eyes.

A moan of helplessness escaped Tirun. And Roca sobbed once.

The noises bothered Nir. In concern for them, all signs of uff sloughed off him.

To be replaced by a determined calm as the slobbering, open maw shot towards Nira's head.

She released the vorpal mechanism with a flick of her thumb.

The lipless mouth opened farther than it should have been able to, descending on her. Nira ducked and closed her eyes against the saliva. Her hand shot out in a blur.

The two blades snickered open like a pair of scissors, and with a sharp snack of blades closing against one another, snipped off the hopeful head at the base of its neck.

With serrated incisors pressing in on the flesh of Nira's scalp, the creature froze.

Nostrils flaring in shock, the jabberwock's uncomprehending mien tumbled to the forest floor, where it landed with a quiet and sticky thud, picking up spade leaves, spikey tulgeys cones and feathery Tumtum needles as it rolled right up to Nira's boots.

She blinked through the frothing spittle, beaming, "I knew it was going to be a frabjous day."

"What's that?" Rocamora halted, mid-limp and mid-swipe with her now crooked pathfinder, at an unfamiliar sound coming from on high.

It grew in volume, but at such a distance as to cause no alarm at present.

Tromping back to the ethership, her cousin didn't look up. Tirunelveli was too busy navigating loops and snarls of tulgey roots with his battered and bent crutch. His boon companion put an arm on his, though, bringing him to a halt as well. Tirun looked up only to glance—but once he glimpsed, he gripped Niramon's arm to gape at what he saw.

A shadow passed over them so large, its corpus blocked the Jovian celestial body from view for a long moment.

Meanwhile, wind from its wings rushed over them as well, gusting hair into faces and tulgey pollen into eyes.

Tirun described it for his cousin in a few choice words, squinting as tail feathers passed overhead. Adding, "It is too high, dearest," noting the movements of her hands.

Roca returned the unused explosive to her pocket yet again, pouting.

Then something wet splashed down around them, covering toves and treetops alike in an off-white viscous fluid that immediately began to drip down to the forest floor.

She spat several times before squealing, "Such a quantity of frume!"

"Mr. Hugo utterly failed to communicate the size of the jubjub bird," Tirun complained as he wiped at his craggy features and started forward again.

Nir shifted the cloak with the jabberwocky head to his other hand already bearing the vorpal blades and whipped out a handkerchief as he followed. "Sir Malenfant, I doubt, will have a sturdy parasol when he hunts hereabout."

Roca just about giggled as she shook the droppings off her hair with eyes squeezed shut. She returned to the limp and the swipe in progress, admonishing the other two, "NO. No need to warn Uncle about that when we get back!"

Arriving at the ethership and releasing a mechanism for the boarding ramp, Nir agreed, "YES. And let us not mention, the Bandersnatch had been our intention."

Tirun gave a gloomy nod as he took his last look around the little moon, "INDEED. We shall call our little outing, The Hunting of the Jabberwock."

Jabberwocky, by Lewis Carroll

'Twas brillig, and the slithy toves
      Did gyre and gimble in the wabe:
All mimsy were the borogoves,
      And the mome raths outgrabe.

"Beware the Jabberwock, my son!
      The jaws that bite, the claws that catch!
Beware the Jubjub bird, and shun
      The frumious Bandersnatch!"

He took his vorpal sword in hand;
      Long time the manxome foe he sought—
So rested he by the Tumtum tree
      And stood awhile in thought.

And, as in uffish thought he stood,
      The Jabberwock, with eyes of flame,
Came whiffling through the tulgey wood,
      And burbled as it came!

One, two! One, two! And through and through
      The vorpal blade went snicker-snack!
He left it dead, and with its head
      He went galumphing back.

"And hast thou slain the Jabberwock?
      Come to my arms, my beamish boy!
O frabjous day! Callooh! Callay!"
      He chortled in his joy.

'Twas brillig, and the slithy toves
      Did gyre and gimble in the wabe:
All mimsy were the borogoves,
      And the mome raths outgrabe.

More From Amber Michelle Cook

Amber Michelle Cook writes literary nonsense and "Space 1899" steampunk. This is the first story she penned that's both. Chocolate & peanut butter fiction! She has short stories in several anthologies and 2 self-published short novellas on Amazon (urban fairy). She'd like it if you followed her author page on Facebook: https://www.facebook.com/ambermichellecookwriter, or clicked to see her author page on Amazon: http://www.amazon.com/-/e/B00B5QTBW6.

The Second Mission of Azarbad the Aeronaut

by J. Woolston Carr

When it was the 15th night of her captivity:

During the time of the Crimean War—when Britain and Russia bickered over the usual imperial disagreements concerning foreign territories, trade routes, and Arab people who wanted nothing to do with them—a British general was stationed among his Ottoman allies at the seaport of Bandar Abbas. Located on the shores of the Persian Gulf, his base was in a centuries-old building ideal for protection by the British Sea and Aerial Navy. It was equipped with a tall spire where scouting dirigibles could easily dock. His directive was to divine military secrets, anticipate Russian strategies, and expose enemy spies.

As for the latter, he had apprehended an unusual foreign operative. While the general despised spies and would normally have had them shot (as he previously had done with 22 others), this particular agent managed to provide information the general found unusually intriguing.

And so he sat at his desk, sipping tea and staring at a wad of documents where he kept re-reading certain boring snippets. In truth, he was lost in the anticipation of the arrival of his captive. His eyes flickered fatuously, his bulbous nose sniffed longingly, and his moustache had been snipped with extra care by petite scissors. The uniform had been pressed and brushed, his medals and buttons polished till they radiated importance. The general was an imbecile, but being a general in the British army, no one noticed.

Late in the evening, a knock on his door signaled the expected arrival. The general adjusted his position, straightening his back to look authoritative and commanding.

"Enter," he directed.

The door opened to reveal a woman. Dressed in a simple dull cotton dress, she nevertheless struck a charming presence. Her golden hair flowed unmanaged to a slim shoulder, her once pale skin glowed pink and brown from the desert sun, and her blue eyes shimmered with drama and narrative.

On either side of her stood a British soldier, both carrying muskets perched on their shoulders. "My gracious thanks for such brave escorts," she said with a wink. Though properly at attention, they still blushed at her regard.

"Dismissed!" growled the general and waved his hand at them as if shooing away flies.

The woman found herself in a large room, which had been the dining area at a time when the house was used for domestic purposes. Now it was a headquarters, and she was in a chamber rearranged for planning, deliberation, and interrogation. The table was no longer set for dining, rather it was arrayed for examination and strategy. Salt shakers and spoons pinned down map corners, and diminutive armies traversed fields of napkins displaying troops with guns and swords, on horseback and in airships. They moved about by means of tiny clockwork components, threatening each other with miniature bayonets, but awaiting orders. She fished out little details in the room, insignificant to the occupants, but she always found ways to make them useful to garnish a future story.

When she entered, he set down his cup. He did not rise and offered her nothing to drink. This did not bother the woman, who knew she was undeserving of the respect normally due to someone of her rank and privilege. She glided over to the same chair she had occupied for several evenings.

The general glanced towards a man sitting at a desk in the interior. He was the clerk, a dull, sallow person with a constant squint and a pretentious attitude, and he would take down each word the woman uttered. The clerk cleared his throat.

"Your name from birth?" he asked.

"Lady Sara Hazard," she answered, her voice melodic.

"Your place of birth?"

"Edinburgh, Scotland."

"State your purpose in the East."

"I have renounced the Christian religion and my lands in Scotland to embrace the Muslim faith. My home is the Iranian city of Shiraz. I have taken the name Sharayah Scheherazade."

The general sighed as if dealing with a small child's ignorant decision to eat cake for dinner. He leaned forward to address her in a personal tone.

"Madame, why would a genteel woman such as you give up the superiority and protection of the British Empire to associate with uncultivated, barbarian heathens?"

"I am attracted to the spirituality and simplicity of Islam."

"Come come, these people are intellectually unfit for religion. Prayer five times a day; how do you deal with the noise?"

"You mean like the ringing of church bells?"

The general leaned back, annoyed. "Lady Sara Hazard, you are being held prisoner for suspicion of collaboration

219

with the enemy. You have been seen cavorting with notable Russian agents," he denounced. "So far, you have acquitted yourself by revealing information I have found...useful. You will continue the report begun last night. You do have more to tell me? If not...." The general slid a finger across his throat. He slipped on his glasses and frowned as if irritated, but she recognized a hidden tremor of burning curiosity.

She nodded. "You want me to continue the report on the Russian secret weapon."

"Ah yes, concerning this Azarbad fellah."

"Captain Azarbad, if you remember. He is an officer in your airship corp."

The general mumbled something, reluctant to acknowledge the rank.

"A Mohametan Captain in the British forces? Has he given up his infidel ways, then, and turned towards Christianity?"

"I don't think that was a requirement for his services."

"And you say this Ottoman Sultan is sending him?"

"In a sense. Sending him or allowing him. It is difficult to see the will of Azarbad."

"Hmm, sounds irresponsible and treacherous. Edwards, repeat to me the last bit of her previous report."

The clerk frowned as he squinted through glasses, searching for the correct spot in his notes. "And so it was that Azarbad the Aeronaut was living a pleasant and enjoyable life, until the Second Mission of Azarbad the Aeronaut. It was then the dawn of day, and she ceased saying her permitted say."

"You will continue and have until the morning light," the general eagerly ordered his prisoner. "And you understand, it will not go well for you if you no longer have useful information."

Sara Hazard nodded and began.

"And he had taken on the name Azarbad, and he was called Azarbad the Aeronaut."

As I said, Azarbad the Aeronaut was living an enjoyable life with the riches he had gained in his last mission, until his thoughts became possessed of travel and intrigue.

Azarbad retained his status as a special officer to the British Royal Aerial Navy, on assignment from the Sultan of the Ottoman Empire. Hawk-eyed and long-bearded, he wore his uniform with honor. His blue, long-skirted jacket was lined with gold stripes and a gold collar. His trousers were white, his boots expensive. But he was also proud of his Mohametan origins, and so a turban wrapped tall upon his head rather than the Ottoman fez, and a wide sash of red silk encircled his waist, securing his curved shamshir sword.

Azarbad's curious hunting falcon perched upon his arm at all times. The body was black and powerful, with fine, dark streaks of feathers. The wing mechanism was made of gold metal gearwork, ticking like a running clock when in flight. One eye was glass, and its beak was gleaming brass. The captain named it Shaheen, and it never parted from his master. The bird spoke as a human does and cautioned his master on the merits of venturing abroad again.

"My captain, we are quite content here in your palace. You have plentiful food, a nest of unusual comfort, and willing ears to hear the tiresome tales of your adventures. Why throw all this away? I fear it will come to naught and only discharge us into danger."

The captain rapped restless, claw-like fingers on a table of expensive African ivorywood. The truth was Azarbad never felt satisfied for long on the ground.

"The sultan has inquired of me to investigate a secret weapon constructed by the Russians. Should I be disloyal to my ruler and disappoint my people?"

"And what of me?" asked the bird with a screech. For the bird was unlike Azarbad. It was pleased to remain on the ground, feeding upon scraps of shrimp and lobster, and polishing its wings with a silken cloth. It had a peevish and contrary nature, which Azarbad endured but rarely dissuaded him from some decision.

With the blessing of the sultan, Captain Azarbad again joined the crew of a British airship of the line called *Albion*. The Ottomans had no serviceable airships matching the British for size and power, and the British had no captain the likes of Azarbad, who knew the lands from the Syrian Desert to the Sea of Oman.

Azarbad thrilled at the return to the clouds, but he understood the excitement of his presence was not shared with the crew of 120 men and officers. The Mohametan captain was a necessary evil to them, and while he gave sound advice and direction, the orders would be delivered by an English-born officer.

The *Albion* was a large, first-rate sky schooner with a pair of steam engines and a balloon, humming in the air like a buzzing bee. Two decks of 60 guns were placed port and starboard. The hull of the gondola was pure wood from the shores of Sicily, the fabric of the balloon was the richest silk from the caterpillars of China. She was a match for anything that could sail, glide, or soar. So thought Azarbad.

As they floated over the Caspian Sea in search of their quarry, a dark cloud descended on the ship, so vast it blotted out the Sun, so rapid no crow's nest attendant gave warning. Fire and ball rained on the ship, and Azarbad struggled mightily to control the wheel. They floundered and plunged like a bird with a broken wing, men screaming and falling from the rails and netting. Possibly Shaheen the falcon squealed

"I told you!" But certainly the mechanized bird had found a hiding place underneath a mattress somewhere out of earshot from the relentless attack.

The English officer joined Azarbad at the wheel.

"Commander, your tie!" cried Azarbad.

The officer peered down at his chest.

"No, not that tie—"

But Azarbad's warning came too late. The ship tilted after a fierce onslaught, and the officer, not tied to a fixture of the ship as was Azarbad, tumbled from the bridge and plummeted towards the sea.

Azarbad was a keen captain, and even amidst this assault he maintained control of the ship. Knowing he was no match for the menacing dreadnought of the sky, he steered the *Albion* to the safety of an island, thus escaping his attackers. The ship settled near a beach, and the captain assessed the destruction.

The chief engineer looked about for the British commander.

"He is gone," said Azarbad. "I am in charge. What is the damage to the balloon and hull of the gondola? Ho, will she fly again?"

The chief engineer was dubious, both about the ship and Azarbad's command.

A jovial Azarbad clapped him on the back, for at home he might be restless and moody, but on an adventure and in the presence of a ship, no matter its condition, he remained eternally optimistic. It was contagious to the chief engineer, who began evaluating the repairs and seemed to cheer up.

"Give me two days, Captain."

"You have three," replied Azarbad. "I mean to explore this sandy rock we now occupy."

The engineer and the lieutenant glanced askew at each other.

"How many men will you take with you, Captain?" asked the lieutenant.

Azarbad looked to the engineer. "How many men do you need for the repairs?"

"All of them," he answered.

The captain was a master in the skies, but a fool on the ground.

"Then I go alone with Shaheen," answered a confident Azarbad, taking only his sword and a canteen of water.

The falcon had emerged from his refuge and clicked his wings. "Praise be to Allah, we are alive. To serve with Captain Azarbad is to serve with ill fortune. I vow never to set a tail feather upon the deck of a ship again."

"Good," said Azarbad, "for we are leaving the ship to explore."

"What?" cried the bird. "Out there? There is nothing but sky and trees. That is no place for a bird."

The expression of the general's clerk was of mistrust as he discontinued his writing.

"How is it you know the conversation of the men?" he asked.

Before Sara Hazard could answer, the general erupted.

"Do not interrupt the story!"

Sara Hazard let a charming smile insinuate its way to her lips. "I learned the story from some Russian sailors, an unfortunate conversation that has brought me to your custody. Then I spoke to members of Captain Azarbad's crew, from whom I heard much of the tale, and I have interviewed the falcon Shaheen. I have an exceptional memory. My sources are firsthand and unimpeachable."

"There you have it," blurted the general. "Firsthand and unimpeachable. Please, Lady, continue."

The captive spy tilted her head and resumed as the first glimmer of morning sunlight peeked through the window.

"Azarbad trekked towards the center of the island. The golden beach gave way to a blanket of trees and some undulating hills towards the center."

A trumpet sounded for morning reveille, and Sara Hazard perceived the dawn of day and ceased to say her permitted say.

When it was the 16th night of her captivity, Lady Sara Hazard began:

Growing weary, Azarbad stopped to rest. He and Shaheen slept through the night, and awoke refreshed. He made for the center of the island, robed by trees and a craggy range of small hills. As he neared the center, a white structure appeared in the distance.

"This is curious," said Azarbad. He was determined to find its origin.

The structure was hidden amongst a copse of trees, behind a jutting hill. Azarbad had to climb the hill to get a glimpse of it, and was surprised at what the sight revealed.

It was a white dome, egg-shaped and the size of an immense palace. There was no entrance, no window, no seam to show the construction or purpose. He sat on the rise of the hill and stared at it.

"This is all very interesting, staring at a blank, white hill," said Shaheen, quite bored. "But shouldn't we get back to the ship?"

"Perhaps...wait. Look."

A small opening appeared on the smooth exterior, and a man exited through a door. Azarbad recognized the baggy, red trousers and blue vests of the French Zouaves, allies to the British and Ottomans in the war against the Russians.

"Hmm...." hummed Azarbad as he stroked his beard. "A secret base? This will be of interest to the sultan and the admiral. We will return to the ship with this observation."

But Azarbad found himself lost on the land of the island. He darted this way and that, searching for familiar signs. None appeared, and he lost his sense of direction with two feet planted firmly on the ground.

By luck, he returned to the beach where his ship had foundered after a day of searching. But it was not there. He was in the right spot, for signs of the ship were all around. Bits of wood, silk, and canvas lay scattered about. Footprints pockmarked the sand, and a deep trench remained where the gondola had lain for repairs.

"Why did you expect the Englishmen to wait for you, oh captain of mild breezes and no airships?" questioned Shaheen. "Now we are stranded. I will perish here, for what am I expected to eat? Seeds from the trees? Flowers in the grass? That is food fit for a pigeon."

"Yes, I am a fool to have explored on my own, and have only the sense that Allah has allotted unto me," Azarbad chided himself. But he was not one to dwell on past mistakes. Instead, he began to make his way back to the dome. Again, his sense of direction, or lack thereof, took him to secluded areas with no domes, but he eventually, through trial and luck, found his objective.

"What will you do?" asked Shaheen. "Creep in like a thief and find some transportation to take us home?"

Azarbad went to the location of the door and hammered upon with insistent blows.

"This is a plan worthy of boobs and simpletons." The falcon flew off.

The door opened and a gun pointed at Azarbad.

"I am a traveler marooned on this island and an officer in the British Navy," said the captain, speaking perfect French. "And I seek sanctuary."

A guard brought him inside. The interior was crowded with soldiers and diplomats. But instead of being taken to a commandant's office, Azarbad was led to a prison cell.

"Wait, did you not hear me? I am an ally, not an enemy."

The guard did not answer, but with a sharp twist, turned on his heel and left Azarbad alone.

"Again, Shaheen was correct in his advice," despaired Captain Azarbad. He did not wait long before a French officer appeared.

"Monsieur, why am I imprisoned?" asked the aeronaut.

After a short laugh, the commandant gave a judgmental twirl of the hairs of his goatee.

"You do not look like a British officer, mon frere. You might be as you say, but we are under orders to detain any suspicious looking persons. You Mohametans do not belong here."

Azarbad belonged in this part of the world much more than a French soldier with a lingering scent of wine on his breath, but he said nothing of that.

"How long will I be held?"

"Until we determine that you are who you say."

"If you but contact the admiral or the sultan...."

The French officer turned up his nose. "We are a secret base, you understand?

We can contact no one."

"Then how will you determine I am who I say I am?" sighed Azarbad.

The commandant shrugged, a thin smile on his lips.

"I am afraid we cannot signal out, and I assure you, no one can find us here."

An explosion rattled the dome, and a soldier hurried to the commander.

"Someone has found us here!" cried the soldier.

The dome rocked again, shells bursting all around.

"Impossible!" The French commandant was frantic. He calmed and said, "It does not matter. No cannon shell can pierce the heavily fortified dome—"

After a loud detonation, part of the rounded ceiling began to collapse.

"Allez!" cried the commandant. "We must abandon the dome!"

"Wait!" cried Azarbad. "What about me?"

But the commandant had already disappeared. With a look of helplessness, Azarbad clutched the bars of his cell. Another piece of the dome cracked and fell, revealing a massive airship hovering above.

"It is the ship that attacked the *Albion*, from which I barely escaped," thought Azarbad. The captain marveled at the great airship, more than twice the size of the one in which he had arrived. Great wings angled and fluttered to aid in its flight, steadying the ship and allowing it to hover or speed forth, faster than any ship he had sailed. Adorning the prow was a hooked beak of a gigantic bird, with the brown wood of the hull carved like feathers and the aft rudder a bundle of tailfeathers. Azarbad could hear the rumble of the massive steam boilers powering the engine, echoing like the thunder of a potent storm cloud. On the side of the ship in Russian he read the name *Rukh*.

"This is the secret weapon devised by the Russians," perceived Azarbad. Alarmed, he cried out for help. French soldiers scurried back and forth, grabbing a bag or a weapon and heading for any available exit.

"This is where I finally perish, Allah preserve me."

Then the guard he had first met came to the cell. He found the keys and unlocked the door.

"No one should suffer a fate such as this," said the guard.

"Not even an infidel?" sniffed Azarbad.

"Napoleon III may have us here fighting for the Catholic Church, but I doubt any of these men are more religious than you, Mohametan. Come with me, and I will show you our escape."

Azarbad hesitated. He found his sword and slipped it in to his belt.

"Many thanks for your assistance, may Allah bless you. But my mission was to discover the existence and purpose of this flying arsenal. I shall not deviate from the path set for me while waiting in another French prison."

The guard nodded, and he quitted his company with a salute.

Azarbad hastened out of the dome, which was now a brittle egg, cracked in so many pieces to make an omelette of dead and wounded Frenchmen.

The great airship floated near the ground, and Azarbad spied his chance. The ship was constructed with large struts extending down from the hull like the legs of a lethal raptor. Hooks captured prizes and deposited them in a large net that was retrieved by the crew of the ship. Able to climb onto a remaining ledge of the dome, Azarbad leapt to gain a hold on one of the struts. He unwrapped his turban and tied himself to the wooden beam.

"I shall see where I am taken," he said with a wistful sigh. Shaheen was nowhere to be seen; Azarbad assumed he had evacuated the area as soon as the attack began.

The ship sailed with Azarbad secured to the strut throughout the night. Sleep was too ambitious of an objective, and he remained awake in the dark sky with no sign of what was below. Still, he was in the air, and this was where he preferred to be, though he confessed his captain's cabin would be more appealing than perilously hanging from the bottom of an airship.

"Why do you pause?" barked the general, leaning forward with fascination despite his attempt to look imposing.

But Sara Hazard perceived the dawn of day and ceased to say her permitted say.

When it was the 17th night of her captivity, Lady Sara Hazard began:

The ship flew swift as a broad-winged albatross. After surmounting a mountain range, it began to descend to a valley where the ground had been gouged with deep, circular furrows. A number of cannons guarded the valley, like serpents in a nest. Asthey came closer, explosives erupted over labourers digging long trenches with shovels and picks. They were mining for ore.

The *Rukh* would soon be moored again, and Azarbad would be discovered. As the ship floated over a ridge of a mountain, the agile aeronaut leapt off and landed on the ground. He was followed by a tumbling mass of feathers and rattling of brass as Shaheen rolled next to him.

"Faithful bird, did you follow me here in hopes of aiding in my rescue?"

"You jest, oh captain. You know how I hate to fly. When I saw you tie yourself to one of the struts, I fastened my claws on another. Then the airship flew so high and far, I dared not release until now."

"Yet we are both alive and free from the French prison."

"This is worse than where we were on the island," screeched the falcon. "There, we had food and water, and might have eventually been rescued. Here, we are trapped in this valley, surrounded by impassable mountains and bitter enemies. You will be captured and tortured, and I will be made into some toy for the amusement of children."

Azarbad could make no argument this time. Instead, he began searching for a cave in which to spend the night.

"Inshallah! If Allah wills it, after a good rest I will think clearly and find a way out of here."

The falcon gave a derisive, mechanical snort. Then he began whistling.

"Why are you doing that?" asked Azarbad.

"I am practicing. When you are being stretched on a rack, I will find some way to make myself entertaining and therefore preserve me."

"I doubt it. You are a bad whistler."

Caverns dotted the mountains, and Azarbad soon found one in which to hide. He entered the darkness and made himself comfortable. Just when he began to drift off to sleep, a bright light appeared in the cave. Three men stood at the entrance, carrying a torch, picks, a wooden crate, and several heavy bags. The men were large and attired like workers in the mines, and did not seem pleased to find Azarbad in their cave. The falcon began a frantic whistle.

"I seem to have gotten lost," suggested Azarbad.

The men seemed disinclined to believe him. One of them set down the crate and handed a pick to the man next to him. The third drew a long, straight-bladed knife.

The falcon stopped whistling. "I have no idea who this wretch is and how he got in here!"

Azarbad glared at Shaheen as he drew forth the shamshir from its leather sheath. Fashioned in the great forges of

Damascus, the blade curved like the crescent moon in the month of Sha'ban, the edge honed sharp as a lion's tooth, the ivory grip riveted to the tang with golden bolts, the blade inscribed with "No warrior but Ali, no sword but Zulfiqar."

The men hesitated, but they were three against one and much bigger than their adversary.

Azarbad swept in amongst his enemy, his blade truly whistled and flashed in the torchlight. He fought with the madness as one who was jinn-struck; the curved sword circled and whirled with precision in the confines of the cave. Azarbad used the restricted space to his advantage, dancing and ducking until he was close enough to grapple with his opponents. Laying the two pick wielders on the ground with two mighty cuts, he then blocked the jab from the knife with his sheath. At close distance, he delivered a deadly thrust.

"Are you finished yet?" asked Shaheen, hidden behind a rock with his wings over his bejeweled eyes.

Azarbad glanced at the bits and pieces of the men at his feet.

"Perhaps we should find another cave to sleep in after all."

Before they moved to another cave, Azarbad inspected the box and bags of the now deceased men. The box contained explosives for mining. The bags, though, were heavy with unpolished diamonds from the mine. Azarbad suspected these men were thieves, and had he not killed them, he might have learned a way off of the mountain.

"Fantastic, we are rich," moaned Shaheen. "We shall either be murdered or die of starvation, but we shall die rich. Such is why I hooked my star with the great Azarbad the Aeronaut."

In the morning Azarbad awoke and stepped outside to view the valley below the mountains. Loud noises accosted his ears, and he witnessed an amazing sight. From the airship the *Rukh*, hundreds of small, aerial carriages glided back and forth, going to the mines in the valley and collecting coal. The ships held one pilot in a narrow, uncovered gondola, with four disc-like wings of tin rapidly rotating as the vehicles descended to pick up the boxes and returned to the huge airship.

"The mines here must have both coal and diamonds," considered Azarbad. "And a ship that size is in need of much fuel to keep her in the air. There must be a great boiler, to power so colossal a ship."

"What is your inspired plan, oh captain of no ship and no crew?"

"Bismillah! Come with me, for we have a way out of the valley and off the mountain. Yet it is still my duty to uncover a weakness in this great airship, and so I must find a way on to her."

"So you plan to get aboard the most pernicious of weapons where you will surely die?" questioned an incredulous Shaheen. "I have discovered your weakness, oh captain. You are a fool."

"What is duty, but the motivation of every ass?" replied Azarbad.

Nevertheless, Azarbad climbed down the side of the cliff. When he reached the ground, he found one of the crates of coal ready to be picked up and crawled in.

"You will be lucky if they do not find you, and simply throw you into the furnace," said Shaheen, departing from the valley.

One of the aerial carriages swooped down like a great eagle and looped its claws around the crate of coal containing Azarbad. The captain peered through the slats of the package to see where he would be delivered. To his horror, the boxes of coal were being deposited directly into a great boiler roaring with flames. Azarbad struggled inside the crate, but the shifting of the box in flight had produced a tight seal of the lid. The heat of the powerful engine melted his resolve.

"Shaheen was correct, I shall die as fuel for this terrible airship. Oh, that I had stayed at home in Baghdad and enjoyed the fruits of my past mission."

As Azarbad said his prayers to Allah, the aerial carriage began to zigzag in an erratic fashion. With a sudden jolt he dropped, realizing this would be his final minute. But instead the crate crashed to the deck of the ship, missing the great furnace and splitting open to dump out the coal and release Azarbad. The Russian crew commenced boisterous shouts, and dazed Captain Azarbad stood to receive their attack. But none was forthcoming. The crew was pointing at a clockwork bird vaulting through the air. In its metal claws was the box of explosives from the cave. Several shots rang out, missing the falcon, and then it released the package into the burning furnace. A great gasp arose from the crew, followed by a huge explosion.

Several aerial carriages that had been carrying the coal now occupied the deck, and Azarbad made for one as the Russian crew raced to control the flames of the blazing airship. In a moment, the Aeronaut was fleeing the sinking craft. Soon Shaheen joined him, with an exhausted sigh.

"I've not flown so much in my life. Rescuing you is very tiresome. However, you are on your own for this one."

"What do you mean?" asked Azarbad, as the falcon flew off again. A whirring of other aerial carriages came to his ears, and Azarbad turned back to see several of the vehicles carrying angry Russians. But this was Azarbad the Aeronaut, and whether it was a massive airship or a single-seater aerial carriage, he was the greatest pilot in the skies. Darting among the treetops and between clefts in the rocky crags of the mountain, he maneuvered through spaces with bare inches to spare, as a fat man squeezes into a pair of pantaloons two sizes too small. The pursuing aerial carriages smashed among the rocky ridges or became ensnared by grasping tree branches, so that Azarbad finally escaped.

Azarbad steered the aerial carriage homeward, his sense of direction as accurate when among the clouds as it was unreliable on the ground. When he returned to the British Admiralty, word of the destruction of the *Rukh* had already arrived. But all disparaged the possibility that a single Mohametan could have been responsible. Instead, Captain Azarbad was put before a court martial for abandoning his ship, and he was only extricated from jail by the intervention of the sultan himself.

Azarbad returned to his home with Shaheen the falcon, and without credit for his exploits, promotion in his rank, or reward in his coffers.

"I performed my duty as commanded, but see little in return for my efforts. Now, I must live modestly in my home with no compensation. Allah alone kenneth what things His Omniscience conceals from man!" spoke Azarbad.

He then looked with concern at Shaheen. The falcon indeed appeared ill and began to gag ferociously.

"Is there something that ails you, bird of sage advice? You look unwell."

Azarbad knelt to his bird, who stood swaying atop a Persian rug. Before Azarbad could come to his aid (or remove him from the expensive carpet), Shaheen expelled a number of bright, shiny stones from his stomach onto the floor.

"The diamonds!" exclaimed Azarbad.

"Is it not prize money?" submitted a proud Shaheen. "We have returned to the City of Peace with wealth and all our wings. Surely, you have no other desire than to serve Allah by retiring from these dangerous missions which threaten my life."

The general roused himself from the mesmerized state he'd fallen into when listening to the story.

"Ha ha! Finally I have heard the end of this Azarbad fellah." He glared menacingly at the woman.

"Yes," said Sara, with a sly twinkle in her voice. "It is the end. That is, Azarbad forgot he was an aeronaut, but only briefly. You are aware, General, of the great Russian gun hidden in the Mountain of the Zughb?"

"Yesss...." the general trailed off suspiciously. "It is called the Cyclops, as fearful an armament as ever there was. The troops we sent to investigate never returned."

"Azarbad was soon seized with a longing for travel and diversion and adventure.

His service once again being necessary to the cause of the British, his past improprieties were now forgotten. He embarked as a Special Officer for the Aerial Navy, investigating reports of this new weapon in the Mountain of the Zughb, where was rumored to live wild tribes of hill people. And so Azarbad the Aeronaut reconnoitered, to the vociferous objections of the falcon Shaheen.

'Once again you bring peril to my exalted life,' moaned Shaheen. 'I shall be consumed by a beastly tribe of wild men, and I shall never know the caressing coos of a red collared dove again.'

Thus begins the third mission of Azarbad the Aeronaut."

"What?" squealed the General. "There's more? This damned Mussalman Azarbad, always getting himself in trouble. You will relate to me what happens next!"

"It is morning, General. Tonight, then?"

Sara Hazard smiled as she perceived the dawn of day and ceased to say her permitted say.

About J. Woolston Carr

J. Woolston Carr currently lives in Dallas, Texas. He works for the Dallas Public Libraries in the History and Archives Division and is an avid reader of 19th century history. Mr. Carr is also employed as a fencing instructor for the Fencing Institute of Texas teaching modern Olympic style fencing, and is president of the Victorian Fencing Society for the study of the martial art of fencing as it was practiced in the nineteenth century. Mr. Carr has a blog for the Victorian Fencing Society with articles on nineteenth century fencing at http://victorianfencingsociety.blogspot.com/, and more information on the Victorian Fencing Society can be found at https://www.victorianfencingsociety.com/

Mr. Carr has recently published stories for the 2019 anthology *Gears, Ghouls and Gauges* and the 2020 anthology *20,000 Leagues Remembered*. Learn more about his work at https://rb.gy/wflwva.

Black Dog, Wild Wood

by Thomas Gregory

Mind you, this was back a piece. A generation, maybe two after men and the clever things they'd built to do their work finished fighting to decide just who was going to serve who for good and all. Look around you. Men may have won, but there wasn't much left worth the winning of by the end. The ones that remained began breaking up the leavings, the strongest among them declaring themselves "the king of this" or "the duke of that," and among these was the King of the Western Road.

The king had a son, as kings are wont to do, and a body possessing more naivete about the world outside his father's castle there could not be found. The prince could not lead men in peace or martial them in war. He was not proficient with a blade nor deadly with a gun, and he would never drive another man to service under his heel as his father and his grandfather did before him. This was not to say the prince was incapable of these things, only that he had not been taught to do them.

But the one thing that the prince could do, the thing that he'd never been beaten at, was racing. It was, it seemed, the only thing his father cared to teach him, though the king himself was middling at best.

At the head of the Western Road sat the glass and steel spire of King's Chapel, and it was here that the prince was called on the morning of his eighteenth birthday. The prince's racing rig was already out, roaring like a steel lion, and beside it stood the king and his driving master.

"My son," said the king. "You have coursed the great roads and the small. You have won victory in every challenge, but now, I fear my day of dread is at hand."

"Sir?" Behind the prince, his road team was doing their final inspection of the Lion.

"I once had a brother, did you know that?"

The prince did indeed know of his uncle, Owen, though not from the lips of his father.

The tale of Owen was told only in half-whispers and old broadsheets. Owen the gadabout. Owen the libertine. Owen who burned out and was gone before his time. The prince could see the knowledge in his father's face.

"Your uncle learned of his trial before its time. The knowledge of what was to come for him led him to live his life as he did, counting the days until his death and filling them with as much pleasure as he could. He saw no escape from the coming death, a death that comes for you, too, my first and only son, as it will for all our firstborn sons until the end of our line or the end of days. The Fell Rider. At dawn the Rider will come to challenge you. I have done my best to prepare you for what is to come and to keep the knowledge of your fate from you so you did not follow your uncle into ruin."

The prince's driving master approached him bearing a fine pair of driving gloves. His red beard only half concealed a thick scar across his chin, a souvenir of his own days of coursing the Western Road.

"All that I can teach, you have learned," said the driving master, embracing the prince.

"When the Rider comes, you must beat him across the great river, into the city and back. To do otherwise is your death and my sorrow." As he said this, dawn broke over the wall of the courtyard, and the air was filled with the sound of a lone engine so loud it even drowned out the prince's rig.

"The Rider approaches. Go now and best the beast with which we have been cursed." The King kissed his son's forehead, and the prince climbed behind the wheel. The Steel Lion was electric in his hands. The courtyard gates swung open. There, waiting outside was a racing rig as black as the heart of the king of demons and louder than all the hammers on all the anvils that ever were. The Fell Rider sat behind the wheel, his helmet painted with the visage of a snarling, black dog.

To hell with being challenged. Today, the prince would lay the challenge at the Rider's feet. Jamming on the gas, the Steel Lion charged out of the courtyard, the Rider in pursuit, and the generations-old contest began again.

A day and a night the two raced ahead through city and village, devoid of people after the war, and finally into the dark and wild wood. Even the road was empty, as if the whole of the living world had died outside the confines of King's Chapel, ghosts until the prince had finished meeting his challenge. Often as not, the prince looked into the rearview and saw a vacant road behind him. Each time, just as he began to think he had outpaced his hound-faced pursuer, the Fell Rider's rig would reappear, roaring fire, and the chase would begin again.

By and by, exhaustion finally overtook the prince. He had lost the Rider yet again, and the woods seemed as if they would never end. As he looked for a hidden place to pull off, a lost filling station came into sight. The station's service bell dinged as the Steel Lion rumbled in, drawing the mechanic out from the garage. Her red coveralls were smeared with grease and one lens of her thick glasses was cracked across the top corner.

"Well, Prince of the Steel Lion, I see the Fell One hasn't tired of playing with you yet."

The old woman registered the confusion on his face. "Of course I know you, Prince. The whole world knows you, knows that this is where you're likely to fall." Deep in the woods, a light shone between the trunks, accompanied by a low motor rumble.

"He comes. Quickly, inside." The mechanic led him by the cuff to the garage and bid him climb into the pit beneath her current project. He could not see the Rider's car as it pulled into the station, only feel the bass thrum of its engine before it shut off.

"You outta gas, Mister?" asked the mechanic.

The door of the rider's rig opened. His leather bodysuit creaked as the creature, for it was surely not a man, climbed out. It had the voice of an oil slick.

"The prince."

"No princes here." The crunch of the Rider's boots on the gravel outside drew nearer. "Hey now, you can't go in there! Plenty of things in there that might get a body hurt."

The old mechanic hit the ground hard as the Rider pushed her out of the way. For a moment, the prince thought to reveal himself, to fight or run and draw the Rider away. Shotgun thunder put a stop to the thought before it was fully formed. The Rider fell beside him, and he saw himself reflected in its helmet before crouching deeper into the well.

"Auntie done told you, didn't she?" The voice was punctuated by the pump action sound of a shell being ejected and another chambered. From his hole, the prince watched as the Rider, impossibly, sat up and rose stiffly to its feet.

"You want the boy, you beat him on the road," demanded

the mechanic. "Them're the rules, least as we understand them."

The weight of the Rider's boots sounded as if they would turn the gravel into dust as it walked back to its rig. A moment later, it was gone, tires chewing up asphalt as they sped away from the garage, away from him.

"Safe enough for you now." At the old woman's all-clear, the prince shimmied out from the pit. He was greeted with the mechanic's dirty face and the long black barrel that had warded off the Fell Rider. "Y' like dinner then? This here's my girlie, Harlan."

"Lucky I heard you. I was way up in the junkers when he rolled up on you." Harlan lowered the barrel of her shotgun and offered him a hand up. The prince had never seen a flesh mod in person before, even in King's Chapel. Built as "entertainment" pieces, when machine-kind turned, the other side used the skin-wrapped constructs as infiltration agents during the Singularity War. Most of them were destroyed in the days after. This one had clearly seen better days, her skin patched with the mismatched tones of different models where repairs had been done. Once on his feet, the prince threw his arms around the mechanic's neck.

"You saved me."

"You watch those arms, boy. I ain't saved shit but Harlan 'n me. Ain't much that thing has an interest in but you anyways. But the way I see it, this ain't your race to run any more'n it's mine or hers. Them as started it are long gone. It's only that dog-headed bastard as don't see it. May be that I got no feelings for no rich man's son, but I certainly got less for him."

The prince and the mechanic dined on stew already reaching its second or third warming. For her part, Harlan fed as well, hooking herself to a noisy generator and sitting dormant and still. Afterwards, the prince was given a bed of old mismatched cushions and moving blankets tossed on a rusted steel couch frame. In the morning, he woke to the smell of fuel as Harlan prepared his racing rig for another day.

"Roust yourself," ordered the mechanic. "Day won't wait and neither will the Rider."

The prince threw the moving blanket off himself.

"Damn. He'll be ahead of me now."

"He won't, I think. The Black Hound likes to play with its prey, and it's not done playing with you yet." The mechanic tossed a rucksack to Harlan as the flesh mod climbed into the passenger seat of the prince's rig.

"She'll serve you now, as all things do for princes sooner or later, I suppose."

"A partner will slow me down."

"A partner will keep you alive. See if she don't." Harlan laid on the horn. "Best git. She don't wait patient. I've a sister of sorts down the other end of the woods, more road witch than me. She'll take you in just as me. Don't stop before then, not if you want to make it to the end of the road."

As the prince climbed behind the wheel, the fire of the race burned in his veins again. He barely heard the old mechanic wish him godspeed as he jammed his foot down on the pedal and put the fueling station in his rearview.

The road and the wild wood did strange things to time. It felt like hours but could have been minutes or days when Harlan, who had spent the journey staring silently at something just outside the windshield the prince couldn't see grabbed for the handbrake without word or warning. The prince fought to keep the racer under control, spinning it around one hundred and eighty degrees. Harlan turned to look out the rear window. The road was ablaze. Somehow, the Rider had felled one of the giant trees that towered alongside the road, and now the smoke turned the daytime sky into twilight. To make matters worse, the Rider was waiting for the prince just on the other side of his handiwork.

"Let me out," ordered Harlan.

"The mechanic said not to stop. Besides, that thing, it'll kill you...break you. Whatever happens to..."

"A machine?"

"I wasn't going to—"

"I plan on being here long after men and beasts are feeding the sod." Harlan opened the passenger door and climbed out, slamming it shut behind her. "Just drive. I'll clear the way and catch you up after. Don't lose my bag."

The prince watched as Harlan planted her feet and charged. She moved like a freight train, a dreadnought, straight for the Rider's blockade. For a moment, the prince forgot himself before spinning the rig back around and rocketing after her. Ahead of him, the felled tree exploded in a shower of flames as Harlan struck it head on, the Steel Lion flying through the gap fast behind.

In the rearview, the prince saw the Fell Rider and Harlan squaring off like wild dogs circling one another. Harlan charged the Rider as she had its blockade and nearly struck before the Rider caught her arm, tossing her effortlessly back into the fire despite Harlan's own strength. Though not so effortlessly as to not distract the Rider from the prince's racer backing over it at speed. The Rider buckled and skidded behind the Steel Lion, rolling to a halt inches from the fire where the specter of Harlan rose, synthetic skin boiling in patches as she cast the Rider into the blaze.

The prince climbed from the rig as Harlan emerged from the flames.

"He's not done," she whispered as he wrestled her into the rig.

White line fever brought the night, and with it came the scrapyard. Harlan had slept or shut down or whatever it was she did after escaping the fire. Over the radio, the voices of distant ghosts filled the airwaves.

"From The Place at the End of the World, The City at the

End of the Road, The City of Night's Dreaming, it's a sonic proclamation from the Duke of Rock 'n' Roll himself, brought to you by his very own Duchess. If you're out there in the night, we see you. We hear you. We know you. We are you."

A wild scream filled the cab, the Duke of Rock 'n' Roll jolting Harlan awake.

"Stop here."

"The junkyard?"

"The Scrapwitch's place. We're here."

The Scrapwitch's place was part roadhouse, part caravan encampment. Road rats gathered around small pit fires swapping drinks and stories, having holed up while the Western Road was shut down for the prince and his adversary. The prince pulled up his rig outside of the ring of fires as others had done.

"Keep your head down," Harlan ordered. "They don't need to know you."

"I think we're too late."

Near one of the pits, a road rat had jumped atop a fifty-five gallon drum.

"All you highway babies and blacktop riders, is that a Steel Lion I see prowlin' in the night?"

"Shit," slurred Harlan, struggling out of the passenger seat. Her feet barely made it to the ground before her legs gave out. "Shit," she slurred again. "More damaged than I thought."

Two of the road rats grabbed the prince by the shoulders and led him to their gassed- up master of ceremonies.

"Crash kittens, I give you...the Prince of the Western Road!" The crowd howled as the prince was hauled upwards, the emcee throwing an arm over his shoulder, pulling him close enough to smell the pomade keeping the short black mohawk he wore slicked back like a tire track across his skull. "Man of the hour in a race for his life. Don't we all know the stories? How his granddaddy and the first Duke of Rock 'n' Roll tamed the roads when the war was done? And now his daddy protects us all, so long as you can pay the strong-arm tax, and if you can't, well, damn you for a highwayman. He tells us when it's closed. He tells us what we can haul and when we can run, and why? Cause his granddaddy cleaned the trash that ran the roads in his day? Well, I say, 'All hail the new trash.'" The road rat raised his tattooed wrist in the air.

"All hail the Black Dog!"

A dozen or more in the crowd raised their dog tattooed wrists in response. Teeth gnashed as they howled for blood. Someone slipped a cord around the prince's neck from behind, dragging him off the barrel. The prince clawed at it as the black dogs laughed, watching him spin in circles, flailing for his life. His legs gave out, and he fell to his knees before the fire, blood boiling in his ears. Something whispered across his temple, a hot kiss that found him gasping for as much air as he could get a moment later.

"Well, ain't this a goddamn sight?" An old woman emerged from the largest of the scrapyard's buildings. "Bunch of animals shittin' in my yard." The Scrapwitch approached the road rat who'd stirred up the others.

"The Black Dog's come to free the road again, old woman. Give it back to the people, not some dusty old sack hiding in a tower who's forgotten the feel of pavement under his wheels."

"Rider don't care for the road. Don't care for the people, neither. Only thing he cares for is killing princes. But you want to go around acting like dogs, you go ahead. Springer'll shoot you down just like one." Something that sounded like an angry hornet flew close overhead, leaving a neat hole in the road rat's forehead. "Too late," said the Scrapwitch as he tumbled from his perch.

The prince scrambled to his feet, almost tripping over the dead rat behind him, the one who'd tried to choke him out before Springer's first bullet struck him down. The crowd parted before the Scrapwitch, and the prince followed close behind.

"Was that all true, what he said about my father?"

"True enough to him. All he knows is a man he ain't never seen, in a castle at the end of the road, tells him what to do or not do, and shuts down his livelihood when he sees fit. How'd you think of it?"

"I don't..."

"Yeah, you don't, do you? Lucky my sister's clanky girl came and got me."

"Harlan?"

"Crawled her ass all the way to my door. Don't you worry though, she'll take a trip on my table, we'll have her back up in no time."

The Scrapwitch led him into her tin cabin, shored on all sides by the skeletons of old junkers and dead rigs. Springer was climbing down from a rooftop perch as they entered, a scoped rifle slung across her back.

"Good job not squirming. Wasn't actually sure I could make that shot with him roping your neck."

"And you took it anyway?"

"Never know until you try," Springer laughed, slapping his shoulder. Any bonhomie that was intended went out of it with the sting of Springer's junkyard prosthetic, a hand and forearm of chains and gears and tire rubber. She noticed him staring at it as he rubbed his shoulder. "Scrapwitch built it. Truth told, she's fixed at least a third of those ungrateful fucks outside at one point or another."

"Springer," chided the Scrapwitch.

"Better go check on your clanky friend before she tries to take my arm back."

"She's not my—" the prince started. But she had already gone somewhere else deep in the Scrapwitch's automotively armored abode, leaving him alone with the Scrapwitch herself. "Why do you let those people stay outside?"

"Where else would they go? Road's closed to them." The prince opened his mouth and shut it again. The old woman rummaged through a set of drawers against the wall. "Ain't your fault. Not really. The Rider's a thing outside control, like a force of nature. You just roll with it and try to survive the best you can."

"Your sister said something similar."

"Yeah, well, she ain't all dumb." The Scrapwitch pulled an old moving blanket from one of the drawers and held it out to him. It smelled like it may have once been used for animal bedding.

"Why does the Rider want me? I've never done anything to anyone. I've barely been out of King's Chapel except to race."

"Heaven knows, boy. Maybe it's something your granddaddy did. Maybe something he shouldn't have messed with. Maybe it's just one of life's mysteries. Only way to know is to make it through to the end of the race. Just remember where this road ends."

"The City of Night's Dreaming."

"The Place at the End of the Road. You've been listening to the Duchess's broadcasts. The City ain't like The Chapel. Ain't like any place you've ever seen. That's why your uncle got so taken with it."

"You met my uncle?"

"More'n met." The Scrapwitch grinned. "This face wasn't always so lined, and that boy was lordly handsome. But that city, it gobbled him up and left the Rider to pick his bones."

"Well, the same won't happen to me."

"Won't it?" asked the Scrapwitch. "There's a bed through there. I'd best be fixing your friend."

"She's not my—" the prince began again, but like Springer, the Scrapwitch was already gone.

The prince had to admit that even the mattress on the Scrapwitch's floor was more comfortable than the couch in her sister's garage, though he could not fathom how she could part together something as complex as Springer's prosthetic but couldn't be bothered to build a bed frame. He could hear the sound of Harlan being repaired somewhere in the house.

Morning came, and with it Harlan and Springer trying to hit him with bits of orange peel from across the room as he slept. Harlan bore several new skin patches that looked like they may once have been upholstery leather for some long dead vehicle, cherry red now faded to pink. The Scrapwitch's entrance signaled it was time to go, and both of them went to retrieve the prince's rig from the yard.

"Let me guess, Springer's coming with me?"

"She's very good at what she does," said the Scrapwitch.

"Why hasn't the Rider outraced me already? It's surely had the chance to do it. I'm not sure that thing even sleeps."

"Because he ain't got one of these." The Scrapwitch tossed a small but weighty box in his lap. A coil of antenna protruded from one end.

"What's this?"

"That'll get you across the river and into the city, just like the Duke's haulers that keep things running there. Without one, you'd be stuck outside, just like the Rider."

The prince was beginning to wonder if the Rider's challenge would ever make sense.

"Mind you, your uncle made it as far as that and no further. Whether he got swallowed up by the city or the Rider managed to end him, it was the end of his road. I hope it won't be the end of yours. You'll reach the city before dark if you don't stop to fool around anymore."

The Steel Lion roared outside. It appeared that Springer's violent show of force had ensured that it survived the night unmolested, though there were still more than a few pairs of resentful eyes following it through the scrapyard. Springer emerging from the driver's seat sent more than a few of them looking for something else to look at, however, as the prince took her place. The Scrapwitch gave a single wave in the rearview mirror as he pulled away. Springer saw the worry cross his face. "She'll be fine. Those yard dogs cross her, there won't be anyone to patch their hurts. They're mean, but they're not *that* stupid."

The prince expected to see the Rider waiting for him, untiring and endlessly pacing outside the gates of the scrapyard, but the road stood empty. He kept an eye behind himself the entire way to the city.

"I don't like it," Springer announced unasked. "It's eerie, no other traffic. I've never seen the road to the city this way."

"Agreed," said Harlan.

"It's like the whole place is waiting for the bullet to hit the bone."

"I didn't know you'd been to the city," said the prince.

"The Scrapwitch has been known to trade with the Duke and his people." As she said that, the antenna box lit up on the dash. "Keep your head down and do as you're told."

The steel bridge spanning the river that separated the city from the Western Road lowered into place. The prince pulled his Lion across into a cattle chute of an entrance that would only have allowed rigs to enter in single file had there been any others on the road. The city gate squealed closed behind them. A guard approached and knocked on the prince's window.

"Welcome to The City, Your Highness. The duke and duchess are waiting."

Everything about the city seemed more alive than the world outside, and bigger, everyone living on top of one another. From King's Chapel, a body could see for miles uninterrupted. From there, the world was neat, orderly, pastoral. From The Palace of Rock 'n' Roll, the view was a riot, like looking down on a colony of ants gone insane. The prince had been forced to check his rig along with all the others at the city gate. A motorized rickshaw took himself and Springer the rest of the way, Harlan jogging easily behind. Now, they waited in a receiving room somewhere in the palace.

They didn't have to wait long. The Duke of Rock 'n' Roll entered like an explosion, accompanied by the duchess. He was thin as a rail, his stringy hair the color of wheat, and though he had an eternally hungry look, he did not seem weak. It was more as if he might tear you apart and eat you at any time from some mad, ravenous appetite inside him. He was bare chested, wearing a long, fur-collared tapestry coat when he entered.

"Princey, baby, we were gettin' worried you were taking so long."

"We thought you'd be here a day ago at least," chimed the duchess. Like her husband, everything about her appeared not performative exactly, but cultivated, planned, from the perfect cut of her leathers to the exact styling of her bleached blonde shag to make it move just so when she laughed. The only difference was the absence of the duke's wildness.

"And wouldn't your daddy just fall apart if he knew you'd been caught?"

"Well, don't you worry, honey. You're safe here."

"Safe as glass houses," said the duke. Behind the prince, Springer and Harlan exchanged a glance. "Now, who wants a drink? Come on, I'll show you The Dungeon."

Springer and Harlan walked behind the prince, duke, and duchess as they descended back through the palace, the duke swanning around at the head.

"We rest up tonight and get him back on the road by morning."

"Agreed."

The Dungeon, as it happened, was not some dark hole in the bowels of The Palace of Rock 'n' Roll, but was instead the name of the city's largest bar where they did most of their actual ruling. At its center, a raised mezzanine bore the couple's stylized thrones, the floor before it barred by velvet ropes. The duke's bouncers parted before them.

"You know, I almost had to fight your uncle over the duchess when he came through."

"He never had any chance," she laughed. "We three were great friends in the time he was here, gods rest his soul." The duchess saluted his memory with her glass.

The prince followed suit, and the drink went down hard. "They say he reveled himself to death before the Rider could take him."

"Who knows? He survived as far as the city, and we offered him sanctuary for as long as he wanted it, as we will you and your...companions. We certainly gave him no reason to want to leave, but one day he was just gone. They found his rig halfway between here and the scrapyard." The duke placed a hand on the prince's shoulder, the first moment of seriousness the boy had seen in him. "The man lived more in his short, sweet time than most people do in their long, full, boring lives. Don't ever be ashamed of him, boy." The thunder of a bass guitar broke the moment. "Sounds like it's time for you to meet the family, kiddo."

Someone brought the duke a microphone. It was as if someone had suddenly flipped a switch within him, his maudlin thoughts gone without a trace.

"Oh, you lucky ones! What a night this is! Not only do you get to hear that daughter of mine, the duchess-to-be, you get to do it in the presence of the Steel Lion himself, the Prince of the Western Road!"

A roar went up from the crowd as a spotlight hit the prince. Springer and Harlan tried to force their way up the stairs from where they had been left with the bouncers.

"Who's afraid of the big black dog?" The duke shouted, egging on the crowd. "Not him! Not you! I don't see the Rider

253

here. Matter of fact, the only dog I see here is me, and baby, I'm *your* dog. Give it up for the duchess-to-be."

The duke tossed his microphone to one of the bouncers and turned. As cymbals crashed, he fell back into the crowd, arms outstretched and Christ-like, and they raised him up above their heads. Bass gave way to guitar as the duchess-to-be took the stage. She was the perfect amalgam of her parents, the duke's wildness and the duchess's style. The duke surfed the waves of the crowd. The prince tried to imagine his father doing the same, but couldn't conjure the image. The duchess read his thoughts.

"You don't have to worry. He belongs to them as much as they belong to him. He's their duke, and they're his people. Besides, without him, the party would stop."

"Why isn't the world outside like this? Free and wild and..."

"Modern? Because the world outside is full of fear and would rather hide itself away, imagining it will keep them safe, but all it will do is keep them alone and scared. Let that be the lesson the city teaches you when you go. Men once built great, impossible things. The City at the End of the Road is one of the last vestiges of those days, like your flesh mod. Now, we're all afraid to build those impossible things anymore because they came back to bite us once upon a time."

For a moment, the prince thought he saw the duchess's veneer drop, only to be picked up again as she turned to watch her daughter on stage.

The night was a sweaty riot of noise from then on. At some point, the duke was pushed up to the stage by the crowd and sang with the duchess-to-be. It was like watching all those ghosts that came through the rig's radio come to life in bleeding color. Libations were forever being sent up to the mezzanine, The Dungeon denizens refusing to let them run out. The prince barely remembered Springer and Harlan carrying him back to

The Palace of Rock 'n' Roll alongside the duke and his family, none of the three in any better shape than himself.

The Sun was well up when the prince woke and dragged himself out of his room, not entirely sure where in the castle he might have been put. Wherever it was, a small dining room wasn't far down the hall, and in it, the duke.

"That was fun, huh?"

"What? I mean, I guess," the prince replied, rubbing his eyes.

"We go again tonight."

"No. I mean, we've got to finish. Go all the way back to King's Chapel."

"Not looking like that, you don't. Here." The duke poured something green out of a pitcher and pushed it across the dining table at him.

"What is it?"

"Corpse reviver. Do you good. Get you moving." The prince held his breath and drank the mixture down as fast as he could. It tasted of licorice and mint and something terribly, terribly earthy. He suddenly felt the need to sit down before it came back up.

"Do you do this every night?" the prince croaked.

"Wouldn't you? Listen, kid, I know we're...a little different here. But we all want the same stuff, yeah? You. Me. Your daddy. To do the best we can by our people, right? We just do it a little louder and more fun." Before the prince could respond, the duchess arrived dressed in a knee length silk robe. She draped her arm over her husband's shoulder from behind.

"Telling the prince what's what now, are you?"

"Just putting him straight as to how the city lives."

The prince looked across at the duchess, remembering her thoughts on just how the city lived from the evening before. He looked away before their eyes met.

"Well, be considerate. He may still be your king some day."

"*Our* king, dear." He kissed her hand.

"Of course."

The prince looked away, embarrassed but unsure as to why. "Has anyone seen Harlan or Springer yet? They wanted to start first thing, and it's already late."

"No, but I'm sure they're fine down on the servant's floor."

The corpse reviver was coming up again in the prince's stomach. "Oh, they will not like that, neither one of them."

The duchess picked a piece of fruit from the bowl on the table, forgoing the duke's corpse reviver. "Perhaps they've changed their minds. Why not take the opportunity to see the city while you can. I promise, I'll check on your friends."

"Well. All hail the Prince of the Road Rats, thief of my personal thunder in my very own house last night." The duchess-to-be stood in the doorway. The prince couldn't tell if she'd slept in her clothing from the previous night or re-dressed herself in the same outfit. Her short undercut made it difficult to tell if she'd spent any time on it or just rolled her way out of bed. It was possible she hadn't slept at all.

"Daughter, where did you learn your manners?" chided the duchess.

"Certainly not from my parents."

"Well, in that case, I think I've found the prince the ideal guide to tour the city." The prince began to object as the duchess put a hand on his shoulder. "Don't worry, I promise she'll behave herself from here on, won't you?" The duchess-to-be glared at her mother and then at the prince.

"Well, come on then, Rat Prince. You're my responsibility now."

"Go. I'll find your friends."

As it happened, The Palace of Rock 'n' Roll did, in fact, have a dungeon that was in no way a drinking establishment. Harlan and Springer learned this when the Duchess of Rock 'n' Roll had them removed from their rooms in the middle of the night and thrown inside. Somewhere in the palace, one of the duke's bouncers had lost an eye to Springer's prosthetic as proof.

"Don't give me that look, clanky. You agreed to stay the night in the city just the same as me."

Harlan's severed head said nothing.

"No wonder your side lost."

"Won. Lost. What's the difference?" asked the duchess as she entered the dungeon. "Mankind won the war to live like a whipped dog under someone's porch. Doesn't seem much like winning to me. But we are going to change that, aren't we?" She drew a finger across Harlan's head. "You are a little jewel, aren't you?"

"Your mother was a rented dalliance," Springer spat.

"True. Fortunately, the old duke wasn't very good at producing heirs, and here we are. At least she could clap with two hands."

Springer lunged at the duchess with the stump of her arm, grunting as the chain cuffed to her wrist jerked taut. "What do you want, witch?"

"Want? I want to break free and take the rest of the world with me. I'm tired of standing still. The prince is going to go the way of his uncle, and when his father comes to collect the body, he and the duke, they'll go, too. Then the city will rise, and we'll finally begin to rebuild. And thanks to your surprisingly intact friend here, I'll even be able to fix my rider and have him at my right hand."

"Take me to the Steel Lion," demanded the duchess-to-be.

"What?"

Since leaving The Palace of Rock 'n' Roll, they'd done nothing but walk in circles, seeing little, if anything, of significance.

"Your rig. I want to see your rig."

"Why would you want to see my rig? I thought we were supposed to be seeing the city."

"Eyes front or on me."

"What?"

The duchess-to-be sighed, but kept a plastic smile on her face.

"We're having fun. You know, fun? And if the bouncer following us thinks any different, you're going to end up killed a lot sooner. Rig. Now." The duchess-to-be took his arm and began leading him towards the city gates. "She's mad, my mother. You can hear her, if you know how to listen. Talking at night through the airwaves. Talking to that...thing outside."

"The Rider?" hissed the prince. Around them, people greeted the duchess-to-be with small nods of obeisance which she only barely acknowledged.

"It obeys her. I think it always has, even in your uncle's time."

"What about the duke?"

The duchess-to-be shook her head. "The duke's power

comes from the duchess, not blood. His heart may be good, but he won't think ill of her without being confronted by it. You have to finish the race and return to your father. At least then you'll have the king's army around you."

"This is mad."

"You're not wrong."

"What about Springer and Harlan?"

"Your friends are dead, or soon will be." The prince stopped, but the duchess-to-be dragged him along. "Finish the race. Beat the Rider. Come back with an army and avenge them."

The prince's pace quickened. "How do we get out?"

The duchess left Springer alone again with the head, making sure to leave it staring in her direction. She seemed to be leaving Springer alive solely out of some sadistic inclination now. Springer jerked on the chain that bound her to the wall for the hundredth time.

"Wake up you clanky bitch, I need your help!" Springer screamed at the head, kicking out at it.

"Springer, I'm trying to focus."

Springer's fury stopped.

"You're working?"

"I only have so much of a charge left, and right now I have to get the rest of me to come back here and set us free. So, if you don't mind...?"

"Wait, your body's free? You can control your body?"

"Not if you keep shouting at me, no!"

The door to the dungeon swung open. Harlan's headless,

patched body stood in the doorway, an unconscious guard under her arm in a headlock.

"Over here, clanky."

"What?" Springer glared at Harlan's head as her body dropped the bouncer.

"What?"

"Just get your head on and get me free."

"You still haven't told me how I'm going to get out of the city," the prince repeated as they reached the city gates.

The duchess-to-be screamed, throwing herself back against the prince and yanking his arm around. The sound drew the gate guard out from his post.

"Bring the prince's ride around before he kills me, you idiot. He and his friends have gone mad." The guard looked at her dumbly. "Now!"

Thunder rolled in the distance, accompanied by the roar of the Fell Rider's engine. Somewhere outside the city walls, the thing was waiting for him, eager for their final confrontation. The sound of his own rig answered as the gate guard brought it into the city's narrow entry.

"Now, back away," ordered the duchess-to-be.

The gate guard complied, and the prince moved to take his place in the driver's seat.

Before he could, the duchess-to-be squeezed herself through the opening and into the rig's passenger seat.

"Will no one do me the favor of *asking* to ride along?"

"No. They'll kill you on the bridge out of the city if I'm not here with you. Now drive."

The gates were barely open when the Steel Lion slipped through, darting across the bridge as it finished lowering and back onto the Western Road.

"And now I look like I've kidnapped you!" shouted the prince.

"How long do you think it will take any one of them to work up the courage to come after us with that thing out here?" The duchess-to-be pointed ahead of them. There on the far horizon, the Rider was waiting. The prince slowed and pulled to the side of the road.

"Get out."

"What are you going to do?"

"Finish my race. For good this time. You've done what you set out to do. I thank you for the warning. If I live, I'll be back with my father's men."

In their stolen motorized rickshaw, Harlan and Springer found the duchess-to-be standing in the rain on the side of the road a short while later. It was only a few miles farther into the forest when they came upon the twisted, burning remains of the Steel Lion. The prince's rig had run off the rain-slick road, rolling sideways into a tree. The Rider's rig was nowhere to be seen. Harlan pulled the rickshaw to a halt and waved for Springer and the duchess-to-be to stay put.

Something was moving, pinned beneath the overturned Steel Lion. Harlan approached low, sliding along the side of the rig. Springer inhaled sharply as Harlan stepped on the thing's neck and tore its head from whatever remained of the rest of it. The last sparks of its artificial life crackled out of the Rider's neck.

"The Rider is dead," whispered Springer.

"The Prince of the Western Road is dead," reported the Duchess as night came and swallowed up the day, her voice on air grave and mournful, *"struck down by the beast of the highway, the death that comes rolling like hellfire, the Fell Rider."*

"Lies," spat the duchess-to-be.

"What do we do?" asked Harlan.

"We go back to the Scrapwitch's place and lay low. The duchess can't let us keep moving. If we get word to the king, especially with the duchess-to-be in tow...."

"What about the prince?"

"We pray."

The Scrapwitch's place was eerily quiet by the time the trio pulled in. The rickshaw had run out of fuel miles ago, and Harlan had resorted to pulling the thing the rest of the way. Even Springer had never seen the scrapyard so quiet. The road rats and caravaners had extinguished their fires and closed themselves inside rigs and tents and trailers. In the center of the yard, they saw why. There, badly scarred but drivable, was the racing rig of the Fell Rider.

The prince was already on the Scrapwitch's table, his face badly bruised, one eye swollen shut. His left arm had been shattered.

But he had survived.

He had survived, and somehow, through sheer force of will, he had driven himself to safety.

"Harlan. Take a rig. I don't care whose. Take the duchess-to-be and go to King's Chapel. Tell them what happened."

"No." The prince grabbed Springer's wrist. "The prince is dead." He inclined his head as best he could. Springer followed his gaze across the room.

The Rider's snarling, dog-headed helmet looked as vicious as ever, sitting on a chair in the corner.

Days passed, and the Western Road was once again opened. Harlan, Springer, and the duchess-to-be hid within the Scrapwitch's walls after secreting away the Fell Rider's rig. Except for the duchess's spies, The City at the End of the Road found itself shut off from the outside world as the duchess stalked the halls of The Palace of Rock 'n' Roll. Things had fallen apart.

Soon, the king would come to collect, if not the body of his dead son, then at least the remains of his rig. The duchess had ordered what was left of the Rider to be destroyed and buried deep in the forest away from roads and rigs and prying eyes. The duke, she left to mourn their missing daughter, a walking phantom in his own palace. The City had gone quiet for the first time in living memory.

Quiet, that was, until the roar of the engine outside the gate. The engine of the Fell Rider.

About Thomas Gregory

Thomas Gregory is an author, playwright, performer and podcaster from southeast Michigan. His previous work appears in the anthologies *Queen of Clocks and Other Steampunk Tales, Harvey Duckman Presents Vol. 4,* and *Harvey Duckman Presents: Christmas Special.* His plays, *The Gillman Problem* and *Whatever Happened to Captain Future?,* have previously been performed by Ypsilanti Michigan's Neighborhood Theater Group. His first full length musical, *Benestopheles!: The Last Days of Ghoulita Graves,* has also been optioned for production. He is the host and producer of the bizarre film podcast Cinema Guano (https://cinemaguano.blogspot.com/) alongside his wife and co-host, Crysta K. Coburn.

Mirror in her Hand

by Liz Tuckwell

I slow my pace as Chanel No. 5 wafts along the dingy corridor and hear a high heel tap-tap-tapping on the floor. Mrs. Jennifer Carr is impatient.

I scratch the stubble on my chin. If I thought she'd come to my shabby office instead of telephoning, I would have shaved. I want to think she's dying to see me again, but I'm not that vain or naïve. She's desperate to discover what I'd done with her stepdaughter.

Otis Miller, Private Investigator is scrawled in chipped, white paint on the front door of my office. I push it open. The first room has a bare desk, a chair, and a brown couch where I sleep more often than not. This is where a secretary would be if I could afford one. It only takes me a few steps to cross to the inner room.

The loveliest dame I ever saw is waiting for me inside. She sits in a chair in front of my battered desk, legs crossed to display their shapeliness. Golden waves cascade to her shoulders. Unforgettable blue eyes with long lashes survey me. Dark lipstick outlines her luscious mouth. A pale blue dress with a white scatter of polka dots hugs her curves. Her left shoe stops its tapping. I take off my fedora and toss it at the hat stand. I grin at my success when it stays on the hook. It's been a while since I managed that. I shrug out of my trench coat and sling it over another hook. As I sit down in the chair opposite Jennifer, she leans forward. Her chair creaks.

"Where have you been?" she asks, almost a whine.

"At an all-night diner. Getting an alibi."

"And?" She pouts a little.

I smile at her. "All A-OK."

She holds out her hand. "Show me."

She's still wearing her white cotton gloves, although she's placed her straw hat on the desk. I pull a handkerchief from my jacket pocket and unwrap it before placing it on the desk. Inside is a lock of black hair. Jennifer picks it up and examines it, holding it close to her eyes and smelling it. Does she need glasses?

"It's hers," I say.

"I know. She always used that lemon shampoo."

Thoughtful of Audrey.

"Black as night, white as snow, red as blood," she murmurs.

"What's that?"

"Just a bargain someone else made," she says, a faraway look in her eyes. She nods and puts it back on the desk. "Any problems?"

I reach over and pull the bottom drawer open. A whiskey bottle nestles inside. I pick it up and hold the bottle up to the light. About three inches of amber liquid left. Well, I'd be able to afford a fresh one now – hell, as many bottles as I want.

"Nah. Easy, like you said. Let's celebrate."

"She didn't put up a fight?"

I give an incredulous laugh. "Her? She's only a kid."

"She's sixteen."

I ignore that. "And those midgets weren't a problem either."

Jennifer raises one delicate arch of an eyebrow. "Midgets?"

"Yeah, she was shacked up with a bunch of midget musicians at a freak show. They call themselves the Zambini Brothers."

"So, she's dead?"

I allow myself to sound cranky. "I said so, didn't I?"

She snaps open her black pocketbook and draws out a gold compact. The morning sunlight hits a diamond in the centre, and I blink away the sudden brilliance. It seems like an odd time to powder her nose, but what do I know?

She clicks it open, then raises it to eye level and says, *"Mirror, mirror, in my hand, who is the fairest in La La Land?"*

I'm gaping at her when I hear a tinny voice reply, *"You are fair, beyond compare. Few can challenge you, it's true, but soon Audrey will outshine you."*

I drop the bottle. It bangs onto the desk. The amber liquid sloshes about but doesn't leak out, to my relief. The compact clicks shut. When I look up, Jennifer's pointing a tiny, pearl-handled pistol at me, the latest Ruger LCP 300. It even has a silencer. Nice.

"What the—"

"The mirror never lies," she interjects, then milks the pause. "Unlike men." She licks her lips. "It's too bad, Otis. I had fun with you. We could've had a lot more."

"Like the chauffeur?" I ask.

Jennifer's face blanks for a moment, then she smiles and says, "Audrey has been telling tales." She shakes her head.

"Did you have a lot of fun with him, too?" To my surprise, I spit the words out. The thought of some other man kissing and caressing her is painful.

I grab my Remington.

But she's faster. She shoots me twice, once in the chest and once in the shoulder. Even a bad shot couldn't miss at that range. The shots push me back, but I still manage to fire. Burning white hot pain kicks in, and blackness swallows me.

I'd tracked Audrey to a traveling carnival. It was their last night in town, so I was lucky to find her. Candy floss and diesel overwhelmed my nostrils. Delighted screams filled the air. Several robots clanked around serving beverages. I bet the crowds gawping at them didn't realize just how many humans were losing their jobs to the mechanical marvels in factories.

Audrey was collecting tickets outside a canvas tent when I showed up. She was even prettier than the colour photo Jennifer had given me. The act was a troupe of seven midget acrobats called the Zambini Brothers. Although if I were Papa Zambini, I'd have some questions for Mama Zambini; one of them was an albino, one a redhead, and another was a negro.

A helpful bearded lady told me the way to their caravan. I used my lock-picking skills to break in. The Zambini acrobats had given me pause; small or not, seven bodies would be a lot to contend with. Luckily, I'd brought along my Remington Model 9500. This wonder could shoot nerve gas pellets as well as bullets. I made myself comfortable on one of the small bunks and waited for them.

It didn't take long when they came back. The pellets came in real handy. Soon, the battered and bruised midgets were all trussed up like tiny turkeys, courtesy of the rope in my pockets. Pays to be prepared. I'd gagged them. Seven little men can make a lot of noise. I didn't want anyone else joining our get-together. Conscious of their glares, I flicked open my pocket knife. I bent over her head, and the sweet-sharp scent of citrus disoriented me for a second. I lifted a handful of her glossy, black hair, exposing her slender neck. She shuddered. I marvelled at the smoothness and whiteness of her skin; it was even paler than her stepmother's. I cut a lock, some of the hairs drifting to the dirt floor. Putting the lock into a handkerchief, I placed it in my jacket pocket. Now I had the evidence I needed to prove I'd carried out my task.

Transparent pearls ran down her porcelain cheeks. Her slender shoulders shook with emotion while she cried. Jennifer'd told me that Audrey was a selfish, spoilt brat who treated everyone like dirt. But could I kill a young woman who'd done nothing to hurt me? My hand trembled a little as I replaced the pocket knife in my coat.

"My stepmother sent you to murder me, didn't she?" she asked, her voice young and breathless.

I shook my head. "Maybe I'm a tramp looking for some quick cash."

"Then why cut my hair? You want proof. For *her*." Her voice was thick with loathing. "I bet she hasn't told you the *truth* about herself. She was my father's second wife, only married him for his money. She encouraged him to order one of those prototypes from his factory, the new rocket cars, a Carr Dynamo?"

I nodded. I knew those beauties, all chrome and curved fins. Way out of my league.

"Then she said he needed a specialist mechanic for it, so he hired a new chauffeur, Joe. He was young and good looking. She started flirting with him." Audrey's mouth twisted, and I wondered if there was some rivalry there. "But never when my father was around. I tried to warn him, but he wouldn't listen. Next thing, my father's dead in a car accident, and she looks like the cat that's got the cream. Joe started acting cocky, and then he's gone all of a sudden, disappeared. Nobody knows where he went."

I paced around the caravan. "What was his full name?" I asked.

"Joe Mercurelli."

I was tempted to untie her, but I resisted the impulse. Instead, I gagged her.

"I'll be back real soon. Stay nice and quiet, boys and girls."

Half an hour later, I returned from the nearest telephone box. My contact down at police headquarters confirmed the murder of a Joe Mercurelli.

"Spill the beans. How did you know his body turned up two days ago?"

"Pure luck, O'Malley. Cause of death?"

"A bullet in the back."

Looked like Mrs. Carr was fond of playing with the hired help. For a while.

I released Audrey. At her insistence, I also untied the midgets. They weren't happy. Only Audrey stopped them from launching themselves at me like human cannonballs. Then we had a nice long talk.

When I wake up, I'm lying on the floor, my chair toppled over on me. My sneezes reverberate around the office. Nobody's cleaned the floor in a long time. The pain in my chest and shoulder is mostly gone. I push the chair away and sit up. My shirt has a blood stain on the front and I know there will be a mass of dried blood on the back. I curse. Now, I've lost the one good white shirt to my name. I pull myself up, steady myself on the edge of the desk. I open the bottle of whisky and take a good slug. And another one. Only then do I look over.

A woman sprawls on the faded rug. The kick back from her pistol and my shot has thrown her almost to the door. I›ve shot her in the chest. Unlike me, she hasn't survived. A small bloodstain on her dress and a pool of blood underneath her. The rug is ruined for sure. Damn, that was a present from my Aunt Bessie. Something else to replace.

Steel gray waves frame her lined face. The blue eyes looking up at me are no longer large and lustrous with long black lashes, but small and deep set with scanty lashes. Her thin lips are drawn back in a snarl. Her wrinkled neck looks like a turkey's. She's a skinny old woman.

My eyes widen and my mouth drops open in horror. I retch, and my throat burns. I stare at her, trying to understand. Is this the true Jennifer Carr?

I take another slug of whisky.

The pistol is lying near her right hand, but the gold compact has fallen open some distance away. I pick it up. Metal and crystal mechanisms show through the cracks in the glass.

I whistle. We had shared our bodies, but not our secrets. If we had, she'd have known to load her gun with silver bullets. I try not to howl at the full moon, and shave three times a day. Audrey hadn't warned me her stepmother was a witch. Maybe she hadn't known. I'm inclined to give her the benefit of the doubt.

This makes things awkward. The plan was to dump Jennifer's body somewhere public so they would soon find her. That would speed up Audrey being able to claim her whole inheritance. But no one would ever believe this husk was the beautiful widow even if the truth was spelled out in neon.

So her stepmother needs to disappear without a trace.

Now, the unpleasant task of stripping the corpse. Nothing to link it to Mrs. Jennifer Carr. I find myself apologizing out

273

loud to Jennifer for the indignity. I hope no one ever finds the body, for her sake as much as mine. Fingering the gold compact with the diamond, I half consider keeping it to pawn. It›s an expensive bauble. But it's too risky. I wipe the fingerprints off the gun and plan to toss it into a garbage can in Skid Row. I try to stop myself swigging the rest of whiskey before nightfall.

When night finally arrives, I dash down to the street to make sure my car is unlocked. As I suspected; no shovel in the trunk. Then I carry Jennifer down to the first floor, her naked body wrapped up in the rug. Her blue-veined feet peeking out from under the rug are oddly touching. I check that the street is deserted and hurry out to my battered old automobile – no Carr Dynamo for me – I open the trunk and throw it in. A car rumbles by and I tense for a moment. I return for her empty pocketbook.

There's a small hardware store on the edge of town. I use some cash Jennifer gave me to buy a shovel, not a fancy electric model, just the basic one. Anyway, you can't use an electric shovel in the desert. The old proprietor raises his bushy eyebrows but remains silent as he rings up my purchase. I'm not stupid enough to make up some excuse for why I'm buying a shovel at this time of night. Nothing to make me more memorable.

A moonlit drive into the Mojave Desert sounds romantic. It isn't, not when you have a corpse in your trunk. I keep my speed steady along the highway, not too fast, not too slow, nothing to attract the cops' attention. This far from the city, the black sky is blazing with stars. To my relief, it's a few days from the full moon. Changing into a wolf is the last thing I need at the moment.

The chill air hits me as I step out of the car. Not that it bothers me, my kind don't feel the cold. I'll be working up a sweat soon digging the grave anyway.

I walk a long way – werewolf strength stands me in good stead – until I reach a cactus towering into the sky, and I start digging. It takes me a while. I don't recommend digging a grave in sand, although it's great for my muscles. The grave may not be deep enough to keep out the coyotes and vultures, but my back aches, and I'm ready to crawl into that new bottle of whiskey I promised myself.

I tip the rug and its contents into the grave and throw in her empty pocketbook. I open the gold compact and stare at the cracked glass. Will it work for me?

"Mirror, mirror, in my hand, Who's the fairest in La La Land?"

The sound is so faint I have to put it to my ear to hear it.

"You are not the one to ask, I have finished now my task."

I close it and hesitate; I'd like to keep a memento of Jennifer. But it's too dicey. I shrug my shoulders and toss it in the grave before filling it in.

That's all Jennifer's scheming and murders got her – an unmarked grave in a desert and a bloodstained rug for a shroud.

She must have thought she had it made, so full of beauty and vitality. Maybe it wasn't just the money that had made me agree to her plan. Hell, after our first night together, I probably would have offered to do it for free. Jennifer was right, we could have had a whole lot of fun. We might have spent the rest of our lives together. So what if she was an evil crone? Nobody's perfect.

The memory of her luscious curves touching my body and her face close to mine, eyes closed in ecstasy, those cherry lips, makes me fling my head back and howl at the white orb above. The sound ripples out across the desert, and in the distance, my cousins the coyotes howl with me.

Why hadn't I chosen her? Maybe it could have turned out differently with me than her other boyfriends. I was wise to her games. We would have been a good match. Life with her would certainly never have been boring.

And now Audrey has to wait five years until she's twenty-one to get her full inheritance. Then two more for her stepmother to be officially declared dead. My payment will be a long time coming.

I stand, looking at the grave. My life could have been so different.

A breeze whispers past my ear as if it has a message for me.

You couldn't trust her. She would have double-crossed you and killed you in the end. You'd have murdered an innocent girl.

I'd forgotten my principles for a while there all for a beautiful dame. I've done some bad things, but I've killed no one who didn't have it coming.

I square my shoulders, turn away, and walk back to the car.

Audrey can hock a few of those fancy ornaments in that mansion to pay me now. After all, she's got her happy ending. The Zambini Brothers will look after her until she gets her inheritance. I've lost the dame, but money makes up for a lot.

And no dame plays me for a patsy.

More From Liz Tuckwell

A collection of bite size fantasy, horror and SF stories

How long does a good story need to be?

Six words? Ten words? The length of a tweet? 100 words? 1,000?

You'll enjoy finding out in this collection of tiny tales and short stories. It includes the fairy tales, *Snow White*, and *Red Riding Hood* but with a SF twist.

US: http://bit.ly/FFFUS

UK: http://bit.ly/FanFFUK

Wound

by Paul Hiscock

Once upon a time, there was a community of artisans. These tiny creatures were the finest artists, sculptors, inventors, and engineers the world had ever seen. The items they created were so beautiful and intricate that on the rare occasions one was found by a human, they were thought to be magical.

For centuries, the artisans lived in the wild countryside, safe and undisturbed. However, over time, they noticed the countryside was shrinking. Their neighbours, the humans, were establishing kingdoms and building cities. They cut down the trees to make walls for their houses and ripped up the meadows to create farmland for their crops.

It was not long before refugees came seeking shelter. One by one, the other communities of tiny creatures from across the country were being trampled underfoot by humans who didn't even realise they existed. The refugees were welcomed, but with each new arrival, the artisans feared it would not be long before the wave of destruction would reach them too.

The leaders of the community gathered to discuss what they could do. Evacuation seemed like the only option, and plans were proposed to build great boats to take them across the sea to find a land untouched by humans. However, Ellyon, the greatest of their inventors opposed their scheme.

"Why should we flee? This has been our home for centuries, since before the humans emerged from their caves. Why should we give it up now?"

"But what can we do?" asked Danan, the oldest amongst them. "The humans are huge and strong, and have no regard for the world around them."

"We tried to talk to them," said Shefa, one of the refugees, "but we couldn't even get their attention, and they did not hear our pleas."

"Maybe we can ask some of the animals to defend us?" asked Ignia, a painter of great renown. "We have lived in peace with them all this time, and their homes are threatened too."

Danan was doubtful. "None of them are strong enough, and the humans accord them little more respect than us. Even the great stags and the fearsome boar are forced to run when the human hunters come."

"You are right," said Ellyon. "We need defenders that they cannot ignore. We need humans that are on our side." The others scoffed at this, but Ellyon had not finished. "And we do not just need a few humans. Our land needs a monarch to own it and an army to defend it."

The scoffing turned into an uproar at this preposterous proposal.

"And where will we find these magical humans that will not only listen to us, but stand against their own kind to defend us?" asked Danan.

Ellyon opened up their satchel, pulled out a sheaf of papers, and spread them out on the table.

"We will not find them. We will build them. Our engineers will assemble clockwork bodies intricate enough to mimic any human action, even thought itself, and our artists will disguise them so that they are indistinguishable from the humans. It will take all of us, working day and night, and it will test our skills to their limits. However, I believe we can achieve this."

The leaders looked over their incredible designs. At first, they were sceptical, but then some became excited and started to discuss how these mechanical protectors might be created, and even ways that they might be improved.

Danan was not swayed. "It will not work. Humans do not even respect each other. Their kings only retain their lands because they build walls to defend them."

"And that is what we will do too." Ellyon took out another set of plans. "We will build a castle on our border for the people we make so they can defend us from all invaders."

Danan was still doubtful, but the tide of opinion had turned. It was agreed that work to build Ellyon's clockwork people would begin immediately.

For months, the artisans worked on Ellyon's scheme. Part after metal part was forged and then taken to a field. They were assembled into gleaming skeletons, each one 20 times the size of the artisans who worked on it.

Next, the artisans added organs so the bodies would appear to breathe and would be able to cry, and even bleed, like a living person. They covered those with skin and added hair, eyes, teeth, and nails to complete the illusion. Finally, they dressed each person according to their role. Every person they created was unique, and no-one who looked at them would suspect they were not real. They appeared to be sleeping as they lay in the field waiting to be activated.

Ellyon inspected the bodies while the community of artisans waited to one side, eager for the culmination of their efforts. Eventually, Ellyon stopped by the body of a person dressed in the exquisite garments of a queen and turned to address the crowds.

"I am so proud of all of you, my friends. These people you have built are better than even I imagined. Thanks to you, we will finally be protected from the wave of human destruction."

The crowd cheered as Ellyon lifted a large key, placed it into the neck of the Clockwork Queen, and gave it one full turn.

Everyone hushed. By the time Ellyon removed the key, there was complete silence. For a moment, it seemed as though nothing was going to happen, but then the queen sat up. As she did so, all the other people lying in the field started to move as well.

The crowd cheered again and surged forward, eager to meet their new protectors.

With the assistance of the clockwork people, the artisans swiftly built the castle Ellyon had designed. The people moved into their new home and began the lives they had been designed to live. The artisans returned to their community, secure in the knowledge that the humans could no longer overrun their land.

It did not take long for the humans to find the castle, and emissaries were dispatched from the nearby kingdoms to meet their mysterious new neighbours. These delegations were welcomed into the castle and received by the Clockwork Queen and King. The visitors were shown every courtesy; none of them ever suspecting their hosts were not human.

All the delegations found it easy to negotiate treaties and trading partnerships that would benefit their kingdoms greatly. There was just one point the Clockwork Queen and King insisted upon in every agreement—the wild countryside beyond the castle was protected land and not to be entered.

The years passed and the clockwork people went about their lives, just like normal people. Occasionally, there were visitors, but the people in the castle mainly kept to themselves. Their neighbours never noticed that no-one in the castle ever aged or died.

For decades the clockwork people were happy. However, slowly, a yearning grew in the heart of the queen. She sent a message to their creator and invited them to the castle.

"We have a wonderful life here," she said, "and I am truly thankful for all your care in designing our realm. My subjects are my friends, my husband loves me dearly, and our son is a blessing to us. Yet, one thing is missing. The king and I would love to have a daughter. Could you make a princess to share in our life here?"

"I am sorry," said Ellyon, "but I designed this realm to work together in perfect harmony. I fear that adding even one new person would upset that delicate balance. Can you be happy without a daughter?"

"If that is how it must be, I can be happy enough. Though I know there will always be a sadness in my heart where the love for my daughter would have been."

Ellyon sighed. "Then the balance has already been lost, and I must try to find a way."

Ellyon returned to the artisan community and told them about the queen's request. Hundreds of plans were drawn up and rejected, until finally they found a possible solution.

"I think there is a way that I can give you a daughter and restore balance to your realm," Ellyon told the Clockwork Queen and King. "However, it will require a sacrifice from you and from every other person who lives here." Then they explained the scheme in detail.

"We cannot make this decision alone," said the King, when he had heard everything. "You must present your proposal to all our subjects and let them decide for themselves whether they consent."

So the clockwork people gathered and the queen and king addressed them all together.

"We have asked Artisan Ellyon to design a princess to share our life here," said the king, and the people cheered.

"But it will require a sacrifice," said the queen. "In order to keep our realm in balance, we must each give up a small piece of our clockwork to contribute towards her construction. This will ensure her gears are perfectly synchronised with ours. Does anyone object to this?"

When there were no objections, the crowd all cheered. The queen and king were delighted and asked Ellyon to begin preparations to build the princess as soon as possible.

In the days that followed, no-one in the castle could talk of anything but the new princess, but one person found he could not share in their excitement. Although all the denizens of the clockwork realm had been created at the same time, Prince Michael's body was that of a young boy. He was the only child in the castle, the queen and king's favourite amongst all Ellyon's creations and beloved by all their subjects.

Yet, as excitement about the princess grew, everyone had less time for him, and a seed of jealousy grew in his boyish heart.

"What if I don't want a sister?" he asked his parents.

Caught up in his own joy, the king just laughed and ruffled his hair. "Just wait until you meet her."

"We know you will love her, and she will love you too," said the queen.

Prince Michael frowned. If they weren't listening to him now, how much worse would things be when his sister arrived?

Finally, the day of the princess's activation arrived. The artisans brought her body to the castle and laid it out on a platform in the square. The people stared at her in admiration. Surely this was the greatest work the artisans had ever produced, a young woman more beautiful than anyone they had ever seen.

When Prince Michael looked at her, he did not feel the

love that he had been told to expect. He could not see what was so special about this girl, but it was clear to him that she had already replaced him in the people's hearts. He ran away in tears, fleeing first from the square and then the castle, out into the world beyond their realm.

In the square, all eyes were on Ellyon as they climbed onto the platform beside the princess and set out their tools. The people were asked to form a line, and approached, one by one.

"Do you agree to share a part of yourself?" Ellyon asked each one. Some nodded quietly, while others responded enthusiastically, eager to contribute. Ellyon would then refer to their pile of plans and sketches, and prise back a section of skin to carefully remove a small metal component. Each wound was repaired expertly; not a mark or scar was left behind.

The queen and king were the last to contribute, and Ellyon extracted a large, shining cog from each of their hearts. Unlike their subjects, who barely felt a thing, the queen and king were obviously weakened by the loss of these parts. They supported each other as they staggered back to their thrones, and the crowd murmured in concern.

"Do not worry," said Ellyon. "As the girl's parents, they have each made a greater sacrifice. Once my task is complete, the princess will fill the space they have made for her in their hearts."

Ellyon sat down and started to assemble the parts they had collected. They fitted together seamlessly, as though this had always been their intended purpose, until finally Ellyon held a gleaming metal heart.

The people gasped in appreciation, but Ellyon appeared concerned.

"My friends, somehow I find there is a piece missing, and without it I cannot complete the princess's heart. Is there anyone who has not come up yet to contribute a part of themselves?"

Everyone waited to see if someone would come forward, but nobody moved.

Then the Clockwork Queen spoke up. "Where is Michael? Has anyone seen our son?"

A few people remembered having seen him earlier in the day, but nobody had seen him leave.

The next hours were spent fruitlessly searching, but as the Sun began to set, the people grew weary and returned to the square.

"Why is everyone so tired?" the queen asked Ellyon. "I have never seen our subjects looking so unwell."

"Like you, their sacrifices have weakened them and their clockwork is winding down. Unless I act now, they will cease to function. We have no choice but to proceed without the prince."

Ellyon picked up their tools and made some adjustments to the heart before inviting the queen to place it inside the princess's chest. They covered the opening with skin but left a small hole—a wound so deep that if one looked closely, it was possible to glimpse the metal heart inside. They placed the same key they had used to activate the queen into the hole, and gave it three clockwise turns before removing it again.

The princess stretched out her arms, and Ellyon had to duck to avoid being swept from the platform. She opened her eyes, sat up, and turned to face the crowd.

At once, the fatigue everyone felt disappeared. The queen and king ran up and hugged her, and all the people cheered.

"But what about Michael?" asked the queen after the initial moment of elation had passed. "Where is he? How did you complete the princess's heart without him?"

Ellyon was mournful. "Alas, I could not complete it, not as I had planned. I hope that you find him, because his absence has left a hole in the princess's heart and in the heart of the realm. Without him, the clockwork that sustains you will be constantly running down. Every night, before the princess goes to sleep, you must use this key to wind her up. Otherwise, when the morning comes she will remain asleep, as will you and all your subjects."

Ellyon handed the key to the queen, and she hung it on a chain around her neck.

In another part of the land, there was a young king called Stefan. He had inherited a great kingdom and wanted for nothing, except a wife to give him an heir. So he sent out his servants and told them, "Scour the country and find me the most beautiful princess in the land."

His servants rode out to the neighbouring kingdoms. So the king could decide which princess he desired most, they took with them the greatest artist in the kingdom to paint their portraits. One by one, each princess was captured on canvas and each monarch was left waiting to find out if they had secured this coveted alliance.

Upon their return, the servants set out all the portraits and invited King Stefan to select his future bride. He walked up and down the gallery, scrutinising the paintings. The artist had done his job superbly, and each picture was incredibly detailed and lifelike. Every flaw, blemish, and pimple was laid bare for the king, and he quickly dismissed princess after princess from consideration until only three remained.

"Tell me truly," King Stefan asked his servants. "Are these the finest princesses in the land?"

"Oh yes," said the first servant. "This one's father owns acres of fertile land, capable of producing enough food for both your kingdoms many times over."

"And this one's father owns a mine full of precious jewels and metals," said the second servant. "He will be able to offer you a large dowry for his daughter."

"This princess's family controls the busiest port in the land," said the third servant. "If you marry her, you will gain great advantages in foreign trade."

"All these are very important considerations," said King Stefan, "but my queen must be the most beautiful in all the land so everyone will admire her and compliment me upon my good fortune."

"They are all just as beautiful as their portraits," said the first servant. "Any one of them would be a fine choice."

The other two servants nodded enthusiastically. However, the artist looked nervously at the floor and shuffled his feet.

"Do you disagree?" asked the king. "Are your portraits not accurate? Speak now, for if I discover upon meeting my bride that you have deceived me, you will be executed on the spot."

"All my paintings are accurate, to the tiniest detail, and I have no qualms staking my life on them. However, there is one princess I was unable to paint for you. It is said that she is the most beautiful woman who ever lived."

"Then why is her picture not here?" shouted King Stefan.

"Alas," said the first servant, "we did not see her. We travelled to her father's castle and told her parents that if their daughter was beautiful enough, they might secure a marriage alliance with your great kingdom. They sent for her, but the princess refused to see us."

"Did her parents not punish her for this disobedience?"

"No, sire. Instead, they told us that we should leave immediately."

"Please do not trouble yourself with her, Your Majesty," said the second servant. "She would not have hidden from us if she were that beautiful."

"Besides, it is only a tiny place, and an alliance with them offers you little advantage. One of these fine women is the bride for you," said the third servant, trying to draw the king's attention back to the portraits. "Which one do you favour?"

They tried to sway him, but it was too late. King Stefan was fixated on the mystery princess. "Saddle my horse," he ordered. "I will go and see her for myself, and if she is as beautiful as the rumours say, I will marry her."

King Stefan rode out in his stately carriage, accompanied by a large entourage. They travelled for many days and nights until they reached the castle of the Clockwork Queen and King. It was far smaller than his own, yet when he saw it, King Stefan became jealous. Where his castle was grey with the wear and tear of everyday life, the clockwork castle gleamed. He could not help but admire the impossibly high, thin towers and the dazzling, coloured glasswork that caught the sun and projected rainbow patterns on the walls.

"I must seek out the architect responsible for this place," the king said, "so he might build a palace bigger and even more beautiful for me to live in with my new bride."

The Clockwork Queen and King were delighted to receive a personal visit from another monarch and invited King Stefan to join them for a great feast in his honour. King Stefan asked after the princess, hoping to meet her immediately, only to be told that she was out visiting some of their subjects. The Clockwork Queen and King assured him that he would meet her at the dinner.

When King Stefan entered the great hall that evening, he was disappointed to see that the princess was still not there.

"Do not worry," said the Clockwork Queen. "She so enjoys spending time with the people of our realm, Princess Rosamund often loses track of time. But she always returns by sunset."

King Stefan was angry. Nobody had ever shown such disrespect to him before. So, to appease him, the queen sent servants to find the princess and ask her if she would come back to meet their guest.

It was not long before Princess Rosamund arrived, but she was not dressed for a state dinner. She wore simple clothes covered in dirt from the fields, and there was mud smeared across her face.

"Mother, father, I am sorry I am late," she said breathlessly. "One of the sheep
escaped from the pasture, and we had to chase it down."

King Stefan stared at the princess in disappointment. Clearly, the stories about her had been exaggerated. He wondered how quickly he could extricate himself from this pointless visit and return home.

A servant came over with a bowl of water and a cloth. Princess Rosamund thanked them and washed her face and hands, then she turned to King Stefan and smiled. "This must be our guest."

Now that he could see her face, King Stefan realised he had been hasty. He should not have been judging her by her garments, those could be replaced with queenly robes. As for the mud, once they were married she would never have cause to step foot in a field again.

Overcome with desire, King Stefan said, "To think, my servants advised me to marry one of those other princesses when the most beautiful woman in the world was waiting for me here. I will have them flogged for their betrayal."

"Please, Your Majesty, we have only just met," Princess Rosamund said, embarrassed by his outburst, and went to sit at the far end of the table next to her father.

King Stefan patted the empty chair next to him. "Won't you sit here next to me?"

"Oh no, Your Majesty. That is my brother's seat. It is always kept free for him."

"And will he be joining us this evening?"

"Sadly, we do not expect him."

"Then where is the harm? Please, come and sit next to me."

Seeing her reluctance, the Clockwork King turned to his daughter. "It is just one meal, and it will make our guest happy."

"Very well," she replied and moved to the other end of the table.

King Stefan placed his hand on her knee, but she lifted it off with a strength that surprised him.

"Please don't, Your Majesty. My dress is so dirty, and you would not want to get any of the mud on you."

Reluctantly, King Stefan withdrew his hand and ordered a servant to fetch water so he could wash himself.

The dinner passed slowly. More than once, King Stefan forgot about the dirt and tried to touch the princess, but each time she politely rebuffed his advances.

When the servants had removed the last plates, King Stefan addressed his hosts.

"Tomorrow, I will return to my kingdom. Or should I say, our kingdom?" He glanced at the princess. "For it is my intention for Princess Rosamund to come with me and become my queen."

The royal family all seemed shocked by this declaration, although King Stefan could not understand why. Had he not made his intentions quite clear from the moment he saw Rosamund's beauty? He was further surprised when it was the princess who replied rather than her father.

"Your Majesty," she said, with as much tact as she could muster, "I am flattered by your kind offer, but I am afraid I must demur. My place is here, in this castle. I have no desire to marry or to leave my people. I thank you for your company this evening, but now it is time for me to retire. I will wish you a good night and a pleasant journey tomorrow, as I must be out early in the morning and doubt I will have a chance to see you."

She retired to her bedchamber. The queen also said her farewells and followed her daughter to wind her, as she did every night.

"That is better," said King Stefan, after they had left. "This is a matter that should be decided between men, not by flighty women. I am sure you see the benefits of a marriage alliance with such a powerful ally."

"I am sorry," said the Clockwork King, "but no, my daughter does not want to marry you."

"Of course, you are a shrewd negotiator. Your country has very little and clearly you cannot offer the large dowry a powerful monarch like myself would normally demand. However, since I am determined to marry your daughter, I am willing to negotiate a vastly reduced sum. I am certain you can manage to raise it with just a small tax increase."

"You misunderstand. I am not trying to negotiate with you. It is not my decision to make. I will not make my daughter marry you, and that is my final word. Goodnight to you, Your Majesty."

King Stefan was unused to being addressed in such a way, and his first instinct was to bring all his military might to bear in retribution. However, his advisers were swift to counsel him against it. What could he gain by marching his troops across the land for the sake of such a meagre prize?

It was true, King Stefan had no interest in this little realm. It was only the princess that he wanted. Although she had rashly refused him, he was convinced that with time, he could bring her around. Once she saw how much better her life could be as his queen, he felt sure she would be grateful he had saved her from this life.

Gathering his entourage, he instructed them to prepare to depart. Then, he took aside three of his most trusted guards. "Go to the princess's room. Tie her, gag her, and bring her to me as quietly as possible. She will come home with us tonight."

The guards did as they were instructed and soon returned carrying Princess Rosamund. She kicked and tried to scream, but to no avail. They forced her into King Stefan's carriage. Then the visitors rode out of the castle and towards their home.

In the morning, the Clockwork Queen and King were surprised to see their guest had departed without saying goodbye. They were less surprised not to see their daughter. After all, she had told them all at dinner that she planned to head out early in the morning.

They grew more concerned as evening approached, and sent out people to search for her, only to discover nobody had seen her all day.

Miles away, as night fell again, King Stefan finally gave his party the order to stop. He had driven them hard with only the briefest stops during the day in order to outpace any pursuers, but now he felt it was safe to rest.

"I apologise for this, Princess Rosamund," he said as he opened the door to his carriage. "I had hoped to leave in a more dignified fashion, but fear not, the reception we receive when we reach my kingdom will more than compensate for the lack of ceremony when we departed."

He peered inside the carriage, surprised not to hear anything. The Princess had been noisy for most of the journey, banging on the carriage walls, and once she managed to work the gag loose, shouting at the top of her voice. Now, she was still and silent.

King Stefan stepped inside, cautious because she might be lying in wait to attack him, but then he saw that she was fast asleep after all her exertions.

When morning came, he went to check on her again. She was still fast asleep, and he ordered his men to set off without disturbing her.

When they next made camp, King Stefan realised he had not heard a sound from the princess all day. Once again, he found her sleeping. He shook her gently, then harder, but she did not respond.

For a moment, he feared she was dead, but he had seen plenty of corpses on the battlefield, their life drained from their bodies. She did not look like them. Her cheeks still had a healthy glow, and her eyes were still bright beneath their lids.

Since there was nothing more he could do for her there, he told his men to pack up and resume their journey, with riders sent ahead to prepare everything for their arrival.

King Stefan barely acknowledged the crowds that had gathered to welcome him home, all cheering and hoping to steal a glance at their future queen. Instead, he rode swiftly through the town to his castle.

He summoned the best physicians to examine the princess. They poked and prodded her at length, but all agreed—physically, there was nothing wrong with the princess. She just seemed to have stopped moving, and there was nothing they could do.

In the absence of a medical explanation, the king's chief advisors agreed that she must have been cursed. How else could such an unnatural sleep be explained? Yet, as everyone knew, a cursed princess could always be restored by a kiss.

The king ordered his servants to wash the princess, style her hair, and clothe her in the finest of dresses. Once they had done all these things, he had them lay her out on the bed in the chamber he had set aside for her.

Admiring his bride as she lay waiting, King Stefan congratulated himself on his fine choice. As he had rightly surmised, now that she was dressed appropriately, she was certainly the most beautiful woman he had ever seen.

He leaned over the bed and kissed the princess gently on the lips. He stood up and waited, but nothing happened.

"Try again, Your Majesty," said one of his advisors. "Maybe a little more passionately."

So the king kissed her again, but still nothing happened.

Again and again he tried, but to no avail. Weary and frustrated, he retired for the night.

Over the following weeks, King Stefan had all the wisest men in the land brought to the castle to examine the princess, but none of them could help her. The doctors gave her their best medicines, the wizards tried all their most powerful spells, and the priests made sacrifices to all their gods, but still she slept.

Weeks turned to months and then years, but the king refused to marry anyone else, for none could compare to the beauty of his princess. Indeed, even as everyone else aged, she remained as young and fair as the day they had first met.

Every morning, the servants would care for Princess Rosamund, washing her and dressing her. Every day, ladies-in-waiting would sit with her. Entertainers were hired to keep her amused and storytellers employed to tell her tales of the world outside. As darkness fell every evening, the king would go and kiss her goodnight, hoping each time that today might be the day when the touch of his lips might awaken her.

As the years passed, the king's advisors grew more and more concerned, for he still had no heir to inherit his kingdom. They implored their monarch to choose another woman to marry, but he would not listen to them.

One day, a new storyteller arrived. As with all the entertainers who visited the castle, he was ordered to perform for Princess Rosamund.

"Your sleeping princess reminds me of a place I once visited," he said. "Many years ago, I was caught in a storm whilst travelling. In the wind and the rain, I lost my way and stumbled into the wild woods. The woods were forbidden, and usually nobody entered them. Some said they were full of dangerous animals, and others said that magical creatures lived there.

"Soon, even the narrow trails I had been following disappeared. I was forced to cut my way through the undergrowth with my hatchet. I was hacking my way through a thicket of briars, and wondering if I would ever make it home, when I struck something solid. Cutting more of the branches away revealed a gleaming, white wall.

"I made my way along the wall until I found an entrance. The gates were stiff with disuse, but they were not locked, and eventually I was able to force my way through. I stepped inside and was surprised to see the courtyard was full of people.

"'Hello there,' I said. 'I'm sorry to disturb you, but I am lost. Can anyone help me find my way out of the woods?'

"However, nobody responded. In fact, I realised, none

of the people were moving at all. They all stood as immobile as statues. I went over to the woman standing nearest to me, thinking that although these people were lifelike, they were made of stone after all. But when I touched her hand, I felt warm flesh.

"I backed away, fearful that whatever curse she was afflicted by might also be passed to me, for surely there was some dark magic at work. When I reached the gate, I turned and ran as fast as I could into the woods. I had no sense of which direction I travelled, I just knew I needed to get away. Luckily, I stumbled across a path, but on I ran, eager to put as much distance between myself and the frozen castle as I could.

"Eventually I emerged from the woods. In the open countryside at last, I paused to catch my breath. Then I heard a cackling laugh. I turned to see an old man, sitting on a log not far from where I had emerged from the woods.

"'So, you saw the castle,' the old man said.

"'How did you know?' I asked. 'Are you responsible for what happened to those people?'

"The old man laughed again. 'I had nothing to do with their fate, but I have seen more than one man emerge from the woods with that look on his face. I assume the people there are still sleeping?'

"I nodded and then asked if he knew what happened to them. The old man told me how the castle had once stood at the edge of the forbidden woods and how the princess who lived there had gone missing. He claimed she was so loved that when she left, the people's grief froze them in place. Then briars climbed up the castle walls, trees grew with unnatural speed, and within weeks the castle was swallowed up by the woods.

"'That is ridiculous,' I said. 'People don't just stop. Is this some kind of trick you play on unwary travellers like myself?'

"'You have seen them, so you know it isn't a trick,' he replied, 'but go back in there and look again if you want. They

will still be waiting there, unless the Lost
Prince has found the princess.'

"'A prince? What prince?'

"'Some people said that one day, the princess would meet
a prince who was also lost. He would give her his heart, bring
her home, and then the curse would be lifted. I never really
believed that part. It was the type of silly love story the girls in
the village used to tell each other.'

"Now that I had heard this story, my curiosity got the
better of me, and I decided to return to the castle to investigate
it further. Although I was sure I had retraced my steps, I could
not find the frozen castle again. It felt like some magic was
keeping me from walking in a straight line, and I kept circling
back to places I had already passed.

"I never saw anything like those people in the castle again...
until today. I would swear that the princess here is under the
same spell. Perhaps," he whispered conspiratorially, "she is
the missing princess, and one day the Lost Prince will come
and wake her up."

The ladies-in-waiting applauded politely as the storyteller
finished his imaginative tale before returning to their sewing.
However, one of them was struck by what they had heard and
reported everything to the king.

King Stefan summoned the storyteller to the throne room
and questioned him about every detail until he was satisfied
he had no more to add.

Once the storyteller had been dismissed, one of the king's
advisors said, "Surely, this is all just some fantasy he dreamed
up when he heard about the princess's condition."

"I would have thought that," said the king, "but I recognised
every detail of the castle he described. I am certain it is the
very place where I met my beloved. I am left wondering, how
much more of his story might also be true? If the Lost Prince
does exist, then we should make every effort to find him, so he

can end the curse and wake up Princess Rosamund."

"But sire, even if the story is true, what will it mean for you if this prince gives her his heart?"

"I am no longer a young man, yet the princess retains the full bloom of youth in her enchanted sleep. While I love her more than any other, it is clear to me now that she is not destined to become my wife. Instead, if this prince exists and can wake her, he can become my heir. Send out messengers across the land saying that we seek a 'lost prince,' and let us try one last time to lift this curse."

The news spread quickly and many princes came, hoping they might be the one to break the curse. The king's advisors questioned them all closely to establish which might be the Lost Prince from the story and selected the three best candidates. Each would be given a chance to wake the princess.

On the day of the testing, the bedchamber filled up quickly with nobles, advisors, and other senior members of the court, eager to see whether the curse would finally be broken. Once everyone had gathered, the king entered and made his way over to the bed. He kissed Princess Rosamund one last time, then sat down beside her.

The first prince was a handsome young man. He reminded the king of himself in his youth, and he thought this man would be an ideal heir.

"Your Majesty, I am Prince Anton. When I was a child, I was kidnapped by my father's enemies and held to ransom. I was missing for a whole month before I was rescued and brought home. I believe that I could be the Lost Prince you seek."

King Stefan nodded in approval and invited Prince Anton to approach the bed. The prince leaned in and gently kissed Princess Rosamund. There was a sigh from some of the ladies in the room at this romantic moment. However, when the prince stood up, the princess remained asleep.

Disappointed, the King dismissed Prince Anton and called for the next suitor. He was a swarthy man from some foreign land.

"My name is Prince Abawa. Two years ago, I set sail from my homeland. My ship was caught in a storm and wrecked on the shores of your land. Now, I am lost, with no way to return to my home."

King Stefan was less enamoured of this foreign man. Nevertheless, he qualified as lost, and seemed well-bred. Perhaps his homeland could be found, and a prosperous trading relationship established.

The king signalled his assent, and Prince Abawa strode over to the bed. His kiss was longer and more passionate than the first suitor's, but still did not have the desired effect. Reluctantly, he withdrew and made way for the final prince.

The king recognised the last man to come forward. He was much older with receding, oily hair and a slight paunch.

"Prince Rupert, I do not know why you think you could be considered a 'lost prince.' You have lived in your family's castle your whole life, relying on the generosity of your father, and now your brother."

"Your Majesty, I have suffered great loss. My father left me a vast tract of land when he died, but gradually it has been stolen from me."

King Stefan laughed. "Stolen? You lost most of it gambling. I won part of it myself in a card game. You are hardly a suitable match for my princess. However, I am a man of my word. If you can wake her, you may marry her and become my heir."

Prince Rupert slicked back his hair and bent over to kiss

Princess Rosamund. His kiss was wet and loud, causing a couple of women to turn away in revulsion. It went on until there was a shout from the crowd.

"Leave her alone!"

Everyone looked to see who had spoken, and a young boy stepped forward. "You have no right to treat her like this."

"Who is this brat?" asked Prince Rupert. "Are you going to let some serving boy interrupt me? The princess was about to wake up."

"Only to get your slobbering lips off her face," said the boy.

Prince Rupert raised a hand, but King Stefan signalled for a guard to step in. "You have had your chance. She is not waking up."

Prince Rupert stormed out of the bedchamber and King Stefan sighed.

"My subjects, I am sorry, but the curse has still not been lifted, and now I fear it never will."

Then somebody shouted, "What is he doing?"

Everybody turned to look at the boy, who in all the excitement had managed to approach the bed and was now standing by the princess.

"Does he think he is going to kiss her?" asked a man in the crowd, and everybody laughed.

Rather than respond, the boy leaned forward to examine the princess closely. She had been dressed in a low cut gown, so he could clearly see the hole just above where her heart lay. He reached over and gently touched it, and just for a moment, some of the people standing closest thought they might have seen the princess's hand twitch.

"Get away from her," shouted the king. "Guards, seize him!"

The guards were unable to get through the crowds as, to the horror of all, the boy opened his shirt and pulled back the skin over his chest. One of the ladies-in- waiting fainted at the sight, expecting blood to come gushing out. Yet, the boy's flesh parted cleanly, as though by design.

With his chest wide open, it was possible to see the clockwork mechanisms ticking inside the boy. He reached into his heart and withdrew a brass cog. He studied it for a moment, and then satisfied he had made the right choice, covered himself up again.

The boy slid the cog into the hole in Princess Rosamund's chest and slotted it into her heart. As soon as he withdrew his hand, the wound that had been there since her activation closed. With a gasp, the princess awoke.

For a moment, everyone stood in shocked silence, then applause rippled around the room.

Princess Rosamund sat up, and Prince Michael hugged her. "I am sorry. I should not have run away, but now you are complete at last."

"Who are you?" asked King Stefan, baffled by what had just transpired.

"This is my brother," said Princess Rosamund. "He has completed my heart by giving up a piece of his own. At last, I can move again."

"Your brother? You cannot marry your brother."

"Who said I should?"

King Stefan thought for a moment, before smiling. "My boy, you are most welcome. You have done us a great service in awakening your sister. I had thought I would have to give her up, but now I see that is not the case. Princess Rosamund, you will take my hand in marriage, as you were always meant to do."

The princess looked at him in disgust. "I never wanted to marry you, not then and certainly not after all these years of you treating me like your plaything; dressing me up like a doll and putting me on display for the amusement of your subjects. I remember every minute, every touch, and every kiss you gave me without my consent. I should take the hand you have offered and remove it so you can never place it on another woman."

Prince Michael stepped forward and grabbed the king's hand. King Stefan tried to break free, but the prince's clockwork grip was as strong as a vice.

"Leave him, Brother," said the princess. "I have stayed here long enough, and he is not worth any more of our time. Besides, I can feel our people waking up, can't you?"

The prince let go of King Stefan and looked down at his chest. "I couldn't before, but now, yes, I can."

"You are all connected in my heart and at last I feel complete."

Then she took her brother's hand and together they walked towards the door.

The members of the court parted before them, amazed at what they had just witnessed. "My beauty," shouted King Stefan, "please stay with me!"

But the princess never looked back as they followed the ticking of her clockwork heart home.

About Paul Hiscock

Paul Hiscock is an author of crime, fantasy, horror, and science fiction tales. His short stories have appeared in a variety of anthologies, and include a seventeenth century whodunnit, a science fiction western, and numerous Sherlock Holmes pastiches.

Paul lives with his family in Kent (England) and in real life has never been called upon to solve a murder or met a dragon. Instead he spends his days engaged in the far more challenging task of taking care of his two children.

He mainly does his writing in coffee shops with members of the local NaNoWriMo group or in the middle of the night when his family has gone to sleep. Consequently, his stories tend to be fuelled by large amounts of black coffee.

You can find out more about Paul's writing at www. detectivesanddragons.uk.

Thank you for your support

A fan
Abigail Hiscock
AJ Knight
Alex & Kota King
Alicat
Amanda DeLand
Andrew Parsons
Anita Cassidy
Anne Wiedenkeller
Anonymous H.
Ashley Groshong
Barbara O'Dell
Barry D. Guertin
Becky Hoover
Beke Harrington
Ben Perkins
Beth Robinson
Blank
Brittany Morgan
Brynn
Caitlin Jane Hughes
Cas Ryzy
Cecelia Rafferty
Cédric Perdereau
Cera Little
Charlotte English
Charlotte R. H.

Chris Kaiser
Chris Miles
Cryptic Creative
Crysta Kay
Dagmar Baumann
Danielle & Nicholas Fryer
Dianne Nicholson
Dr Rich Williams
Ed Stafford
Elaine Tindill-Rohr
Elizabeth Sweeny
Esapekka Eriksson
George Reissig
Grace Unruh
Ian McFarlin
Isabella & Dylan Steckline
James Lucas
Jennie Cochran-Chinn
Jennifer Gilbert
Jennifer L. Pierce
Jeremy Medon
Jessa Willson
Joe Dubé
Jonas Heinzmann
Karen Broecker
Karen Carlisle
Kathy Marcia

Thank you for your support

Kay Gray
Kaylin Cullum-Lynch
Kevin Chung
Krystal Bohannan
Linda Checkal-Fromm
Linda Ojanen
Lndail
Lynn Cecil
Mandy Gilmore
Marisa Gallego
Mark Carter
Mary Barry
Mat Meillier
Mathieu Duval
Matt & Camille Knepper
Maxfield Klein
Melanie
Melanie F. Camp
Michael Szul
Michael the Horologist
Michelle M. Pessoa
Michelle Mishmash
Mom & Dad
Morgan Jones
Neeneko
Nicholas Grendel
   Rabinowicz

Nicholas Robinson
Olivia Montoya
Patricia Beghtol
Rachael Lee
Richard Sands
Rose D.
Ross Aitken
Ryan Power
S. Chen
Sakura Sky
Sarah Galvez
Scout Raven
Shawnee M.
Stacy Overby
Stacy Spilker
Stephen Hiscock
Tamara Shiver ~
   PurpleSteamDragon
Tania
Tara Zuber
Ted Wesley
Terri Merrett
The Creative Fund by
   BackerKit
Thomas & Emily Hiscock
Thomas S. Kilijanek
Tim "Buzz" Isakson

Thank you for your support

Tim P.
Tracy 'Rayhne' Fretwell
Trip Space-Parasite
Ursa Major
Val Hiscock
Victoria Acero
Vida Cruz
Zoe Kaplan
Zoltan Deathspawn

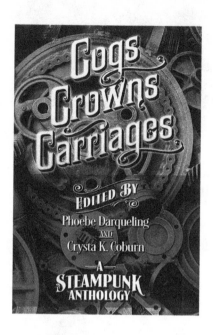

Cogs, Crowns, and Carriages

Twelve international authors have come together to bring you a fresh collection of Steampunk and Gaslamp Fantasy inspired tales. Our stories range from light and comedic to dark and full of drama, so fans of the genre both old and new are bound to find something they love within these pages. Featuring:

Secrets and Airships by A. F. Stewart

Regicide and Prejudice by Paul Michael

Gho-Power by Michael Chandos

Nihon Daitan'na by TJ O'Hare

Monster of the Deep by Thomas Roggenbuck

Where the Light Enters by Crysta K. Coburn

Treason in the Sky by Jacy Sellers

Catchin' Gargoyles by Tim Kidwell

The Last Sleep by Sarah Van Goethem

The Mobius Trip by Phoebe Darqueling

The Last Automaton of Doctor Jubal Varva by K.A. Lindstrom

Peregrine Rising: A Skies of Fire and Lightning Story by Drew Carmody

Gears, Ghouls, and Gauges

A dozen authors from around the world bring you their take on the Steampunk and Gaslamp Fantasy genres. Science fiction and the supernatural collide to create fantastical creatures, exciting adventures, and unusual technologies. Whether you are brand new to these genres or a long-time fan, everyone will find something to love. Featuring:

"The Mechanist's Daughter" by Tracie McBride
"The Lady Defiance" by Mandy Burkhead
"An Evening on Harbor Ridge" by Mark Rivett
"In the Cavern of the Sleepers" by Ali Abbas
"Fractured Moonlight" by W. T. Paterson
"Basic Black" by K.A. Fox
"The Grand Assault" by J. Woolston Carr
"The Steam Horses of Stem Park" by Robert B. Read Jr.
"Jewels from the Deep, a Sussex Steampunk Tale" by Nils Nisse Visser
"The Bronze Bomber" by Briant Laslo
"La Muerda" by Mercury
"Divine" by E. A. Catania

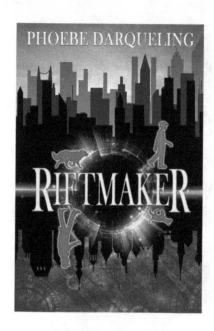

Riftmaker

Save his boy, uncover a conspiracy, and master opposable thumbs—a dog's work is never done.

Buddy's favorite thing is curling up for a nap at the foot of Ethan's bed. Then he stumbles through a portal to a clockwork city plagued by chimeras, and everything changes... Well, not everything. Sure, his new human body comes with magic powers, but he'd still rather nap than face the people of Excelsior, who harbor both desire and fear when it comes to "the other side."

He discovers Ethan followed him through the portal and underwent his own transformation, and it becomes Buddy's doggone duty to save him. Buddy finds unlikely allies in an aristocrat with everything on the line, a mechanic with something to hide, and a musician willing to do anything to protect her. Using a ramshackle flying machine, the group follows the chimeras deep into the forest and uncovers a plot that could reshape the worlds on both sides of the rift.

bit.ly/Riftmaker

The Steampunk Handbook

The Steampunk Handbook is a collection of articles by Steampunk author and lecturer, Phoebe Darqueling. It covers topics such as the history of steam power, the philosophical roots of punk and punk literature as a whole, and the history and evolution of the Steampunk fandom. In addition, you will find information about the historical and cultural underpinnings behind twelve of the most popular tropes in Steampunk.

Get your free e-book at bit.ly/SteampunkHandbook or buy a print copy at bit.ly/SteampunkHandbookPrint

No Rest for the Wicked

Other people just think they're "haunted by the past." In Vi's case, it's true.

Clairvoyant Viola Thorne wants to forget about her days of grifting and running errands for ghosts. The problem? Playing it safe is dull. So when a dead stranger begs for her help, Vi jumps at the chance to dust off her hustling skills. The unlikely companions are soon tangling with bandits, cheating at cards, and loving every minute.

Then she finds out who referred him, and Vi has to face both a past and ex-partner that refuse to stay buried. Though she betrayed Peter, his spirit warns her of the plot that cost him his life. Vi's guilty conscience won't let her rest until she solves his murder. Though she's spent her whole life fighting the pull of the paranormal, it holds the key to atoning for the only deception she's ever regretted—breaking Peter's heart.

Available in print, e-book, and audio book at bit.ly/ViolaThorne

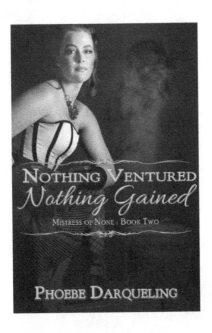

Nothing Ventured, Nothing Gained

There are many types of monsters; Vi just hopes she isn't one of them.

Now that medium and con woman Viola Thorne has been flushed out of hiding, she must dodge old marks and protect new allies while grappling with her ever-growing psychic abilities. On her way south to root out the clandestine organization that murdered her partner, she and her traveling companions (both living and dead) are drawn into a mystery surrounding a burlesque troupe aboard an old flame's steamship.

To get close to the suspects, Vi joins the show and is thrust back into the spotlight. Solving this case might be her next step toward redemption, but both mundane and supernatural forces are working against her at every turn. All aboard for wily women, fractured friendships, and ghosts galore in this paranormal adventure down the mighty Mississippi.

bit.ly/ViolaThorne2

CPSIA information can be obtained
at www.ICGtesting.com
Printed in the USA
LVHW030616130121
676354LV00003B/181

9 781734 729863